Dear [illegible]
Thanks [illegible]
I hope you like it!

ST. MARY'S
PRIVATE DANCER

Blair

A SHEPHERD MURDOCH MYSTERY

BLAIR HULL

APOCRYPHILE
PRESS

The Apocryphile Press
1700 Shattuck Ave. #81
Berkeley, CA 94709
www.apocryphile.org

ISBN 978-1-944769-42-0

Printed in the United States of America

DEDICATION

This book is dedicated to my first grandchild, Riley. If, in some way, I have made your life a little better, it has been my honor. Being part of your comings and goings, and ups and downs for these past eighteen years has been a blessing. Riley, you make me a better person, pastor and friend. May God bless you in all you do.

~~~

St. Mary's Private Dancer is also for all the women and men who feel life has been a disappointment and a confusion, but who are willing to seek a way beyond the difficulties, maybe one friend or one book at a time.
~~~

THANK YOU...

First, I want to thank everybody in my world who has ever loved me, challenged me, and walked with me as a friend. Thanks for every song I have ever sung. For my parents Casey and Bill; for my brothers and sister; for my daughter Kate, who teaches me about myself; and for my son James who always has my back. For Chicago Theological Seminary, and the United Church of Christ who said I was worthy to be a pastor. For God at my shoulder.

There would be no book were it not for Write By the Lake, a summer writing program at the University of Wisconsin—Madison, Wisconsin. For my first mystery teacher, Jeremiah Healy; my writing sisters: Bibi Belford, Cheryl Hanson, Julie Holmes, Lisa Kusko, Roi Solberg, and our amazing mentor and teacher Christine DeSmet—whose books I hope you read.

Thanks to the wonderful people from Holy Wisdom Monastery, Middleton Wisconsin, who helped me center myself, and where I wrote the first pages.

Thanks to every friend who took time out of their busy lives to read my words as I was just beginning, especially Lisa Dahl, Ann Little Hull, Rev. Barbara Bolsen and Jeanne Whelan.

Thanks to Chrissy Hansen who has been so helpful to me. She reads my mind better than me at times and is currently writing the screenplay.

Thanks for the rest of my amazing circle of friends who make my world better every day. Especially Rev. Roger Dart, Rev. Carol Barriger, Cynthia Fremling, Donna Dorl-Adams, Rev. Betsy Bueschel, Sara Turnbull Gray, Julie Hamilton, Jan Krist, Maggie Deas, Janine Poehlman, Elizabeth McKee, Janine Veto and many more.

Thanks to Rev. Dr. John Mabry, who read *St. Mary's Private Dancer* and said he'd love to publish it! John you have been so helpful to me—telling me to breathe and remember that all will be well, when I wondered if I should read it one more time. You are the best!

Thanks to Pat McHenry Sullivan and Chrissy Hansen for your editing. Dear readers please know that any mistakes found here are completely mine!

Last, but not least, thanks to Mark Knopfler, who gave permission for me to use the words to his amazing song, "Private Dancer." And thanks to many I have forgotten to mention—I could not have done this work without you.

Blessings,
Rev. Blair Ann Hull

PART I

CHAPTER 1

"He puts a gun on your pillow every night?" I repeated, not sure I'd heard her right.

"Pretty much." She fidgeted with the ruffles on her skin-tight mini skirt.

Brushing garden soil off my hands onto my coveralls I led her into my office. It was just an old door, covered with a glass top, balanced on two low file cabinets stuck in the middle of the greenhouse.

She was thin, average height, with disarming blue eyes, and dark wispy hair. The early morning sun behind her made her look like some twisted avant-garde version of Our Lady of Guadalupe in a mini-skirt.

"A friend gave me your name," she was saying, "but you don't look like a minister."

"No, what does a minister look like?"

"I don't know." She twirled a strand of her hair with a well-manicured finger. "You are," she glanced at a scrap of paper in her hand, "Reverend Shepherd Murdoch, right?"

"Yes."

We sat in the moist greenhouse and both waited for more.

My property hugs Lake Michigan, on the southeast edge of Evanston, Illinois, just north of Chicago. Easy to see on Google Earth, but in the real world, no one can find me without detailed instructions. So she'd had help finding me.

Two years ago I quit ministry. I'd let go of what had become an overwhelming burden of taking care of others and decided to instead grow flowers in this greenhouse sanctuary I'd inherited from my grandmother.

"In this house we hide in plain sight," I'd heard her say once. I was grateful for the stone house that came with the greenhouse but I spend most of my time here with the growing things that don't talk back. Growing flowers was better for my soul than being a stand-in rescuer for St. Jude's hopeless causes. One of which had just walked through my door.

To look at her I could tell this would be complicated. Overdone make-up, ratted hair, and skimpy clothes. Bare feet. She held Jimmy Choo stilettos in one hand and had a small purse hanging from her shoulder. It was big enough for a cell phone, lipstick, cash, and condoms, but not much more. This uniform announced she was most probably a sex worker who had an occasional wealthy client and was just coming off the late shift.

She was attractive in a cheap kind of way and probably much younger than she looked. Why anyone with her looks would need to sell her body was beyond me. I could be wrong about how she made her living, if you could call it that, but I doubted it.

"My birth certificate says Marnie Cooper," she blurted, "but I haven't used that name in years."

"Marnie Cooper," I said, as I pulled my long hair up off my neck and fastened it with the hair clip I had in my pocket, "that's two confessions so far. Before we go any further, have a seat." I pointed to a plastic chair, next to a row of cream white gardenias just coming into bloom.

The glorious smell of the fragile buds permeated the air and filled the greenhouse with perfume.

"I might need some...help," she said as she sat down, trying to keep her knees together while pulling at her skirt at the same time.

"Who is he?" I asked.

"What?"

"The guy with the gun."

"Right," she said, startled, as if she'd forgotten she'd said anything about a gun. "He's my, uh, boyfriend."

"What's his name?"

Her eyes widened and morphed from caution to terror. "Shit. He'll kill me..."

"Well," I said, "You got my name from an anonymous source. You tell me your boyfriend puts a gun on your pillow every night, but you don't want me to know his name. Right?"

"Pretty much."

"How long has this been going on?" I asked, taking the bait.

My heart was racing. *Here we go*, I thought, as I caught a reflection of myself in the mirror next to the door. No make-up, dark brown hair, with gray woven throughout that seemed to have recently come from nowhere, just like Ms. Marnie here.

It was easy for me to be sucked into the adrenalin rush that comes when I think I can help someone in trouble. For the last two years, hiding with my flowers had helped keep my adrenalin addiction at bay, but obviously, I wasn't hiding well enough. At the moment, I'm not sure who needed Co-Dependents Anonymous more, Marnie, or me. And the big question is, why not give this woman the name of a good therapist and send her on her way?

I straddled an old wooden chair sitting directly across from her and started tapping my fingers, waiting for her to answer me.

"I can't remember when it wasn't bad," she said. "I thought I could handle it all myself." Her hands were closed into fists in her lap. She jiggled the balls of her feet so her knees bounced up and down in a nervous rhythm.

"Are you trying to see if you can trust me?" I asked, a little softer this time.

"Trust?" With a grim, tight smile she shook her head. "They told me I could talk to you, but trust? Don't think so." She reached for her purse and looked toward the door.

I leaned forward, knowing better than to ask who *they* were. I touched her arm—she didn't flinch. "I don't need to hear more to know you're in trouble. You need to go to a safe place with people who can help you."

Marnie tensed and looked around to see if someone else was listening. "You mean a safe-house? I did that once," she said, whispering, "It's not that simple."

"Understood," I said gently. "Seems to me you need to make some decisions." I paused waiting for some kind of reaction; "I can take you to a place in Waukegan." Again, there was another heavy silence.

I reached out to take her hands. Neither of us spoke for a long time. The birds were waking up singing their morning songs and the heavy warm, fragrant smells of the greenhouse helped me say what I'd been told a long time ago.

"Evil changes you forever. Evil slams into you and affects everything about you—your openness, your ability to love and trust, to make good choices—it all changes. You're numb. You're suspicious of everyone—mostly yourself."

"You muddle through each day, knowing you are on your own and you couldn't get help even if you needed it. But you're here, talking to me. That's a start."

Marnie's eyes filled with tears. She pulled back from me, shaking her shoulders, trying to revert back into the composed character, which only minutes earlier had walked in my door.

"If you don't get help, you could be dead soon," I said quietly.

Marnie's tear-streaked face became confused and suspicious at the same time. "No," she blurted. Her body trembled as her chest started to heave. "Dying never mattered—most days it would be a relief, but," she sobbed, "I'm pregnant."

I put my arms around this skinny young thing and held her until she stopped crying. "Let's go," I said, heading for my car.

"Is it really a safe house?" she asked.

"Yes," I said, and hoped I was right.

CHAPTER 2

Bad news comes in the middle of the night, and it's always an emergency. Seminary taught me about theology, the Bible, and history—lots and lots of history, but, except for weddings and funerals, we never learned much about the real world demands of ministry—like how to fix the furnace, deal with church fights, or respond to horrific life altering emergencies. I think I got called after midnight more than my colleagues. Somehow it was common knowledge that I was a knee jerk, adrenalin junkie, and any time was fair game for me. I never said no.

Bleary-eyed, I'd jump up, like I was on autopilot, and hurry to the hospital to be with any person in crisis who'd asked for a minister.

Like a few hours ago, when the hospital called, and asked me to be with this out-of-town traveler who'd killed a kid dressed in black walking down the center of an unlit highway.

While holding the driver's hand, I knew all the compassionate listening in the world wouldn't help him feel less guilty, but I did my best.

"They feel better after talking to you," the nurse said, as I headed toward the door.

"Birdie, what part of *I quit* don't you get?" As an over dedicated ER nurse, she would never understand my need to grow flowers and leave all this drama behind me.

"Shep," she said, "ministers are like nurses. We never quit caring for the lost and the broken. Besides, you're too good to quit." She gave me a hug. "Thanks for coming."

With a weak smile and a wave, I pushed the big square button on the wall to open the emergency room door.

Back home, in bed, I could not have been asleep for more than a few minutes when the damn phone rang again. Twice in one night—I wasn't going to answer this time—the clock said four a.m., but the phone kept ringing. I'd forgotten to turn on my antediluvian answering machine. I loathed that thing, why I kept it, or this stupid landline, was beyond me. Most were messages I didn't want to hear anyway.

"Hello," I said, none too cheerful.

"It's Marnie."

In the years I'd known Marnie, she'd never called in the middle of the night. Never. She'd catch up with me after her story was rehearsed and her defenses were in place. It was no secret that Marnie had lousy taste in men. Every problem she had was, without exception, because of some guy. In the six years since Max was born, I thought her life was better—not perfect, but better.

"What's the matter?" I pinched my cheek to wake up.

"He's tearing up my house."

"Who?" I turned on the light.

"Can you come get us?" Marnie was whispering. "On my way." I pulled on the clothes I'd just thrown on the floor an hour ago. I ran down stairs, jumped into my old Subaru, and drove like hell, mumbling prayers.

I felt like such a fraud. Why did people think I could help them? To be honest, I loved the rush, but that was so disingenuous—dishonest maybe. Not good for a minister to be dishonest, or was I just too hard on myself? Or maybe I was just tired.

It took five minutes to get to Marnie's. That's way too fast for the twisty part of Sheridan Road, even for me.

Except for an eerie, supernatural light coming from the backyard, the house was dark.

I got out of the car and walked slowly up the driveway. As I moved into the flood of light on the back porch I was hoping to see her sitting on the stoop, nursing a beer, doing damage control. But I could see the garage open, and empty, and there was no Marnie to throw her arms around me and say, "False alarm."

I opened the screen door and stepped into the bright kitchen.

"Oh, God," I gasped.

There were feathered sprays of blood on the walls of the daffodil-yellow kitchen. Blood was on Max's school pictures taped to the refrigerator. There were small brown semi-coagulated globs on the floor near the sink. Fumbling for my phone to call 911, I heard a tiny little-boy whimper, and it made me jump.

Max!

The light shining from the kitchen made it hard to see as I looked into the dark living room. There at the far end, cowering near the overstuffed yellow-and-blue wing chair—was Max, holding his six-year-old fists up against his mouth.

"Shhh," I put my finger to my lips, not knowing if the perpetrator was still in the house. Lowering myself to the floor, I started to crawl the length of the living room, so as not to spook him any more.

Then without warning Max made a flying leap and knocked me over. I grabbed him as he wrapped his arms around my neck. "It's okay honey, everything's okay," I lied.

We ran out the front door, into the blinding lights of a police car just pulling in the driveway. Swirling red, white, and blue swaths of light lit up the near dawn.

"That was fast. I hadn't called," I said, out of breath, cell phone in hand.

He was the image of the perfect cop, very blue and over-ironed for so early in the morning. He stayed in the car, gave me a *you-are-so-guilty* look, and jerked his thumb toward the back seat.

"Get in, Miss."

I held Max with my left arm, and opened the door with the other. "No door-opening gallantry, kid and all?" I mumbled.

The cop's response was to pull the bulletproof shield closed between the front and back seats.

Inching Max and me into the squad car, I blurted loud enough for the cop to hear through the little holes in the plastic shield, "I didn't see a body, but there's blood in the kitchen."

Briefly his eyes grabbed mine in the rearview mirror, but otherwise he didn't acknowledge me as he spoke into his phone.

I knocked on the locked plastic window between us. "Officer, I'd like to take this boy to my house. He doesn't need to see more." The cop ignored me.

My captor opened his door and got out. "Don't go anywhere," he said, without looking at us, and slammed the door.

Don't go anywhere. Very funny. Everyone who ever watched a cop show on TV knows these doors don't open from the inside. I tried it anyway—no luck.

"Shhh, Max," I whispered to the little boy whimpering in my arms. "I've got you honey, shhh." I rocked Max in my arms and watched the morning sun inch its way up over the horizon. Normally he'd say what a big boy he was, and how being held like a baby was 'inappropriate.'

Tiny whorls of pink mixed with yellow merged with blue and white as the sun inched upward over the deep dark water of Lake Michigan. Most of the time I'd have found this reassuring, like the constancy of the sky was a sign that God was paying attention to me. But at the moment, for Max and me, I had to slow down the panic I was experiencing.

Feeling one with God would have to wait.

Over the past six years I thought I knew Marnie. Now, locked in this squad car with Max's warm little body leaning into mine, and the harsh taste of fear in my mouth, I wondered what I knew about her. Max's need for me to comfort him was a welcome distraction from the bile creeping into my throat.

"God, help us here," I said too loud, startling Max. "Sorry honey, don't worry, it's okay," I lied again. "Just praying, go back to sleep." I had to get myself together, for Max, if not for me.

Under different circumstances sitting in a police car with Max might have been a fun field trip. But now he was shaking and I was holding my breath. Stroking his fresh smelling hair, I held him closer and started to sing.

"Little boy kneels at the foot of his bed." For years I sung this lullaby to my own children before they went to bed. I'd sing it to Max, too, whenever he came over to spend the night. We knew it by heart. Hearing the music now helped calm us both down. Music is an inside healer for me, and at the moment it was working.

Max nuzzled into my neck. The dinosaur jammies I'd given him for Christmas smelled clean. I knew Max had both a bath and a story before Marnie put him to bed. She wanted to give him the kind of normal childhood she'd never had. Guess she has blown that charade for good now—for nothing about tonight had anything to do with any remote concept of *normal*.

What had Max seen and heard? Whose blood was in Marnie's kitchen? Still singing, with Max's head tucked under my chin, shielding him in some small way, I watched as multiple emergency vehicles parked on Marnie's manicured lawn. Various uniforms swarmed over the property. I'd seen enough, yet trapped in the squad car I couldn't help but watch the drama unfold. I touched Max's arms and legs, checking for injuries. He stirred; opening his eyes he stared at me with great seriousness.

"Does anything hurt, honey?"

"No."

"You want to tell me what happened?"

Without answering, he squeezed his eyes tight again, as if trying to make everything go away.

"Sweetie, maybe later." I kept singing. Neighbors were coming down the street—some walking dogs in their bathrobes, making no pretense at decorum. The sun was now too bright to look at and increasingly more yellow than pink. Finally, as unmarked police cars and empty ambulances pulled away, I thought perhaps the worst was over, but whom was I kidding?

"There's nobody in there, just a mess," the officer said, sliding back into the squad car. At the sound of his voice Max jumped again. "So, miss, you want to tell me what you know?"

I kept rocking Max in my arms, saying all that stupid stuff, in-between sentences to the cop, like "It'll be alright honey, everything will be fine." There I was lying again.

"Marnie, that's Max's mother, called me around four a.m. She said someone was in the house. She asked me to come get her. When I got here her car was gone. I went around back, stepped in the house, and saw the blood. I heard Max cry, I went into the living room and found him hiding behind a chair. We ran out just as you arrived. That's it."

He took notes.

"Son," he said to Max, "what happened?"

Max squeezed his eyes shut again, and dug his head under my arm.

"For God's sake, give the kid a break. Can't you just leave him for now?" I said.

"How well did you know her?"

"*Do* know her," I snapped, too tired to be nice. "She's my friend, this boy's my godson. He stays with me when she goes to class. My name is *Reverend* Shepherd Murdoch. That's my car," I said, pointing. "I'm no threat to you. Why don't you just let me take this kid home and put him to bed?"

"Whoa, slow down. We know who you are. We ran your license plates," he said, now in a more compassionate voice. "That guy says he lives down the street, heard a commotion and called us."

The young man he was pointing to, in jeans and a t-shirt, was facing my side of the car. He smiled at me and waved.

"I've never seen him before," I said. "Max, do you know this guy?" But Max was having no part of it, and kept his head tightly pressed into my neck.

"For some strange reason I was also told you can take the boy home. I hear the chief knew your grandmother. Procedure is to have the kid turned over to the Department of Children and Family Services, but they have a waiting list, and besides, I guess when you're a Murdoch, exceptions are made."

If he only knew how little I'd known my grandmother! But I kept quiet.

"DCFS has been notified, and someone will call you about arrangements." The officer continued to write things into his tablet, noting, I presume, the non-verbal exchange between the good looking stranger outside, and myself.

"You need to come to the station this afternoon. Bring the clothes you're wearing in a clean plastic bag for forensics. Ask for me, Sergeant Patrick Kelly. Reverend Murdoch? You got that?"

"Sure. I got it." My stomach was churning. Who was the guy in the t-shirt? The only neighbors I could remember Marnie having were all over eighty. I stared at the James Dean look-alike who blew me a kiss. Bile rose again in my throat.

"Reverend Murdoch?"

"The station on Lake Street?" I managed to ask.

"Only one in Evanston, Miss."

"Right. What about him?" I cocked my head toward the guy walking away.

"We took his statement and have no reason to hold him at this time. We'll check him out, like we'll check you out. Anything else you'd like to add?"

"No."

"You'd better go take care of the boy," he said, with a smidge of kindness, as he opened the passenger door and helped us out of the squad car.

I carried Max to my car. "I want my Mama," he whimpered.

"It'll be all right, Max." I choked back tears. "We'll go to Mama Shep's house. Rupert will make you pancakes, and you can go to day camp with Crystal after breakfast. You can see your friends." I was jabbering.

Sliding into the driver's seat, I bumped my head.

"Shit," I blurted. I glanced at Max in the back seat, ready to promise a dime for swearing, as was our agreement, but he'd already fallen asleep.

Driving home more slowly now, I was afraid for Marnie. "*Men take what they want from women and dump the rest,*" she'd said once, out of the blue.

"Not all men are like that, Marnie," I'd said, but she looked at me like I was stupid.

"Never forget, if I end up dead, Derek did it." Derek.

CHAPTER 3

Twenty years ago, in one short cold winter afternoon, my life changed and I stopped being my naive self.

After an exhausting therapy session that morning, we drove home in silence.

"My back is killing me." My husband said, coming in from his engine repair shop, slamming the door with a louder bang than usual.

"Hey, quiet, the kids just fell asleep."

"God, Shep, its always about those damn kids."

He didn't mean that about damn kids, he couldn't. Maybe if I'd rub his back we could talk about what happened at therapy. Of course, now it was going to be a back rub for him and ostensibly nothing for me. "So, would you rub my back for me?"

"Shepherd," the therapist had said this morning, "at some point you have to soften up and not protect yourself so much." So, I agreed to rub his back. Really, as bad as things were between us, Jack is the father of my children, and they deserve us to work things out. I could rub his back for five minutes, I told myself, as I checked my watch.

My husband had taken off his shirt and his jeans, leaving on his boxer shorts, with the sheet over his bottom but his back exposed. We talked a little bit about the morning session, but most of the time it was quiet. Deciding to finish the back rub, I glanced at my watch and saw more than twenty minutes had gone by. This is good, I'd thought. Now maybe we were getting somewhere.

At first I'd been repulsed touching him. But I kept saying to myself *we have to get this together*. The back rub was a small thing, but it seemed to be a good start.

"I want to have sex," he said.

"You are kidding?" I said, "Just because I rubbed your back doesn't mean sex."

I was shaking. I'd been so revealing that morning, saying things in therapy that I'd only whispered to myself.

Jack gave me a blank look. His hand then caressed my neck, and I was relieved. I relaxed. I let my guard down. Here he was, my Jack.

Then his look turned suddenly hard, as if some malevolent being was taking over. He was intertwining my hair in his fingers and then around his hand until my long hair was knotted around his fist. With this thin-mouthed grin he moved my head a little one way, and then the other, pulling harder each time I resisted. He was like a boy torturing a baby rabbit he'd found in the grass in the backyard.

"Open your mouth," he said, as he yanked on my hair, holding my head just where he wanted it. I started to disconnect and began to feel like I was floating away. I was no longer connected to my body or what was happening.

Seemingly from outside myself, I watched what was happening to me. Why didn't I bite and kick and scream, claw, do anything to get away? Why couldn't I move? Held in his grip, I was just waiting for him to be finished.

I'd read about women who were raped—forced to have sex. "I just went through with it," they'd said. "It seemed safer than fighting back." I always thought that was such a lame excuse. Now I understood.

Soon the kids would be up from their nap. I would just wait him out. I was grateful to feel disconnected and calm. But I was cold—cold, like death.

When he was done, and let go of my hair, I went to stand up, but he grabbed my shoulder, flinging me forcefully on my back. I managed to sit up, but he held my arms.

"So," Jack growled low, "Now, I want to talk to that little girl inside you. The one you were talking about this morning," and he started to laugh. "The soft little pink one, the vulnerable one you've been protecting. Guess you aren't doing such a great job at that now, are you? So let me talk to her."

I used all my strength to turn out of his grip. "Not on your life, not now, not ever. You just completely broke this family in two, you stupid, stupid man." I moved to the side of the bed and started to stand up.

Everything was off-kilter. I was still half out of my body. I tried to get up, to make my legs work, to get out of that room, to get away from him. Getting up, I was off the bed and trying to get my balance but I wasn't looking behind me. Jack used his full long reach to punch me hard in the middle of my back, and I lurched forward hitting my head on the wall. I managed to catch myself and walk out of that bedroom, down the stairs.

Standing in the kitchen spitting into the sink, with my hands resting on the ledge, I knew I was different. My head hurt from having my hair pulled so hard and then hitting the wall. I don't remember starting to cry, but now I couldn't stop.

On this bitter cold February afternoon, everything bright and beautiful had just been sucked right out of me. Everything naive or sexy or hopeful or pretty or happy was gone.

Jack came into the kitchen. This had been no accidental random act of violence from a perpetrator invading my home. This was my husband, the father of my children.

Jack said something. Maybe he said he was sorry, I'm not sure. I was too cold to hear or feel anything—everything smelled bad.

That feeling of empty cold would stay with me for a long time. I was broken.

After the kids woke up, I bundled them up in snowsuits, mittens, hats, and boots, and went for a long walk to my pastor's house where I told her what happened.

Our kids played together in the living room of the manse, and she held me in her arms for a long time. Neither one of us knew quite what to say.

CHAPTER 4

No matter how exhausted I was from all these old emotional memories, the best place to be rejuvenated and get back into the real world was in my greenhouse.

I started across the yard and saw Rupert, my right-hand man, jogging to catch up with me.

"You look terrible," he said, as we walked together into the greenhouse.

Rupert was a tall, light-skinned, attractive black man, who I'd guess was in his early sixties, but who looked at least a decade younger.

"Right. Well, Marnie's missing, maybe kidnapped or worse. Max is upstairs." I reached to turn on the ultra sensitive baby monitor in my greenhouse office. I fiddled with the volume control until I could hear Max breathing.

"What the fuck?"

"Can you give me a minute?" I asked, putting my hands up.

Rupert gave a terse nod and retreated to the small kitchen at the back of the greenhouse. Soon he came back with two extra-large mugs of steaming hot lattes.

"Could you bring Crystal to the house in a few hours to take Max to camp? And could you make him those chocolate chip pancakes he loves so much?"

Rupert and his soul mate Crystal are my closest friends. They are the envy of all who know them—a model for what it means to be in a committed relationship, to say nothing of being successful at dodging the difficulties of interracial marriage. Even in Chicago, where this was more common, it still wasn't an easy road for either of them. But Rupert and Crystal made it work. It would be hard to imagine one without the other.

Crystal is attractive, compassionate, and loving. She couldn't have kids, so she compensated by being the best teacher of preschoolers that St. Mary's Early Education Center would ever know. She was also the director at Max's summer camp. To the chagrin of the St. Mary's church board, Crystal went out of her way to arrange full scholarships for her poorer students so they could have quality day care and a safe place to be in the summer. No one cared for these kids like Crystal. Although there were government programs, many of these kids were illegal in one way or another. Off the radar. So there would be no Kid Care Illinois for them, and Crystal knew it.

It was my good fortune that Crystal and Rupert had come as lifetime employees at the property I'd inherited from my grandmother. For years these two had taken exemplary care of things for my grandmother, who they'd affectionately nicknamed Livy. At first I was hesitant at having strangers intimately involved in the everyday ins-and-outs of my life, but now I depend on them. Crystal and Rupert are like family, not only to me, but to Marnie and Max as well.

Crystal was accustomed to taking Max to school or camp twice a week on the nights Marnie took classes at the local community college and Max stayed with me. After I moved into Woodstone, both Crystal and Rupert had accepted me right away but were protective and hesitant, if not downright negative, about me helping Marnie, saying something about my bleeding heart.

"Sorry," I said, coming back to our conversation.

"No problem." He sipped his coffee. Patience was Rupert's long suit.

"Max had a bad night. Not sure what he saw. Marnie called at 4 a.m. When I got there, there was blood in the kitchen. Maybe knives got grabbed out of the dish drainer. Shit, I don't know. I found Max hiding behind a chair. Cops came, and now I have to go to the station later. Max and I are pretty shook up."

“We’ll do whatever you need.” Rupert was crazy about Max, even if he was never quite sure what to do with him.

“I don’t know much more. DCFS is going to call to set up a home visit. If all goes well, Max can stay here until this gets figured out. I can’t have him going to a foster home.”

“Got it.” Rupert furrowed his brow. “Shep?”

“Yes?”

“How are you?”

“Not sure.”

Rupert put his strong brown hands on my shoulders and kissed my forehead. “You know I am not a huge fan of Marnie, but this is as close to family as Crystal and I have had in a long time. We’ll get Max fed and to camp. It’s the least we can do.”

“Keeping some routine for him is a good idea, don’t you think?” I asked.

“I guess there are no rules on stuff like this.”

“Thanks. I’ll stay in here for a while. I need to think—or better yet, not think.”

Rupert nodded, looking as if he wanted to say something else, but instead he walked out the door toward the cottage he and Crystal had shared for many years before I’d known them.

It was unexpected for the usually cool and collected Rupert to get personal and say things like we were family. *Family?*

After my twins grew up and moved away, I'd let go of the idea of family the best I could. There were occasional long telephone calls on birthdays and other momentous occasions, like a new job, or when they needed to talk over some sadness with their mom, otherwise that was it.

The exception was on Christmas Eve when they both would make sure they came back to be with me. We'd decorate, cook, and say wonderful things to each other for a few days, and then they'd head back to their own lives.

Max's part time presence these last few years had helped me get over Connor and Sinead launching themselves into the world so successfully, and doing it completely without me.

"That's a mother's job," I'd told Marnie a while back. "We don't have kids to make *us* feel whole. Being a mother means you raise your kids so they're independent, capable of taking care of themselves, and if we're lucky, ironed and clean with good manners when they face the world—all with an occasional kiss on the cheek for their mother." I didn't say how much you'd miss them when they're gone; that reality comes soon enough.

I sat down at my old beat up desk and I was just trying to breathe. Not too long ago Rupert had said my grandmother would hate it if she knew I was doing greenhouse business instead of writing sermons. "That's bullshit," I'd told Rupert. "Livy never saw me preach, so what difference does it make what I do with the desk?"

"Are you sure?"

"About what?"

"That she never heard you preach?"

"Pretty sure." I shrugged.

Until last week this makeshift desk had been covered with piles of papers and seed catalogs. Then, in preparation for the summer season, I'd cleaned up everything including old paid invoices, catalogs, and flower arrangement ideas torn out from magazines. Under the heavy glass top, that covered the now clean desk, I was looking right into the smiling faces of my kids, from yellowed photographs taken so many years ago. I left the pictures there to remind me of what love looks like. Shifting my gaze beyond the desk, I saw the long shelf of gloxinias just starting to bloom. I inhaled the smells of fresh dirt and new flowers, and I started to cry. Crying wouldn't help any more than duct-taping a broken hoe, but even so, I welcomed the tears.

This trying to help the lost and lonely was making me sick. I didn't want to do this anymore. It tore me up inside. I knew how guilty I'd feel when I couldn't part the Red Sea or heal the sick from their infirmities. But now that it was Marnie who was missing, this new wrinkle was too close to home to ignore.

Procrastinating, I again read the newspaper article I'd also stuck under the glass. There was a big picture of me in my coveralls, hair a mess, sitting at Livy's desk. *The Chicago Tribune* editorial by columnist Heather Foster was writing about me inheriting Woodstone. I was grateful the column was not too gossipy.

> Murdoch is not a new name in Chicago society, and neither is Shepherd Murdoch's name new to the religion section, but only recently have the two been identified together.
>
> Well-known society matron Livy Murdoch died ten years ago, leaving her will and vast fortune undistributed until last month.
>
> It was a surprise when her famous home, along with an undisclosed amount of money to be held in trust for property expenses, was left to her granddaughter, the Rev. Shepherd Murdoch.
>
> Shepherd Murdoch, the fortunate new owner, is an ordained minister. She is known for speaking out against sexual abuse and the death penalty; as a champion of marriage equality, the just peace movement and civil rights; years earlier she'd been a singer in local jazz clubs. Shep, as her friends call her, was hardly the one expected to inherit the Murdoch mansion. Most presumed it would have been given to the Chicago Botanical Society, where Olivia Murdoch was a long time board member.

Architect Leona Hutton, who'd been a Frank Lloyd Wright protégé, designed the famous Murdoch mansion and greenhouse. Leona and Livy (who never liked being called Olivia) were great friends and named the mansion "Woodstone" because that's what it is made of—wood and stone. While the greenhouse has a stone foundation, it is mostly glass walls that are well positioned between thin steel supports. The property, on Sheridan Road, just into Evanston, directly east of Calvary Cemetery, is well camouflaged by high hedges that now hide a beautiful, sturdy, Prairie School-style wrought iron fence.

When asked about her grandmother, Rev. Murdoch said, "I didn't know her very well. I remember seeing her at a family gathering when I was about six. After high school I got a degree in horticulture. My interest in flowers is something Livy and I would have had in common, it must be in the DNA," Murdoch added with a grin. "I'm most grateful for her generosity. Woodstone is a beautiful place and a most unexpected surprise."

With her new inheritance Rev. Murdoch has decided to leave her church responsibilities, renovate the greenhouse that has been left to languish in the years since Olivia Murdoch's death, and grow flowers like her grandmother.

Again, Rev. Murdoch: "It's a little eerie that there was a caveat in the will that I not turn the house into a homeless shelter for single mothers and their children. Which means my grandmother actually must have known a whole lot more about me than I knew about her."

Well, I thought, looking again at the ready-to-pop, cherry red and pink buds of the gloxinias lined up on greenhouse tables across from my desk; I guess that wasn't bad reporting for the *Chicago Tribune*. I've had worse. At least this journalist got most of the quotes right. Funny though, that part about taking a leave from pastoral duties, what leave?

As I headed back to the house, the sky had suddenly turned a menacing green-gray and the wind was picking up. I loved the fresh clean smell that announced a big storm was coming, followed by the swirling clouds in hundreds of shades of gray in Turner-like configurations, all galloping at great speed across the sky. This storm looked to already be moving east over Lake Michigan, which most often meant the violence would pass by, saving us from taking cover until another day.

Most of these storms were harmless and rarely became ferocious enough to be killers, but when the occasional tornado hit, lives changed forever.

Coming out of the shower, washed clean, I knew I'd gone over everything I knew about Marnie. Now, I was left only with gut-sinking worry. But I was sure that she knew at least two things about me. Marnie knew I'd take care of Max, and that I'd do everything I could to find her.

CHAPTER 5

"Reverend Shepherd Murdoch to see Sergeant Kelly," I said, to the young cop behind the bulletproof glass. I tried to look relaxed as I walked into the Evanston Police Department at the appointed time, because I sure felt anything but relaxed.

"You mean *Detective* Sergeant Patrick Kelly," she said, as she picked up her phone and dialed. "A *Reverend* Murdoch here to see you."

"He'll be with you in a minute," she snapped, pointing to a beaten-up orange molded plastic chair bolted to the floor. What was she so snippy about? And why were these old ugly chairs bolted to the floor? Who in their right mind would want to steal them?

It was only last night Marnie had called for help. I was tired, my stomach ached, and I couldn't believe any of it.

I'd so been enjoying my freedom, meditating, doing yoga twice a day, and playing in the dirt. But here I am once again, helping sort out another person's crap.

It's as if I have a flashing sign over my head that says, *Shep will drop everything in her life and take care of yours—no charge.* And here I was, waiting at the police station to be interrogated by a cop.

I'd debated the best way to dress in order to be taken seriously and had settled on a navy suit, crisp white clergy shirt with a clerical collar, which I almost never wore, and low heels. I was looking for recognition of my authority as a minister and I was hoping that somehow this getup would help give me some credence. But that was hilarious, since I was at a police station.

Sergeant Kelly came into the waiting room. "Please follow me, Reverend Murdoch. My office is down the hall."

"Last night you were in uniform, but you are a detective?" I said. "Oh, right, I remember reading something in the *Evanston Review* about detectives having to do street duty in order to give some beat cops their summer vacation because of the finances. That you?" I was blabbering, but who cared? That had nothing to do with why I was there.

He nodded.

In the bright fluorescent lights that lined the hallway, Sergeant Kelly appeared to be in his early 50's and he looked as tired as I felt. Unlikely either of us had gotten much sleep.

This afternoon his crisp chambray shirt and pressed slacks seemed to be just as much a uniform for the good sergeant as the blues he'd been wearing last night.

Sergeant Kelly had that military look. If he'd seen combat, with those shiny shoes, my guess would be Marine Corps. Even my USMC father years later had the habit of shining his boots every day before he put them on to go work at the telephone company.

Sergeant Kelly's office was small with regulation gray walls, a darker gray steel desk and chairs that looked older, by a decade, than the orange chairs in the entryway. Nothing in the room revealed anything personal about him.

I took a deep breath and leaned forward.

"So, what have you found out so far?" I asked, as if I were there to interview him.

He sat quietly at his desk, looking me over.

"Do you know if the blood was Marnie's? Do you think she's alive?" I was nervous. Exasperated I said, "Do you have *any idea* what happened?"

"What kind of Murdoch are you, Scot or Irish?"

"What? Irish. What kind of Kelly are you Cork or Donegal?" I quipped.

The sergeant smiled for the first time. He had that Irish sparkle in his eyes that some are blessed with. I could see him playing Santa at the Evanston Police Department's family Christmas party. Or better yet, I pictured him at Children's Memorial Hospital, handing out stuffed animals and telling stories to sick kids to brighten up their day.

With his elbows on the table, the sergeant rested his chin on folded hands and looked straight at me. His gaze threw me off. He just stared and I marveled at his interesting kind of Zen interrogation style.

Looking at him full on, he did have great eyes, but it was his hands that were most revealing. They were big hands with beautiful fingers that looked like they could caress a woman or change a tire equally well.

"Reverend Murdoch—that is what I call you, right? Reverend Murdoch?"

"Shepherd or Reverend Murdoch is fine." I combed my fingers through my hair, trying to soften up just a bit.

"You can call me Sergeant Kelly." He dropped his smile. "So, Rev—er Shepherd, where were you last night before we saw you running out of Marnie Cooper's house with her son?"

I was startled by his question. "Shouldn't this conversation be about Marnie and not me?"

"Sure, Rev, we'll get to that, but if you could answer the question, that would be great."

"You can't be serious. I'm a suspect?" I quickly sucked in air and coughed. "Never mind, ask away," I said, irritated at his condescending manner. We were in his element, not mine. I was used to claiming spiritual authority, not legal. I was out of my depth.

"Listen, before you bite my head off again, I'd like to suggest you relax," Sergeant Kelly said. "I'm not happy about this either. I retire in two months. The last thing I need is to get tied up in a case like this that already points to bad news."

"So, why are you even talking to me? Shouldn't you be passing this on to someone else and cleaning out your files?"

He raised his eyebrows at my insolence, and then nodded, waiting to hear more. Even nice-ish cops like this one made me nervous. I hadn't talked to a cop up close and personal for a long time, except at peace rallies and that was different. At a rally I was speaking to the crowds while wearing my old Marine-Mom-Against-War sweatshirt, and the cops were around to keep peaceniks like me protected and, well, peaceful.

Just then his phone rang, interrupting whatever game we were playing.

"Excuse me a minute."

What *was* I afraid of? I thought, reacting to his question. I was at the ER last night. I have an alibi. I had no reason to feel afraid, but fear was crawling into my stomach, threatening to make me sick. It was true, I was afraid of lots of things. Like having my blood drawn, being found guilty of something I had or hadn't done, and I was afraid of what any man over sixteen could do to me without my permission.

Shit, that crazy-making thought hadn't crept into my consciousness for decades, and what could that have to do with Marnie's disappearance? Just when I think I'm finished with some demon or other, it shows up again to haunt me.

These back-and-forth conversations I had with myself were normal when I was working in the greenhouse or on a long drive in the country alone. But to pop up while talking to a cop in the police station where I needed to be on my guard and ever vigilant? Clearly I was running low on my internal reserves.

Hanging up the phone, the sergeant continued, "Let's start with an easier question. Why the greenhouse? That's a long way from chaplain at Northwestern University Hospital."

I just sat there and smiled, picking imaginary lint off the jacket of my suit. "Sergeant Kelly, that was an internship. It seems you've found my resume. I still think we are talking an awful lot about me. Can we talk about finding Marnie?"

"Well," he said with his pencil poised to write, "how about starting with how you met her and what you know. Tell me everything, even if you don't think it's important, right up to what you were doing last night before you got to her house. Don't try to protect her. You don't know anything that'll hurt her if she is dead."

"Right. That was blunt. Ok, you want details, or high points?"

"High points at the moment."

"The beginning it is." I launched into the first time I'd met her and ended with last night, surprising myself by leaving out very little. "It has been made quite apparent to me that I don't know Marnie Cooper very well after all," I said, finishing. "But I do love her, shortcomings and all."

He nodded just as his phone rang again. Putting his hand over the mouthpiece he said, "Be with you in a minute."

"Sure. I think I'll find the Woman's Room."

Sergeant Kelly looked quizzical then smiled, pointed to the door, gestured toward the left, and then nodded as he went back to his call.

In spite of the air conditioning I was perspiring and my blouse was sticking to my back. In the bathroom I studied myself in the mirror and splashed some water on my face. My eyes were puffy, and I looked tired.

After finding my way back to his office, I walked in just as he was hanging up the phone.

"Now, where were we?" He smiled.

"Not sure. I think I have just told you everything I know about Marnie Cooper."

"You mean Margaret Mary Cooper, Honey Sue Jackson, or Shana Smith?"

I was not shocked Marnie had official aliases. I knew she had a past that wasn't pretty, but I'd made a decision a long time ago not to pry if I could help it.

"That's what the call was about?"

He nodded. "She hasn't been arrested for six years, just kind of dropped off the radar screen after lots of activity for ten years running."

"Has she been in jail?"

"Seven years ago or so she was arrested with a street punk named Derek Johnson. And no, she never did any hard time because she testified against him. He got out a few months ago—on good behavior. It's amazing how they change when they're locked up and not doing crack."

"I've heard the name Derek Johnson. I presume he's Max's father and the one who terrorized her years ago. I suspect he was at it again last night. When she called she said Derek was making a wreck out of the house.

"You know, I thought I knew this woman, but there seems to be a lot I don't know. Besides there's the boy."

At that he got serious. "We need to talk about that. I told DCFS you'd be here today. They'll contact you, but a caseworker said they were backed up. I vouched for you as temporary guardian and said that you'd tell us if the boy said anything that will help with the case. Correct?"

"Yes, of course, I'll call." I said, grateful he was beginning to trust me a bit and was calling it a *case*.

"The question is," Kelly asked, "are you willing to take care of the boy until we find his mother?"

"I love that kid, and I'd be happy to take care of him. Right now Max is at day care," I volunteered, "as usual."

"Think carefully, Reverend Murdoch. Did Marnie say anything else you can think of that might help us find her?"

"I am pretty sure she had a pattern of abusive relationships. She never gave me details. We just talked in generalities about men and how they treated women, that sort of thing. She rarely went into specifics."

"I want you to call me day or night if you think of anything else. Here's my card." He pushed a crisp black and white card across the desk.

"Detective, if Marnie is a sex worker, then her disappearance can't be much of a priority. Nobody cares about what happens to a hooker, right?"

"If she's already turned states' evidence against this Derek guy, they are all through with her. By the way, was she in a witness protection program?" I asked, thinking out loud.

At that he flashed his great smile again. "I doubt it. Look, we don't get this kind of stuff often. We handle parking tickets, speeding violations, a little B&E and gang related stuff. Reverend Murdoch, your concern for your friend and the fact there's a child involved makes me want to keep following what few leads we have. How's that with you?"

I yawned. The earlier call about the who, what, where, and why of my public persona and resume seemed to have made us more colleagues than adversaries. I had no other real explanation for his sudden friendliness.

"Now I have to go see the forensics guy about the DNA and hand over those clothes you brought in. I'll see if I can jump start them into action."

Then as an afterthought he asked, "You want to tag along?"

For the second time in less than twenty-four hours, I was sitting in a squad car. Only this time I was graced with the front seat and appropriate door holding. Exhausted as I was, the possibility of finding new information out about Marnie gave me new energy and I was glad to tag along.

We turned left on Lake, toward Sheridan Road and the city of Chicago. "Mind if we turn on the radio?" I asked. I'd done enough talking, and my mind needed a rest.

"Sure." He switched on the radio,

"I'm your private dancer, a dancer for money. I'll do what you want me to do. I'm your private dancer, a dancer for money. And any old music will do." Tina Turner's raspy voice painfully filled the car.

The irony was too profound. Sergeant Kelly and I glanced at each other, and I reached over and turned the radio off, and then we both looked straight ahead.

"Did you know Mark Knopfler wrote that originally for Dire Straits?" I said.

"Nope."

The idea of 'sex for money' made it sound like a clear-cut barter proposition, an even trade where both parties benefited—but that was hardly the case. I am sure that for Marnie, or any sex worker, it was rape, every time. And now it seemed I was accepting the obvious about her.

Many women, down on their luck, thought if Julia Roberts' character in *Pretty Woman* could find Prince Charming by sleeping with rich men, then so could they. All this made me shiver with grief and sadness for my friend and anybody else who believed that bullshit. But Mark Knopfler had it right. For a guy I'm not sure how he knew this so well, but he was right, and Tina did this song justice.

We took the elevator to the basement of a nondescript building on Clinton Street away from the glitter of the Loop. It was clean and cold. A strong odor filled the air. After high school biology you never forget that formaldehyde smell. It permeated the air. In this era of new discoveries, I couldn't imagine they were still using that awful stuff. Maybe the smell had just seeped into the walls from years ago. There was also the familiar clean smell of bleach that seemed to make it all right some how. Bleach made things clean in this cold, cold place that was all about death.

"Morgue?" I wrinkled my nose.

"Just passed it." Patrick said. "In there are poor schleps down on their luck. Dead from drugs, accidents, and gunshot wounds; homeless body after homeless body piled up with a numbered tag on their toe." He pointed down another hallway. "Forensics is to the left."

"The others, the more regular folks who die a more civilized death, go right from the hospital to the funeral home. They have loved ones crying or praying, or maybe mad as hell. But the ones lined up behind that wall—well, probably not too many people are crying for them."

We walked from office to office, listening to different technicians who said the same thing. The DNA wouldn't be back for days and they had lots of cases in front of this one.

"Sergeant, all we have is a crime scene—no body, no weapon, hard to know too much this early," the last technician said, as he shook Sergeant Kelly's hand and gave me a nod. With no new information we turned to walk back down the formaldehyde-bleach hallway.

"So, since there's no dead body, this isn't a priority," I said, more as fact than question.

"Something like that," Sergeant Kelly said. "Given her past, there's nothing to say that she didn't stab someone who got away, and she has just disappeared."

"Marnie wouldn't leave Max. Whatever else she might be, she's a devoted mom."

"But she has left him, hasn't she?"

I couldn't argue with him there. We drove back to the police station in silence.

"I'm sure I will see you again, Sergeant Kelly. Here's *my* card. Not that you need it since you seem to know a lot about me already. But, if you hear anything, I'd appreciate a call."

"Shep," he said as I opened the car door ready to be away from all this, "I'll start the paper work for missing persons. Are you sure she has no living relatives except for Max?"

I shook my head. "I don't think so. But honestly, I guess I don't really know."

CHAPTER 6

I was nervous. I felt dirty and crazy. I hated this feeling and the best prescription for me was to go for a run along Lake Michigan and get my body to stop shaking from the inside out. After a few minutes of running, beads of sweat dripped off my forehead and I headed for the lighthouse.

Surprising myself, I turned left at Foster Beach toward Marnie's townhouse instead of taking my usual path north toward Northwestern University.

Ducking under the yellow-and-black crime scene tape strung across the entrance, I walked up the drive and checked under the blue enamel flowerpot next to the back steps, and there was the extra key, right where it belonged. That felt good. At least something was in its right place.

I wanted to get this over with and be home and relaxed when Max got back from camp. I didn't have a lot of time to play detective so, I thought to myself, the basement might have some good information.

Marnie hated basements so much she had a washer and dryer installed in the kitchen pantry on the main floor. Once in a while she'd send me down here for something or other, but that had been a while ago. I'd never known Marnie to ever go into the basement herself.

Making my way down the dark stairs there was another smell, besides that dank old basement moldy smell. This smell was crisp, fresh and out-of-place, and I'd never noticed it before.

As usual there was a pile of mismatched, lopsided boxes, all softened by basement-dampness, and labeled in black marker in a bold hand—*books, baby clothes, journals, maternity, toys*, and the like. Marnie would never come down to get anything. Once a box landed in the basement that was the end of it. Still, she never seemed to throw things out. Marnie saved everything, *just in case.*

On the opposite wall, across from all the abandoned cardboard boxes, were wooden crates all neatly arranged on those expensive, heavy metal shelving units you see in professional kitchens. The wood was new and that was the smell I hadn't noticed before.

I couldn't read the writing on the crates, but I was pretty sure it was Latin or Italian. The whole setup looked fishy. I was positive that whatever was in these boxes, it didn't belong to Marnie. She'd said she was going to night school but, to my knowledge, she wasn't taking any languages except English, which was hard enough for her since she'd hardly ever gone to school.

After what I learned this afternoon, it was obvious that all those evenings I was watching Max and thought she was in class, she probably wasn't. My cheeks flushed hot. The boxes were locked, so I couldn't check the contents.

I went upstairs to the kitchen. Obviously the investigative unit had dusted for fingerprints. Graphite was brushed all over everything, revealing lots of fingerprints, but whose? And why graphite? I thought they used those little pieces of tape, or digital imaging to pick up prints these days.

The blood on the floor and walls now had a web of white strings going from one spot to the other and then tacked in place. It looked like some eighth grade science project. As I followed the strings, I could see what officers were trying to do. The spatters didn't look as if they were coming from one direction, nor were they just on one side of the kitchen. Connect the dots? And it sure looked like a lot less blood than it had last night.

It was hard to tell what they were looking for, or what these strings meant, but I bet it had to do with trajectory and number of participants, and who got cut. Arteries spurt bright red blood and the victim could die if not attended to quickly. Cut veins tend to pool, and the blood is darker. That much I knew from being on call at the ER. There was not a lot of spurting blood here, but someone was cut. That was for sure. Maybe this kind of investigation could help determine the kinds of weapons used. While it was a fool's errand, my money was on kitchen knives.

Last night, I hadn't gone upstairs since getting Max was my priority. Now I avoided the web of strings and went up the back kitchen stairs two at a time.

Everything on the second floor looked pretty normal except that the sheets and blankets were thrown back from both sides of the bed. Maybe Marnie had a boyfriend I was unaware of, but even if she did, Marnie had a hard and fast rule to never bring men to her house.

"For Max's sake," she'd said. Marnie wanted Max to have a good home life without all the "uncles" she'd had to put up with. The person on the other side of the bed couldn't have been Derek. There must have been someone else. She'd rather die than let Derek have sex with her. Or maybe she didn't let him. Maybe he just did what he wanted like she said. Maybe she did die.

The clock next to the bed read 4:30 p.m. I had to go. I hoped Marnie had been in bed with a great guy who was crazy in love with her. Or maybe Max had crawled in with her after a bad dream. But, wouldn't he have crawled out on her side? And I don't think Max would have thrown the covers back like that.

I heard voices out front. Sneaking down the back stairs, I closed the door to the basement just as I heard voices in the front of the house.

I stood there for a few minutes and caught my breath.

"We'll dust upstairs today and if it's warranted," I heard one of them say, "we'll get to the basement later."

Releasing my breath, I let myself out of the basement and locked the door behind me, hoping the investigators wouldn't look out the upstairs window to see me sneaking away. I put the key in my shorts pocket since I might need it again. No one would think I hadn't always had this key since I had the others to her house. Except for Marnie, of course, since, come to think of it, she'd asked for my basement key back not too long ago. Maybe that's because she was storing contraband in her basement and didn't want me snooping around. Or maybe she needed to lend the key to a repairperson. I'd believe anything at this point.

I jogged toward home and felt my own demons chasing me. Instead of endorphins coming to relax me, the adrenaline rush from almost being discovered by the cops was kicking my butt in more ways than one.

For the right or the wrong of it, part of becoming a pastor had been about getting free from the craziness—literally and figuratively. My family of origin was hard to predict. Bigger question was why did I turn to seminary and Marnie to the streets? At times like these, when my bad memories resurface uninvited, like reruns of a bad movie I can't turn off, I know I am in trouble. The memories start slow, like a migraine, and once they start I am in for the duration.

Marnie's disappearance brought back memories I wanted buried and forgotten. "Stuff like this never goes away," my spiritual director had told me. "It lives submerged in the recesses of the psyche and can reappear when you are under stress." Intellectually, I knew about the posttraumatic stress that lived in the ganglia of my brain. When it slipped back to torture me, I was at its mercy and it had to run its course.

Exercise helped, but the stress of the last few days had left me wide open to demons. Running past Sheridan Square and into my gate, I was grateful to be home and I realized for the first time that Marnie must have experienced this kind of thing with great regularity. I ran into the bathroom and threw up.

CHAPTER 7

Fifteen years ago my grandmother hired Crystal and Rupert Bristow and set up a perpetual trust that would pay them as long as they were living at Woodstone. I wasn't privy to Livy's finances, but now money was deposited into my account every month for expenses.

Rupert and Crystal were a perfect couple in a strange sort of way. Childless, they poured their love and devotion into Livy. This came easy for Rupert. He often said he respected love as an intellectual construct, but his real goal, short of really knowing what absolute love was, was to take care of people who needed him. The only thing Livy thought was wrong with Crystal and Rupert was that they couldn't grow a thing. Not flowers, vegetables, or even babies. When Livy died, the mansion was well taken care of, but the greenhouse and the gardens died with her; and these were my first and top priority. I enjoyed studying her detailed plans and getting things back the way my grandmother had them outlined in her notebooks. Sort of made me feel closer to her.

When I'd moved into Woodstone, it was in perfect shape. If Rupert didn't have a green thumb, he compensated with the magic he worked on the building. Brass handles on the tub and sink in the bathrooms were always polished and shiny; any rotten windowsill or warped floorboard was always exquisitely replicated. Rupert could even sew. But he couldn't tell a daisy from a gardenia and he didn't care.

My biggest decision about making changes to the house was to modernize the kitchen without losing its charm and to add another bathroom. I didn't want to drag greenhouse dirt upstairs, so a convenient shower right inside the kitchen door made the house perfect. Even if there are already six bathrooms at Woodstone, this made sense to me. Each of the six, now seven, bathrooms has a thick terrycloth robe hanging behind the door. Nice touch, Grandma, I thought as I got out of the shower and grabbed the bathrobe.

After making a cup of tea, I went to sit in the library while I waited for Max. It was easy to get lost in this cozy room of elegantly carved built-in bookshelves and cabinets. Livy had kept a little TV in here, hidden behind a carved cupboard door. I switched on the news. The local station was reporting a fire on Sheridan Road, a mile south of the mansion, not too far from St. Mary's church and the daycare center. With the fire, traffic would be tied up for miles and I was sure now they'd be late. I turned off the

TV and leaned my head on the cool, dark red leather of my favorite wing chair, closed my eyes and slept.

Max woke me up with a hug and a sloppy kiss but it lacked his usual enthusiasm. I was grateful for the interruption from my panicky dreams about Marnie. After the requisite hugging, Max curled up in my lap and stared out the window.

"Hey, buddy, how was your day?" I asked. He shrugged his shoulders and gave me that look only a six-year-old can manage, like *what do you think my day was like?*

"Right, stupid question."

"Mama Shep?"

"Yes, dear?"

"We don't say *stupid*."

"Right, honey, you're right, sorry. How about getting some dinner. Are you hungry?"

Rupert had already slipped out of the house, but not before he had set out a big veggie salad for me and rustled up a kid-friendly dinner for Max. A note next to my bowl said, *I'm having dinner with Crystal. See you later.* Max and I ate in silence, which was unusual for us.

"How's dinner?" I attempted. "That *macrioni* looks good."

Max gave me a bored look, as if I were talking beneath him. "It's mac*aroni*."

"Well, smart stuff, that's what you used to call it before you were such an eloquent speaker. Macrioni."

"What does eloquent mean?"

"Very classy-talking, with a lot of style."

He wrinkled up his face and shrugged. "Can I watch TV?" Now this was my old Max, trying to get something he knew he wasn't supposed to have. He loved to play two-ends-against-the-middle when it came to Marnie, the rules, and me. He also knew there was no TV after dinner, only a bath and books.

"Max, TV time is on Saturday, day after tomorrow, right?"

He smiled at me for the first time that day as we headed upstairs.

Max collected toys for his bath that included some of his action figures, alphabet letters that stick on the wall, and his collection of various sized rubber duckies. And I drew his bath.

"I've got this, Mama Shep," he said, tossing his cache into the warm water. "I'll call you if I need you."

I went to lie down, and I could hear him talking to his toys. It was all toy-talk; nothing revealing about yesterday seemed to come out. After a long soak he yelled, "Mama Shep, I'm ready for you to wash my hair." There was comfort in routine. He was trying to be chipper but he looked so sad. As Max stepped out of the tub, I wrapped him in a towel and started to dry him off.

"What happened to Mama? Where is she?"

"I don't know where she is, but I'm going to try and find her. Max?"

"Yes."

"Do you remember what happened last night?"

Tears started down his cheeks, "Mama left me."

"Who was she with?" I asked, even though I didn't want to make things worse for him.

"I don't know. They had hats on their face, the kind you wear when it's winter." He was sobbing.

"Honey, it's going to fine. We'll find her. I know it's hard. Can you remember anything else?"

"She was crying. She told me to be very quiet and hide until you came."

"And you did a really good job at that. If you think of anything else, will you tell me?"

"Okay, Mama Shep. Mama Shep?"

"What honey?"

"I love you."

"I love you, too."

Sitting on the tile floor in that big bathroom, with those little arms sticking out of that huge towel wrapped around his body, Max leaned against me and sobbed, and I cried with him.

"Let's get ready for bed and find a book to read. I think we've cried enough for tonight. But Max," I said, looking at his sad little face, "I want you to know that crying about stuff like this is a good thing." He, of course, didn't know what I was talking about. For a six-year-old, when it is time to cry you cry, you don't think about whether it is a good thing or not.

"Mama Shep, can I sleep in your big bed tonight?"

"Sure honey."

It had been a long day for both of us. With his head on my shoulder and our arms wrapped around each other, we finally got some sleep.

~~~

Crystal picked up Max at 8:30 a.m., the following morning on her way to day camp. "He hasn't eaten much," I said, feeling a little guilty.

She nodded, "They'll have breakfast at the church."

Kneeling down to give Max a hug, I said, "Tonight you and Rupert are doing something together. I think you're going to the movies."

I glanced at Crystal, who said, "That's right, you lucky guy," as she ruffled his hair.
~~~

"By the way, that fire yesterday? It was in the basement of one of the priest's residents over on Albion, near our center. I'm sure I'll hear more about it at work. Bye. See you later. Come on Max, let's go or we'll be late." They headed for the door, hand in hand.

Crystal and I were both pretending everything was fine. It was curious she'd mentioned the fire last night. Lingering over my oatmeal and blueberries, my mind wandered to the bits of information I had so far, but I couldn't seem to find any thread to pull it all together.

Greenhouse work was the best therapy. It was time to get back to the flowers and leave investigating to the professionals, but before I could get my coveralls on, my home phone rang.

"Reverend Murdoch, this is Sergeant Kelly. I hear you've been doing a little sleuthing on your own."

I was glad he couldn't see me blushing. *Busted*, as Max would say.

"And good morning to you, Sergeant Kelly."

"I'm not going to beat around the bush. We need to talk. I'll be at your place at noon. And by the way, why haven't you been answering your phone?"

"What are you talking about? I just answered the phone."

"Don't you have a cell phone?"

"Lost it. And really what concern is that of yours?"

"Got it. I'll see you in a few hours and just so you know, I don't eat fish or most vegetables, other than a green salad every now and again. Usually I don't eat with someone unless I know them, but you have friends I trust and I am starving."

"So an exception is being made?" My voice was hard. "Well, how kind of you. If I didn't know better, Sergeant, I'd think this was a social call."

"Think what you want."

"Isn't the word *trust* an oxymoron for a cop? I mean where would you be if—"

"I'll see you in a few hours," he said, cutting me off. "And maybe you need to stay home this morning and not go running up and down the lakefront or delivering potted plants to little old ladies. I'll be there at noon." And at that he hung up.

What! Who did this jerk think he was, inviting himself for lunch and giving me orders? Why didn't I just tell him to go to hell and forget the good Sergeant? But I was getting more curious about this guy. Plus, he was the only possible help I might have in finding Marnie.

I pulled on electric blue coveralls and went looking for Rupert. I knew I'd find him in the greenhouse. He'd said he was going to fix those few panes of glass that cracked after a tree limb fell in the last storm. My plan for today had been to repot baskets for my front porch and get the Presbyterian Home deliveries ready. Every time I had a new crop of flowers come into bloom, like these fabulous gloxinias, I gave most of them away to neighbors and folks in nursing homes, but how'd Kelly known that?

"Rupert, you know everybody around here. What do you know about a Patrick Kelly?"

"Lots of Kellys, this *is* Chicago. Second largest population of Irish illegals—"

"Next to Boston. I know. This Kelly is an Evanston cop."

"Oh, *that* Kelly. I know him. Why?"

"He invited himself to lunch. Says he doesn't eat fish or vegetables."

At that Rupert laughed. "Well, that's all you eat. Shall I make him a PB&J?"

"He'd deserve it," I said. "What do you know about him?"

"First Gulf, Marines, crack cop, honest. Divorced. We went to high school together."

"Well, isn't that a coincidence?"

"Like you said, I know everybody around here."

"Is that why the good sergeant seems to know more about me than I've told him?"

At that Rupert put down his glazing gun and got serious. "Missus, I never talks about you or yo' gran unless I be under a subpoena or tortured."

"Quit that, Rupert."

He continued his stare. "Sorry. It's just that the guy seems to know things about me, he's getting under my skin—I almost told him to fuck off. And when I start thinking like that, I'm way off my game."

"Pat and I have had our disagreements over the years, but he's a straight shooter. He knows I worked for your grandmother. And how does he know about you? Shit, girl, this is the 21st century. You used to be a regular item protesting for one bleeding heart cause or another. All he has to do is go to the great oracle and Google you."

"Right, sorry for snapping."

As he turned back to glazing windows, I went to the front of the greenhouse to check on the new African violet propagations and got lost in the beauty of good work.

"You know Rupert, if God had a smell, I think it would be like the inside of a greenhouse like this," I said, an hour later. He gave me his characteristic little wave, pointed at his watch and headed for the house.

After our interchange this morning Rupert was being more cool than usual. He was more than a handyman, he was a chef extraordinaire, and most important he was my friend and confidant, but when he was mad he did his best to remain silent. I don't know how I'd manage without Rupert, but I was pretty sure that underneath all that control he had a dark side I didn't want to see.

I knew Rupert went in the house to make lunch, as ordered, and I kept planting hanging baskets. There would be no dressing the part today. No more pretenses. For Patrick Kelly from County Cork with the sparkly eyes and great hands.

CHAPTER 8

"Morning Shep," Sergeant Kelly said, ducking down to get his 6'3" rugged-looking self through the short door of the greenhouse, "Rupert said I could find you in here."

"Reverend Murdoch to you, Sergeant Kelly."

"Testy aren't we?"

The stress was getting to me. All of a sudden my semi-tranquil, well-managed life was turning in on itself. Now, this cop who'd interrogated me yesterday, is coming for lunch and telling me how to manage my time.

"You're right. Come on in. I'm forgetting my manners. This has been tough. I'm not myself, or maybe too much myself. Would you like a look around the greenhouse?"

"Maybe another time. I'm on my lunch break and I thought we should talk about your friends disappearance before you get yourself into trouble."

"Well, Sergeant Kelly, let me at least wash up and we'll have that lunch you ordered."

"Patrick."

"Good saint to be named after. I like St. Patrick, even though he was English and went to Ireland to save the heathens. And of course it was the English who were the real snakes, isn't that right?"

"Something like that," he said.

Now I prayed for help, or maybe instead of a prayer, I needed two fingers of Redbreast. Might help civilize me quicker, but I never drink whiskey, or much of anything else in the light of day. "I'll just be a minute." I washed my hands in the work sink by the door, climbed out of the overalls, down to a tank top and shorts, and started toward the house. Well, one couldn't call it a house—it was so much more than just a house. I wasn't used to living in anything bigger than what my mother called a Mayor-Daley-bungalow, and this was definitely not that.

Entering the newly reconstructed kitchen, feng shuied by my daughter on her last Christmas trip, the illusive Rupert was nowhere to be seen, but he'd put a wonderful lunch on the table.

"Forensics has a bit of news." Patrick sat in front of the huge sloppy hamburger. "But it's hard to tell if fingerprints are from the night Marnie disappeared or older. Blood samples indicate we are looking at two, maybe three people. There isn't enough evidence to presume there's been a murder yet so this is moot, don't worry. They rushed it because I asked, but I am not sure this information has helped much."

"Sergeant Kelly, please don't pat my hand and say 'don't worry,' I hate that. Yesterday you said this isn't something you're putting much effort in—what happened to change that?"

"Note to self, she hates it when someone says 'don't worry.' And you're right, there doesn't seem to be much official interest in finding your friend, at least not yet." He had such an engaging expression on his face it was hard to dislike him, even if he was a cop.

Rupert had made me a big green salad dressed with Meyer's lemon olive oil and red apple balsamic vinegar, topped with grilled organic chicken breast marinated in something yummy.

"Great burger."

"Yah. I keep that crap on hand for you red-meat types."

"Hey, cut me some slack." He put the burger down and wiped his hands with a napkin. "I like you, and for some stupid reason I want to help. I'm here, even if it's against my better judgment. Besides, I love being around a damsel in distress. Aren't you going to eat?"

The twinkle in his eyes made me laugh, "I'll ignore the damsel remark for now since some help is better than no help. I'll eat eventually. What else have you learned?"

"Still more questions than answers. I was wondering did Marnie have any friends, or a regular visitor?"

"Not to my knowledge. I've wondered if there was a guy in her life, but she never talked about it. Maybe this Derek Johnson was jealous, seeking revenge or money. Could be that simple. Lots of folks are killed by a jealous lover."

Since he was back to wolfing down his burger, wiping his chin along the way, I kept talking, "But really, to my knowledge Derek never came around."

"He got out of jail last week."

"Really? Well, that can't be a coincidence. I do know that Marnie wasn't one to have boyfriends at the house. She'd go out from time to time, but foolish me, I thought those were dates. It never crossed my mind she was, well, doing something else.

"Besides school, Marnie went out only once or twice a month at best. She kept that part of her life pretty secret, obviously. But, from my vantage point she was home more often than not."

"That's good, with the boy and all. How's he doing by the way?"

"Sad. He chatted a bit last night and said the men were wearing ski masks. I was going to call you with that, but I figured that's not all that helpful. Coffee?"

"How about tea, with caffeine?"

Now I laughed, "At least you don't fit the black-coffee-cop stereotype. How about some Barry's Red—I think it's the best black Irish tea I can find stateside."

"That'd be great."

Kelly was finishing his lunch when his cell phone played *Four Green Fields.*

"I'll get there when I get there," he growled to whoever was calling.

"I hate this thing, but it saves lives. Got any milk?" He asked, stirring sugar into his tea. "Shep," he said, leaning forward, "we can do this one of two ways. As friends—together—or me alone. But you can't be doing this *on your own.*"

"Why do you want to work with me? I'm a green-thumb retired pastor and a pacifist to boot—and friends, we hardly know each other. Isn't all this against regulations?"

"Yes and no. You know a lot about Marnie, and you want to help. It appears you are going to follow your nose no matter what I say. So, do we have a deal? We do this together?"

"I still don't know what that means."

"Can we talk more about this when I'm off duty? Like tomorrow night, for dinner?"

"Dinner?"

"Gotta pay you back for the great burger. We can go wherever you want." He put his napkin on the table and pushed back his chair.

I picked a classy, loud upscale Mexican restaurant. "Dinner, sure, Sergeant Kelly, Frontera Grill, on Clark, downtown, at what, 7 p.m.?"

"How about you call me, Patrick? Kelly is so formal," he said smiling.

"Patrick." I said, wondering what this would mean? Probably nothing.

He pushed the chair under the table, like a gentleman on his best behavior. "Great choice, I'll meet you there. We'll have lots of time to talk since the line is so long and they don't take reservations. I'll call you if anything new comes up. You, too?"

"Sure." I wondered if either of us meant it.

Patrick Kelly walked out of the kitchen door just as Rupert came back in. It was as if they'd planned it that way. Nodding to each other, they changed places at the back door.

"Hi, how ya doing?" Patrick asked.

"Good. You?"

"Good, thanks. Great burger. You always were a great cook."

"You ain't bad yourself."

Patrick backed his squad car out of the driveway, and Rupert was leaning against the doorway, cleaning his fingernails with his pocketknife, grinning.

"Rupert, you could have eaten with us."

"I had to get more glazing caulk at the hardware store. And they don't have the kind of glass we need for those last panes. I'll go to that glass place on Pulaski. How'd it go?"

"He didn't say much about the case. He said we had to *work together*, as friends, metaphorically of course, since we're hardly friends. He busted me for poking around at Marnie's yesterday, but not bad."

"What the hell, Shep. When were you going to tell me about this breaking and entering?"

"Oh, get real. I have keys, and so what if I keep looking for Marnie on my own? He'd what, lock me up?"

"I doubt it."

"Oh, knock that smile off your face. You're enjoying this too much. He'd have already figured I'd try anything I could think of to find her—so he's just trying to divide and conquer."

"Patrick's a good cop, one who still believes his first charge is to protect folks and keep them safe. That means keep you safe, too."

Squeezing Rupert's muscled arm, reddish brown from the summer sun, I said, "With the two of you worrywarts hovering around, how could anything happen to me?" He gave his signature wave and headed toward the greenhouse.

Back in the kitchen I made a cup of the same strong black Irish tea I'd served the good officer and turned on the kitchen computer. I had an idea on where to get some more information and maybe to find out more about finding Marnie. I clicked on, *Women's Shelters/Safe houses in Chicago/Northern Illinois.* It was a logical guess that Marnie'd gone to a local shelter or a safe house before I took her to Waukegan six years ago.

Fresh and clean, showered and dressed in blue jeans and a white pullover cotton sweater, I again went looking for Rupert, who wasn't too hard to find.

"I want to run something by you—windows look good by the way," I said, feeling a pang of guilt I wasn't attending to the greenhouse. "Are all the sprinklers and timers working yet?"

"Working on it," he said, as he came down the ladder. "Me first. I'm dying to practice my new profession as a mind reader. Let's see, Pat likes you, he's going to help find Marnie, and you are a bit interested in both ideas but too busy at the moment to find time to date with your new field work assignment as a first-time sleuth."

"Go on, Dr. Phil." I smiled back at him.

"No more. Really, just an astute observation."

"You know I can't sit still when there is something I might be able to do to help. When I first met Marnie, she'd admitted to going to a shelter. There are five around Chicago for abused women, so I'm going to go visit a few and ask questions. Then if you'll keep an eye on things tonight, I want to see Judith at the monastery and spend the night with the nuns."

"Say *hi* for me." Rupert and Judith had met once or twice. He kept his distance from religious types, except for me, and I didn't fit the mold.

"Of course, I'd rather go dig around in Marnie's basement, but I think the good Sergeant wouldn't approve, something about messing in police business. Instead, I'll do what I know and check out these shelters."

"Sure, no problem, we'd be happy to watch Max. I promised him a movie tonight anyway. Let me see your list. An old friend of mine works at one of those shelters." He glanced at the paper I handed him, "I think Pricilla works at Lydia's House in Uptown. I'm going to the glass place, in that direction. I'll stop in and see if I can learn anything."

"You know that place? I've never been there, but I met the director at a seminary lecture. It's a safe house for sex workers, not a shelter for battered women."

"You want me to check it out or not? Your call, you're the detective in training."

"Very funny, but sure, give it a try."

"You know Marnie would never leave Max unless she had to."

"Maybe they threatened to hurt the kid," Rupert said.

"Knowing we'd take care of Max, maybe Marnie felt she could take off with Derek, but this still doesn't sound right."

"Presuming it was Derek," he said in a quiet voice.

"Right. This reminds me of that old gag: I go in the back door and they go out the front. Rupert, am I being used?"

"By Marnie? Maybe. Hard to know what's up, but when you see Patrick again, tell him what you're thinking. You visit your list of shelters, and I'll see what Pricilla has to say. By the way, did you look into any dance clubs? That might be another place to look. Before you gasp at such an idea, I am out of here." Rupert said, smiling at me, "And for God's sake stay out of trouble."

CHAPTER 9

As I pulled up to the first woman's shelter on my list, I'd already decided that the only way to do this was to play it straight. I didn't have energy for games. I had a list of five shelters and lots of talking ahead of me, so why not use the direct approach?

The first shelter was nestled in a suburban neighborhood northwest of Chicago, and it was nothing fancy. It was an ordinary house on an ordinary street, but what went on inside was not ordinary. This was a place where they worked to help women and their children have some kind of a future. I wondered what their success rate was, or if they even knew.

There were no frills. Everything was donated—discarded by those who took the donations off their taxes. Nonetheless the place was homey.

I gave my name to the receptionist. Colorful children's drawings graced one wall and were the only decoration. Some were framed; some were just tacked up on the walls. It was as if the pictures needed to be looked at just a little longer before they were filed away where no one would ever see them again.

There were also a few photographs on the wall of women and men in suits, maybe contributors from a fundraiser or two. The minister in me thought maybe one or two might have even needed help themselves. "You need a reason to smile for a camera," I remember saying years ago to a friend trying to cheer me up after I'd landed in Chicago with two kids and no money. I knew how abuse took all the smiles away, sometimes forever, and there was no segment of the population that escaped this.

"How can I help you, Reverend Murdoch?" the director said, with an edge in her voice.

"I'm looking for some information on a woman who might have been here a while back. Maybe six or seven years ago, maybe pregnant at the time."

"You must know that all our files are confidential. They always have been, and now with the Health Insurance Portability and Accountability Act, doubly so. We can't reveal information without a warrant, and maybe not then either. I can't help you," she said, still standing by the door.

Me think she protesteth too much, I thought, as I was determined to forge ahead. "I guess I knew that, Ms...?"

"Doctor, Doctor Cassandra Anderson." In a perfunctory motion, she shook my hand while at the same time she checked her watch, a clear indication I was interfering with her day. "Kids are due back from swimming lessons any minute," she said, "I have to greet them when they come back."

"Sure. I'll make it short. I'm looking for Marnie Cooper." I watched her. The good doctor shook her head left to right. Looking over her reading glasses at me, as if I were stupid, she said, "I couldn't tell you if I knew anyone. I told you that." But had Dr. Anderson's eyes involuntarily bugged just a bit when I said Marnie's name, or was that my imagination?

"Name doesn't ring a bell, can't help you," she added, without missing a beat.

"Maybe I could jog your memory a second." She looked trapped but motioned with her hand for me to continue as she checked her watch again.

"Marnie's pretty granola—most of the time, an earth mother, gorgeous with or without makeup, a recent feminist type who'd go to any length to give her son the best food and current educational advantages she can afford. I bet she nursed him even longer than she admitted to."

"Marnie has chestnut hair, cropped short now, she mostly wears jeans, cotton T shirts and sandals, even in winter, and she has a body to die for. Well, I hope not actually die for. You'd remember her, Dr. Anderson." I started to choke up. "We're friends—she's disappeared, kidnapped perhaps, but I am not sure."

"She has children?" She seemed to soften around the edges.

"A boy. A terrific kid who's six going on ancient, a very old soul."

"Sorry," she said as if she meant it. "She's lucky to have a friend like you."

"I appreciate you talking about Marnie in the present tense. It is easy to see that you care for these families, Dr. Anderson, thanks for your time. I won't keep you any longer, but if you think of something, here is my card."

We watched the kids straggle down the hall, coming in from their swimming lesson. The receptionist came over and handed Dr. Anderson a piece of paper.

"Most of them don't know how to swim," Dr. Anderson said, glancing at the paper then nodding at the receptionist. "Living near Lake Michigan they need to learn. Red Cross and the local YWCA help us out."

As the kids walked by, hair still wet from the pool, any observer could see that there wasn't much joy in their faces. Dr. Anderson whispered, "Swimming lessons don't make up for living scared that someone is going to hurt you, or hurt your mom, but every little bit helps when people are trying to get their lives back." The concerned director shook my hand again, this time with more sincerity.

She was the consummate administrator, and I was glad I hadn't laughed when her receptionist scurried up to us again and handed me a packet of literature on the shelter. Dr. Anderson was waving at the children and shaking my free hand at the same time. Handshaking was perfunctory for her, as much a part of the job as protecting her clients.

"If you'd wait a minute, Reverend Murdoch, I'll give you a tour of the place." I was interested in her increased warmth and sudden change of heart.

"Dr. Anderson," I said, "I can see you have your hands full. Maybe another time."

Smiling too much, she filled my arms with more brochures that another woman had brought from around the corner. "You're Olivia Murdoch's granddaughter, aren't you?" She said, holding up the note. "We recently sent a grant application into the Murdoch Foundation."

"Oh, I'm sorry to disappoint you. I don't manage the foundation. I'm a fortunate beneficiary of my grandmother's generosity myself. I'll put in a good word if they ask."

Dr. Anderson stopped smiling so much. I could see she didn't believe me, but she should. I used to think I'd like to be a philanthropist and give money away to starving artists and single mothers. Now, I decidedly liked being a recipient myself, rather than answering all those pleas for money. If I had the money it would be hard for me to ever turn anyone down.

I backed out of the driveway and tried to figure out if I'd learned anything about Marnie from the appropriately tight-lipped Dr. Anderson. It was only when I'd mentioned Marnie's name that her eyes remotely showed some surprise, but that could just be my imagination at work. Nevertheless she was good. If Anderson knew Marnie, she wasn't saying.

I visited all five shelters on my list to no avail. The trail was cold. I hoped Rupert hadn't come up with anything either. Lydia's House wasn't a place I felt comfortable, even though I had been there for a fundraiser. It was a safe house for prostitutes. But I was probably living in la, la land. Whatever Marnie was, she was, and I loved her anyway.

CHAPTER 10

I'd had enough sleuthing for one day. Now I needed to go do some serious praying and let someone take care of me. As if on autopilot, I drove to the Benedictine Monastery outside the Chicago city limits and slipped into the sacristy just as evening prayer had begun.

Chanting hymns often helped me clear the unnecessary from the necessary.

I dipped my fingers in the perpetual baptismal font at the entrance of the chapel. The water felt so clean and fresh on my forehead as I crossed myself Catholic-style. Noticing there were only a few seats in the front row, I took a deep breath, bowed to the cross, sat down and began following the liturgy. My Benedictine sister friends would say nothing about my tardiness nor would they make eye contact until we were finished with the service.

As we chanted the refrain from Psalm 32, I wanted to empty out the events of the last few days and pour all my grief into prayer and music, to give it to God and let her take care of it. *Steadfast love surrounds those who trust in God.* The message was clear as I began to concentrate on the prayers and not my fears.

As prayers concluded, the others slowly left the intimate chapel, leaving the one red candle still lit as if for me alone. I stayed behind, and in the beauty of this holy place, I couldn't hold back the tears any longer.

Salty drops fell in my lap. Alone in the dusky light, with the waxy smell of snuffed out candles and lingering incense, I cried. It was as if I needed to purge myself to make more room in my heart for whatever was to come next.

Shit, hadn't I just done this crying stuff yesterday? This crying crap wasn't going away. Now, I was getting scared.

Sister Judith, my spiritual director, colleague and friend of many years, returned to the chapel and stood behind me. Putting her all-knowing hands on my shoulders, she comforted me with that gentle touch of hers. She stood behind me until my tears subsided.

Judith wasn't a touchy-feely type, but she was tender and she had a healing touch. Not saying a word, she moved around from where she had been standing, sat down in the seat next to me, and held my hand until I was calm.

"Shep, what is it?"

Judith had been my mother confessor, even though most Protestants don't have such things. She knew my mistakes, my junk, and she loved me in spite of myself.

"This isn't about me. My friend Marnie," I said, glad I could talk now without sobbing, "is missing, leaving behind her six-year-old son Max. There are no clues about what happened or where to find her."

"I've been going to women's shelters today looking for information. Everyone I talked with seemed like they knew her name without admitting it. How many shelters had she been to anyway? I think I'm coming apart. Yesterday, I had that awful memory about what happened with Jack, and now I am afraid it will start again when I least expect it."

Judith had been the person who'd helped me unravel my own shit. One day during spiritual direction she asked just the right question and, as if in a trance, I told her everything as I'd remembered it.

"Go ahead, tell me again," she said. "The more you talk, the less power the past will have over you. Let's go over it before it gets you at another time."

"Now? We'll miss dinner and I'm starving," I lied, laughing and trying to wiggle out of the inevitable encounter I must have known was coming the moment I pulled up the monastery drive and saw Judith's sturdy station wagon in the lot.

"We'll raid the refrigerator," she said. "Now tell me, what is starting again, which part?"

"How do you always say the right thing at the right time?"

"I've got lots of help." She nodded toward the beautiful wrought iron cross in the front of the chapel. This was such a great place. Even Jesus, from his obviously disadvantaged position on the cross, looked like he was trying to help me.

"Judith, you make me feel like I'm the most important person in the world."

"Right now, you are dear." She patted my hand. For not having any kids of her own, Judith was a great mother. With her hands around mine, I felt safer and more together than I was.

The sun was setting and it was getting dark. But the red eternal candle on the communion table in the front of the chapel stayed lit, day and night.

I told Sister Judith my story again, revealing myself to the only other person who knew what had happened to me all those years ago. Each time I started at another place and told a different part of the story. Each time she listened and assured me that this was all necessary.

"I don't see how going over this again will help me find Marnie," I said. But I knew Judith was right. Marnie's junk was creeping into me, and I was confusing her junk with my junk. As usual Judith was the wise one. It's always good to have someone around who's a little closer to God than you are.

"Shep, my dear sister, before you can help Marnie, you have to get out of your own way."

I trusted Judith would help me do that, but first I knew I had to go over the pain again and again until it was wrung out of me. Until I felt whole and clean.

"It was in February, and it had been a colder than usual winter."

"Instead of going to graduate school, as planned, I'd agreed to stay home with the kids for another year, on the condition that my husband would go to marriage counseling, which we did. But the marriage was getting worse, not better, and we were getting farther apart."

"Jack was brittle and meaner by the day, often slamming doors and hollering words like you-stupid-fucking-asshole to me and the kids."

"Therapy was good. I was making progress—I could feel it. You know what that's like when you emerge into the sun after being under a rock for so long? Trusting that therapy would bring us closer, I began to open up. Once a week he saw Mr. Dr. Hoffman and I saw Mrs. Dr. Hoffman. The following week we'd all meet together. At a joint session in early February, Dr. Hoffman looked my husband in the eye and said, *Jack, Betty and I have come to a few conclusions, and we'd like to push you a bit. We think Shep's made a major behavioral shift in her therapy and it behooves you to do the same.* Listening to that, I could hardly breathe. Then Betty asked me to tell Jack about my two little girls."

"Believing they knew what they were doing, I talked, in front of Jack, about what I had discovered working one-on-one with Betty."

"There's this photograph I showed you, the one of me pulling my cousin in a wagon. I'm tall and strong, with dark hair and a Dutch-boy haircut. In the wagon is a small-boned, ethereal looking girl with wispy blond hair and a faraway smile," I told him. I hesitated. "*Go on,*" Betty had said.

"I told him that I realized both girls were me. The soft side I don't like or trust is the wimp in the wagon. She's weak, small, and easily taken advantage of. But the other one is strong and capable of everything. Everything, including taking care of the weak one."

"I was proud of myself for merging the two. Betty said it was the wimp, as I called her, who sang and loved and trusted. The tomboy, on the other hand, was going to protect the weaker one and wasn't going to let her be too vulnerable or love too much."

"I was so pleased to have made the connection," I said. Judith and I sat in the silence for a few long moments; she knew I wasn't finished.

"We drove home after that session, and I could see that he was clouding over. He'd said he wasn't feeling well, that his back hurt."

"If there would be any way to get back to liking each other, or to making love again, I was all for it. But sex for me has to be a connecting place that's only possible when there's harmony, affection and love. Sorry about the sex stuff, Judith." I turned to look at her.

"I might not know much about sex, but I know about intimacy," Judith said.

"Right. So at that point I started to be afraid. I was trying not to be too worried, and hoped that being so transparent wasn't going to hurt me. But that metallic, scary taste of fear began to creep into my mouth. You know, like just before a situation is going to get bad and you can sense it? I don't have to go over all that part again, do I?" I asked her, as if I was a child seeking permission. We both knew I was done talking for now.

"You got more out this time." She smiled. "Soon you'll be done with it. Hungry?"

In the huge monastery kitchen, we raided the fridge and found yummy leftovers. Poached salmon with dill, a tossed salad, and fresh chocolate chip cookies just baked that afternoon.

As we ate, I told Sister Judith what had been happening the last two days. She patted my hand. "That's how it goes with post-traumatic stress. And it is why your demons paid you another visit. The more you attend to your demons, the less power they have over you. Now go to bed. You look terrible. I'll take care of the kitchen. And Shep?"

"Yes?"

"This, too, shall pass."

CHAPTER 11

The granite countertops and stainless steel appliances in my kitchen seemed opulent compared to the utilitarian facilities at the monastery. Nonetheless, the kitchen was my favorite room in the house. Maybe because, next to the new bathroom, the kitchen was the one thing I'd changed in my grandmother's house for myself. I just wish I had more time to cook.

On the counter was a drawing for me from Max. It was done with black crayon on big spongy, manila paper. It was a picture of a scary dragon with sharp pointy teeth, menacing eyes, and its head was very much out of proportion to its body. Then there was a person who looked like a little boy with a turtle shell on his back and a mask on his face that was pointing a long stick, what looked like a spear, at the heart of the dragon. What made the drawing so eerie was not the anger the picture conveyed, but the big red nasty looking triumphant smile on the boy's face. There was also a note from Crystal.

We're fine. There were a few tears, but we talked with him, read to him—he was better. We are off to the beach so prayers for the teachers are appreciated! We love you. Crystal

P.S. Rupert wants to see you.

Tonight, I would have to tell Crystal how much I appreciated her.

The light was flashing on my ancient answering machine indicating I had three messages. I pressed *Play* and flipped through the snail mail Rupert had left for me on the counter. First message was Sergeant Kelly confirming tonight's upcoming dinner date, which I'd already regretted agreeing to. The next two calls were hang-ups.

Feeling that sick, panicky feeling, I tried to catch my breath. Was that Marnie? Why didn't she leave a message? It was such a 'girl' thing—to think better of a call and hang up.

I called Kelly to report the calls and got his answering machine. "You have reached..."

I hung up without leaving a message and collapsed in a chair at the kitchen table just as Rupert walked in. "Hey, what's the matter?"

"I just got two hang-ups. Maybe it was Marnie. I called Kelly at the office, but he's not answering."

"Not much you can do except hope they call back. Guessing isn't worth much, but neither is wishful thinking. We'll do better with what we know."

I gave Rupert a dirty look, but he was right. Getting emotional was not productive.

"Speaking of knowing things, how'd it go yesterday?" Rupert asked, changing the subject.

"So, just the facts huh? No speculation, no emotional reaction? You ask a lot."

"Yup. About yesterday, what'd you find?" Rupert said, as he opened the refrigerator and took out brown farm eggs, butter, fresh veggies, cheese, and parsley – all organic.

"Omelet?" he smiled, trying to cheer me up. "I'll cook, you talk."

"Sounds good. I got a whole lot of nothing. Everyone was suspicious as soon as I started asking questions. They all were into their HIPAA privacy thing, a very convenient way to play dumb if you ask me. All I got was a few poppy eyes when I mentioned her name. Most seemed genuinely sorry they couldn't give me more information."

"Folks are protective of people they are trying to help. You should know that, being a minister and all." Rupert said, as he retrieved the cutting board from on top of the fridge.

"Right, that's why I thought I could get some information. But being a minister of any stripe doesn't carry the influence it used to. How about you? Was your friend helpful?" Watching him chop the vegetables, I felt useless. "Can I help? I'll chop anything but onions."

"I'm fine here." Rupert lined up asparagus spears and chopped them with the short, fast movements of a professional chef. "Well, unlike the shelters you visited, the girls at Lydia's didn't give a rip about privacy after my friend Priscilla introduced me. My hunch was right—a few of the girls know Marnie." He set down a glass of fresh-squeezed orange juice in front of me. "But you relax and listen to me. It isn't pretty."

"As long as there's food. You know I listen better with food." I smiled. "With you around I could forget how to cook," I added as Rupert beat the eggs.

"A few of the girls told me that they knew Marnie from the street—years ago. Said she was likable but had a few enemies too. I couldn't get any details. I'm guessing she's alive, and maybe held by people she knows. Survivors like her don't go belly up without a fight. By the way, one of the girls knew about your friendship with Marnie."

"What?"

"Good news travels, just a little slower than bad."

"What good news? You know, I never did find out how Marnie had heard about me in the first place—she just showed up."

"One of life's mysteries," Rupert said, finishing up the omelet.

"Many times I've kicked myself for getting so close to her. I have a soft spot for the wounded who want to make something of their lives in spite of the crap."

"Like you?" he asked, as he buttered an English muffin for me.

"I can do that," I said.

"What?"

"Butter my muffin."

"Guess I am overdoing it, sorry. Where were we?"

"We were at the part where you suggested that my interest in Marnie was some how self-serving. My question is why does she have friends who are in a safe house for sex workers? That is what they are, right?"

"Mostly, I guess." He put the finishing touches on the omelet, sprinkling it with chopped parsley and grated Parmesan cheese.

"Why would they want to be my friend? I never gave Marnie money or a place to live."

"People do what they do. Besides, you gave Marnie more than money. You gave her friendship."

"So, from what you learned yesterday, she kept in touch with these women after she had the baby?"

"That didn't come up, but a girl named Candy told me to tell you she'd be glad to take Marnie's place." He smiled. "Don't look so shocked. Any one of those girls would love a friend like you. Here's breakfast." He put the luscious veggie omelet and another buttered muffin in front of me and sat down across the table from me.

"*Women*, Rupert. Given what they've been through they are hardly girls, no matter what their age." I said, savoring the delicious food and trying not to eat too fast.

"*Women,* okay? But most of the hookers I've met over the years act more like young girls than *women*. When they want chips they don't buy a bag, they buy out the store. Just in case they don't have money in the future for chips. That kind of thing. "

"I wouldn't know. And I won't ask how you happened to meet them or know this stuff. Anyway, befriending the lot of them is out of the question. Remember what my grandmother said. I can have the mansion as long as I don't turn it into a home for wayward teens. I suspect that would include sex workers. So, at least for today, I'll follow this one rule and not invite them all home for lunch."

"Well, Ms. Prickly, these *women* dream everyday of having someone like you to care about them. They're injured and desperate. Including Marnie, they have all been in trouble up to their ass."

"Why would they know Marnie? Her abuser was her boyfriend, wasn't it? I don't see what this has to do with Marnie? Women who are tired of getting beat up go to all kinds of shelters. She must have met them at one of those."

Rupert looked at me, puzzled. "You aren't serious. You must be a more puritanical wishful thinker than I'd ever imagined. Pretty white to think all that."

"I admit the thought creeps in every now and then. But really, Sergeant Kelly told me there were no real or consequential arrests for Marnie. And just because she has a few aliases, it doesn't have to mean she is or *was* a sex worker."

"You might not be ready for this," Rupert said, as a pre-storm thunderclap rumbled through the sky. "Your granola-bar girlfriend has been taking money for tricks for some time. She was picked up off the street as a kid, maybe twelve, by some pimp creep named Rocky Lewand. That was a year or two after her mother had already initiated her into the life. Marnie moved her way up the ladder and was more successful than most, maybe because she avoided drugs, which is an anomaly in that business. She seemed to get free from hooking around the time she first talked with you—or she was under the radar. The girls—ah, women—didn't think she could do it, but thought she might have. She's like a folk hero for these women."

"Everyone was sad when I told them about her disappearance. Not just for Marnie but for themselves. If she'd beaten the life, so might they. She was a role model, until now."

"Rupert, how in the hell did you get all this? I got a millisecond of eye fluttering when I said her name, and you got the whole biography. Questionable as it might be."

"What can I say?" He smiled. "Guess I haven't lost the old charm! Besides, with your white-bread looks and seeming naïveté, they just didn't want to shock you."

"Are you telling me Marnie may have gotten away from all that crap right about the time she found out she was pregnant with Max?"

"Something like that."

"I admit, I guessed that was what she was doing when I'd met her, but I never asked. I didn't want to know—even at the first."

"Denial frees you up to believe what you want." Rupert cleared the table.

"I guess we can presume the pregnancy was the main motivator for not going back to the old way, but any success might not last long without love and support," I mused.

"Don't you think that's where you come in?"

"I guess. But if she was a sex worker, and I still hate the idea, she *has* stopped for six years. Six years is a long time. So why did they kidnap her?"

"For God's sake, what rock have you come crawling out of? How do you think she's paying her bills? You yourself saw her all dolled up that night. What do you think she was doing, going to play Mahjong with the girls?"

"Seeing her dressed to the nines once in six years doesn't make her—" I stopped. Marnie was dressed pretty wild the night I'd gone back to her house for a few of Max's things. "Could you be wrong?"

"Outside chance, but I'd bet the farm on it."

"Maybe what you're saying is true. That's what Kelly said the first time I talked with him. I hate this."

Rupert nodded as he loaded the dishwasher. "The girls said in the early days she used to drink too much, but, strangely, she had the reputation for never doing drugs. You can sort of feel good about that part. That's rare. Must have been awful in some ways for her, these women take drugs for a reason. It's all about survival."

"Right. I didn't want to believe she was selling her body, but that's me ignoring facts. Guess it's my ignorant-wishful-stupid-white-girl self that is thinking I could accept all this better if I thought she'd stopped. Any chance on that?"

"No. I doubt she quit. Not unless she hit the lotto or is doing other dirty stuff, which is always possible."

"Now *you're* guessing. Let's stick to facts." I smiled. I was surprised that I was ready to contemplate these possibilities when only a day earlier I was in total denial.

Rupert returned the smile as he washed the glasses that didn't go in the dishwasher. "This is tough for all of us. I love her too, in a way."

"I know. Thanks for the fabulous breakfast. Always tastes better when somebody else cooks. And you're right again, the morality monger in me was hoping for a different result."

"Speaking of morality, I got you something." He handed me a new cell phone.

"Thanks, but this is a waste. You know I'll just lose it."

Rupert nodded, pointing and wagging his finger at me. "Just until this is all resolved. I'll feel better knowing I can find you."

"Fair enough." I put the thing in my pocket and knew it would be another in my long line of lost cell phones.

"Non sequitur," he said, changing the subject, "I picked up the glass for those back panels in the greenhouse, and they are installed, glazing done and it all looks great. Now, I'm ready for the next thing on your list, which I think is to update that damned sprinkler system."

As he left the kitchen for the greenhouse, I went for my jogging clothes. This time I took my backpack and the key I had taken from Marnie's house two day ago. What was I forgetting as I continued my foray to the dark side? That big black flashlight under the sink would have to double for a bludgeon and a light saber in case I needed either.

It was a beautiful day for a run, but steaming hot already. The sun would be overhead by the time I finished, so *no lallygagging*, as my mother would say. Jogging up Sheridan Road past the cemetery, along Evanston's lakefront, and unlike last time, all my stress and tension seemed to fly off with every step. When I reached Marnie's house I was calmer than I'd been since the night she disappeared.

There were no cars parked near the house and that was strange unless they'd all just been towed. Street parking was limited so you could always see visitors coming and going. Parking tickets were a primary source of revenue for the City of Evanston. Plus this stretch near the beach was well monitored except that there were no cops cruising by at the moment. The yellow crime scene tape had been removed from around the house. Was forensics finished? Was this no longer a crime scene? Were Patrick and Rupert right, and this case is just about the disappearance of a sex worker who left her kid? And would they call this child endangerment and not kidnapping?

I fished around the waistband pocket of my running shorts for the key. That pocket was a nice convenience for runners or, in my case, burglars. I headed down the six exterior concrete stairs to the basement door. Bright red geraniums and glossy ivy in dark blue glazed pots sat just above me on the small porch by the kitchen door. Inside I waited for my eyes to adjust. My nose tickled from the basement's moldy smell, and I sneezed. I listened for noises but was pretty sure I was alone this time.

The wooden boxes looked untouched. Why hadn't the cops at least carted off a box or two? These boxes were out of place compared to the rest of the mess. This had something to do with why Marnie was taken, I was sure of it. The foreign words on the boxes reminded me again that I'd forgotten to call Father Sawyer. The other day I thought I'd seen a cardboard box off to the side marked "journals" in black magic marker. It had been sitting askew and right out in the open. The hefty wooden boxes seemed suspicious, and I don't think it had been this dark down here before. I dug around in my backpack for the flashlight and turned it on. Much better.

While I looked for the box of journals, I wondered who else, besides the cops, could be trying to find out what I wanted to know.

Then I saw the old cardboard box I was looking for, but it was set farther back than I'd remembered. The box was yellowed and softened by the moisture that seeps into everything in the basement of an old house. This time it was half covered with a musty old rose-patterned comforter like someone was trying to hide it but had to leave in a hurry. As I started to open the box—taped with that ubiquitous multi-purpose duct tape—I heard a creak, like an old floorboard or a door with a rusty hinge. I could have kicked myself for being so cavalier: the noises above made it clear that I wasn't alone.

Well, get smart Shepherd, and back yourself out the way you came in. Tonight, I'd tell Kelly my idea. I bet this box of journals or diaries would help get more information about what kind of trouble Marnie was in, and who might be out to hurt her.

I threw the comforter over the box and hoped my half-hearted attempt at camouflage would not make this box of interest to anyone else unless they'd already looked.

Leaving fast was out of the question. Now I heard more little sounds, like someone trying to sneak up on me, but I couldn't figure out from where. Was he in the kitchen and coming down the stairs, or were the noises outside?

Holding my breath, I inched toward the basement door, praying and admonishing myself at the same time. I had that heavy black flashlight in my hand, now turned off. My main goal was to get out of there in one piece.

Each step seemed to take an hour, opening the door slowly was agonizing. Then it was just up the steps to the outside. He was right in front of me, that cute stranger I'd seen from Kelly's police car the night Marnie disappeared. He must have come through the kitchen back door to meet me at the top of the basement steps. I recognized his face just as he started to swing what looked like a baseball bat.

Running toward the street, my heart was pounding. If I got out in the open where there was traffic, I knew I'd have a better chance of getting away. He was taller than me, lanky, and a good runner. I turned slightly. He was only a few feet away. I threw the flashlight, grazing his left cheek, just as he thwacked me hard below my left shoulder with the bat. As I fell, in slow motion, I thought I could feel him close to me. *What was that smell,* I wondered as I hit my head against one of the huge granite rocks that lined Marnie's long blacktopped driveway, *that old man smell?*

CHAPTER 12

Waking up in a tiny little cubicle in the emergency room at Evanston Hospital, I heard sounds of the monitoring equipment and saw a nurse fussing around me. As my eyes began to focus, three worried faces stared down at me.

"What happened?" I mumbled. My mouth felt like it was full of cotton and the pain was profound.

"You didn't come back from your run, so I went looking for you," Rupert said.

"Guess we aren't going to dinner, Patrick." I said, stating the obvious and wincing at the pain.

"Is it broken?" I asked Rupert, who was closest to me. He was still in those coveralls we both liked to wear in the greenhouse. He looked angry, and his eyebrows were knit together against the center of his brow. "Your head?"

he answered, "Yes, it's broken, Shepherd Mary Murdoch, stupid broken."

"Shut up." The pain in my arm was now beating time with my pulse, but my head felt like a train was running right through me. I didn't know if it hurt more to talk or listen.

"For God's sake, Rupert, go easy on her." Crystal leaned over me, smelling of fresh air. "He blames himself, Shep. You know Rupert. It's his way.

"Just in case you were wondering, Max is at the after camp program. I'll get him later." This was a long monologue from Crystal who preferred talking to children rather than adults.

"When can I get out of here?" I asked, trying to get oriented.

"You scared the crap out of us." Rupert patted my hand.

"Me, too." I said, and tried not to move. Patrick said nothing.

As the ER resident pulled the curtain open, my crew of friends listened and I closed my eyes, praying the doctors wouldn't keep me. Time was critical. People were getting desperate and doing stupid things.

"Reverend Murdock," the doctor started, "is it all right with you if your friends hear what I have to say?"

"What? Oh, you're doing that HIPPA thing. Sure they can hear it all."

"Your arm is seriously bruised but not broken, you have a slight concussion, you are somewhat sun burned, would have been worse if you hadn't used sunscreen, and you are dehydrated."

Turning to my band of worrywarts the doctor said, "We're giving fluids and we'll do a CT scan to double check the scope of her injuries. We need to keep her a few hours for observation. I don't think the scan will show much since she's regained consciousness and isn't throwing up. We'll give her something for pain," he rambled on in medical monotone, sounding bored, and ended with words I was pleased to hear: "We won't be admitting her."

There was a collective moan from Rupert, Crystal and Patrick.

"You were hoping they'd keep me. Is that so you could solve this case yourselves?" I asked, with my eyes still closed. "It's my left arm, not to worry. Nothing a few hours sleep and maybe a chocolate-covered donut won't cure. You've got to get it together. I'm fine. It just hurts."

The doctor smiled and said, "The pain will be better in a few days. The nurses say you're an on-call chaplain for the ER. Guess today the shoe is on the other foot." I nodded, as the doctor pulled the sick green-colored curtain aside and left the cubicle.

Patrick, who'd been standing back while Crystal and Rupert hovered, leaned toward me and touched my forehead with his fingertips. Even with the pain, that little touch felt so tender and genuine, I teared up.

"There's something I want you to do," I said, to no one in particular.

"She's back in charge," Patrick said, with a thin smile.

"Kelly, whatever made you think that wasn't true?" Rupert said angrily, responding to Patrick, but Rupert was looking right at me. "Flat on her back, on this hard-ass black plastic covered gurney, after being assaulted and lying in the heat for God knows how long, she's giving orders. There's no doubt here who's in charge here.

"As long as I'm at it," Rupert said turning to Patrick, "you'd better know with this woman, what you see is what you get. Like they say if you can't stand the heat man," Rupert paused, talking to Patrick but again looking at me, "get out of the fucking kitchen." Patrick's tender touch had not been lost on Rupert.

"Thanks for the vote of confidence, Rupert, but will you just calm down?" I said, as the nurse walked in with a syringe that I knew was for me "Hey, Birdie," I said, recognizing the nurse who often called me to the ER for some tragedy or other. She nodded, looking worried like the rest of them. "Would you wait with that for just a second?" I asked.

"Patrick," I said waving him closer to me. "The guy who hit me was the guy in the driveway the night Marnie disappeared. He smelled like an old-man smell. I can still smell it."

"That's enough, Reverend Murdoch, let's get you a little pain relief." Birdie said as she pushed the painkiller into the butterfly-contraption taped to the back of my hand. At first there was an uncomfortable cold, burning, stinging sensation that made me arch my back in pain, just before my hand and everything else started to go numb and I faded into that place where it still hurts but the drugs help you pretend it doesn't.

"Patrick, get the journals from her basement," I said, garbled at best.

"I can't do that," Patrick said, smiling. "It's against the law. Detectives got a box yesterday. It was diaries, girl stuff." Patrick gave the expected party line for a cop and shrugged.

"Rupert, you go." I was slurring my words. My audience was grinning, holding back giggles. Like when a child is talking gibberish and you don't want to laugh or hurt her feelings.

Patrick and Crystal walked toward the curtain to leave, but Rupert bent down and cocked his ear near me.

"It is a box in back." I concentrated on getting the words out. "Old comforter. Key pocket." My eyes were slits now and I knew I'd be sleeping hard soon. No longer in control, I tried to get the rest out before it all went black. "Pink flowers—" It was like a bad dream where you want to move but you can't.

Rupert squeezed my hand, "I'll be back in a few hours."

Finally back home, Crystal helped me upstairs and propped up the pillows in the huge cherry wood canopy bed my grandmother had shipped from England so many years ago. I slipped off my grimy running clothes as Crystal dropped the light cotton nightgown over my head. "Go home, get some sleep yourself." I said, carefully lying down on my good shoulder.

"I'm staying here tonight, for Max. I'll be close by." She blew a kiss.

"Crystal? Thanks."

She nodded, and left.

Sleep came easy at first, but it wasn't long before the pain woke me and caused me to toss and turn the rest of the night. My shoulder throbbed while the blood beat a rhythm of torture against my temples. My head hurt more from the painkiller after effects than from the lump on the back of my head. I hated pain. I believed that my survival depended on me staying in control. It was hard to be in pain and in control at the same time. Total oxymoron. But control and all those other things I learned to protect myself with were like necessary old friends and I depended on them. Especially in a crisis.

Ten years ago Sister Judith told me I had more defense mechanisms than anyone she'd ever met. I'd been stung by her frankness. "And," she'd said before I could object, "you needed every one of those things to survive. But maybe now you can begin to let go of them. One at a time."

"Is that possible?" I'd asked.

"It's like the choice-of-no-choice—change or keep living in misery. *For that which serves you too much can kill you in the long run.*"

Focusing my eyes across the room on the window that faced Lake Michigan, I could see it was another stunning morning. Trying to sit up, I felt the full impact of my injuries and sank back against the pillows into another fitful sleep.

Then, I smelled coffee.

As the door clicked closed, I knew it had been Rupert. He was a good mother. Next to my bed was a steaming cup of coffee, toast with jam and butter, that cell phone he'd bought me and Marnie's key. He must have dug through my clothes they'd shoved under the gurney at the ER and found the key. Good for Rupert.

Inching to a seated position with my good hand for support, I was glad Rupert wasn't there to watch me grimace. Sipping the steaming coffee with frothy milk and grated cinnamon, I saw Rupert had done what I'd asked. The box from Marnie's basement was next to my bed.

On my nightstand was a newish looking leather bound book that Rupert must have culled from the box. I took the towel that had covered the ice pack last night and laid it over the end of my bed so as not get the basement dust on my white comforter. I picked up the first few books and went to work.

Sitting cross-legged I prayed, "God of all great things, help me." Help me what? Find Marnie? Do your will? What was I praying for here? Sitting in silence I meditated and let my usual meditation words wash over me and calm my spirit. *Be still and know that I am God, be still and know that I am God ...* Repeating these words again, and again I could feel my heart slow down, and the pain start to subside just a bit.

Trusting my all-good-God to be with me made me feel stronger. The only problem was, I thought, I don't have a direct line to God, no matter what anyone thinks. *Be still and know that I am God ...*

God was at my shoulder, as she had been many times before, but that never prevented me from getting hurt or doing stupid things. At that I opened my eyes, said *amen* and meditation time was over.

The books next to the bed were in amazing shape for how old some of them seemed to be. Each was marked with a number, and they were stacked in numerical order. They all were blue leather with a gold filigree design around the cover. The pages were numbered and lined in light blue with pinkish red lines making columns. I started with the one Rupert had picked out, number 55.

In Marnie's handwriting were dates, numbers and dollar amounts. She seemed quite good at keeping records, maybe too good. If people knew about this, would one or more of these *numbers* want her dead? Or was this about something else besides turning tricks? Rupert thought she might be doing something else—selling drugs maybe? But this looked more sophisticated than selling weed to kids in the suburbs or meth addicts on the street. Nonetheless, Marnie was obviously deep into something secretive and crummy.

This was not what I expected. I'd been thinking these would be years of personal journals talking about the angst and pain of Marnie's life. Maybe that had been the box of "girl talk" diaries Patrick said the detectives got yesterday. I'm surprised they didn't get this one, but with a basement full of junky mildewed boxes, it would have taken them a while to find anything.

The only thing personal in these ledgers was an occasional hen-scratched word in the margins amplifying her feelings about a specific entry: "never again," "talker," "sweet," "boring," "dangerous." But most of the entries were just number identifiers and dollar amounts.

I couldn't decipher the numbering system. While I didn't want these to be drug dealers she worked with or tricks she'd turned, I was pretty sure they were something like that.

Some numbers repeated and others had only one notation. This couldn't have just been for Marnie. Maybe she kept track of others, too. God help me—a madam? No, I'd have noticed that, wouldn't I? Or am I just that naïve?

In each book it felt like there were too many clues to decipher. I felt like I was back at square one and lost in a maze at the same time. From what I could tell there must be another book—the key that gave names to go with these numbers. A book like that could explain everything. No one this detailed would have left these records without a key or a legend.

Picking up the last and oldest ledger, a torn picture of a skinny, beautiful Marnie fell out. On the back was written, "The Dream." There she was, thin as a rail in a simple red strapless dress and black high heels, her hair long to her waist. She must have been about sixteen. She looked both worldly wise and innocent at the same time, just like when I'd met her. Men are known to like a woman who knows a lot about sex but pretends she doesn't.

Once in a while, people cross your path and change your life. Marnie was one of those people. She and I had started to get acquainted the day she came to my greenhouse and asked for help. She was striking to look at, and I'd wanted to know all about her. I wanted to know how she stayed so strong and seemed to be secure, even though her background would indicate she should feel otherwise. Marnie made it easy to be her friend.

When we bumped into each other at the grocery store a few months after I'd taken her to the safe house in Waukegan, Marnie was very pregnant, and her cart was filled with fresh vegetables.

"Hi Marnie," I'd said, "looks like you're eating good these days."

"Oh, good to see you Rev. I saw the doctor and she said eat lots of vegetables so I needed to get some." I could tell from her cart that unless she was feeding a big family or knew how to freeze or can, most of the food she had in her cart would go to waste.

"I've been meaning to call you," she said. "I have a question."

"Shoot." I expected her to ask for another counseling session.

"Would you be my baby's godmother?"

I laughed out loud—not only out of surprise at her openness and candor but because I knew no good logical reason I should answer "yes" to her question.

"Don't you think you should interview me and find out if I'd make the right kind of godmother?"

Startled by the ragged sound of the land line ringing, I snapped back to reality and answered the phone—dropping the book on the floor.

"Hello?" Pain shot through my shoulder so hard it took my breath away. "Hello?" Nothing on the other end but light breathing. I knew I'd grabbed the phone before the caller ID had time to register the number.

On a hunch I said, "Max's fine." There was a short quick gasp on the other end of the line.

"Marnie?" I whispered, as who ever it was hung up and the phone went dead.

That sour taste was gathering in my throat. Oh, I was worried, sure, but suddenly I was getting pissed at

Marnie's total disregard for *my* life and *my* feelings. It was time to shift gears.

I jumped out of bed and winced at the sharp shooting pain in my arm. To hell with the pain, I thought, I needed to go to the greenhouse, to get flowers ready for the weekend, to breathe in the garden smells. It was almost time for the Evanston Art Fair, and I'd planned to have a booth on flower arranging.

My grandmother was known for her flower arrangements. She would donate marvelous collections of flowers to charity events, and I was hoping her reputation would continue to carry on through me. It was the least I could do for her. Besides, getting back to work would give me the break I needed from this cat-and-mouse game of *where's Marnie—who's Marnie?*

My heart was growing tired of this investigating shit. Next time I saw him I'd tell Patrick all my little bits of information and be done with it. I'd come clean, turn it over to him and give up. I didn't care who was in the other part of the torn photo, or when it was taken, or what the hell *the Dream* meant.

The new cell phone Rupert had gotten me yesterday for "emergencies" started playing "Take Me out to the Ball Game." It was, of course, Rupert, the only person who knew the number.

"Hey, Rupert it looks like you've been doing some breaking and entering of your own. Thanks. And how'd you avoid the troll with the baseball bat?"

"If he's as skinny as you say, he took one look at this buff bod and took a pass."

I smiled at the thought. Just by looking at Rupert you could see he'd win most skirmishes, especially with a punk kid who'd already pissed him off. "By the way, I gave this number to Pat just in case he needed to get in touch."

"Now it's Pat?"

"We go back—high school, we even enlisted together, the whole bit. I told you. We used to be tight. Will you just relax? Anyway, I've something to show you. Can you make it out to the greenhouse?"

"I hate when people tell me to relax. At least you didn't say, *don't worry* on top of it. I'll be out in a minute, there's no good reason to stay in bed. My arm and my head will hurt lying down or arranging flowers. Got another call coming in."

I clicked a button on the cell phone. "Hi there, this must be Patrick, before you say one word, I am in a foul mood and I am not responsible...for anything."

"Gotcha. You know, I was thinking, as I close in on retirement, I hate stuff like this. I like what makes sense right in front of me, like how many boxes of paper clips we need at the station for the next month. All that hotdogging about *who shot John* is for young cops full of idealism and faith in their ability to get the bad guy, with no thought that they'll ever get shot."

"Are you are in?" I asked, cutting the chase. At the moment I had no patience for small talk.

"Why not? I am beginning to think you have a point or two that makes this worth looking into. Besides, I like you."

"Please don't do this to do me any favors." I knew I was not being fair. I was mad at Marnie, not Patrick. But he was laughing

"Right, sorry. Look, I gotta go. How about we finish jousting later? Since we missed dinner last night I finagled reservations at Le Petite Gourmet. I'll pick you up at seven—after all, a girl's gotta eat. How about it?"

I hesitated. This quick fast date making stuff was not my style. I liked making a date a week in advance, think about it and usually canceling. But, I told myself, this was a little different. "Sure, but I'll meet you there."

"Ah, the fast getaway factor. Sure, no problem." He'd hung up before I could jump all over him again or wonder why I had said *yes* to dinner in the first place?

Hands down, Le Petite Gourmet was the best restaurant in Evanston. Usually it takes months to get in to Le Petite Gourmet, but maybe Patrick's job curries reservation favors. How could I resist the invitation? I hoped I'd have an appetite by evening. Admittedly, Sergeant Patrick Kelly was starting to grow on me, but the last thing in the world I wanted was a cop boyfriend.

CHAPTER 13

I struggled into my coveralls to go see what Rupert had for me. I was starting to hobble my way downstairs, and the damn landline started ringing again.

"Shep's Happy Home for Nuts," I answered, but regretted it right away. Again there was a dead silence, like the person on the other line was listening to me breathe but not breathing herself. I'd answered too fast again and she was gone. Like a little bird flitting around, brushing carelessly up against my soul, wanting me to brush up against hers. This time I wasn't angry at her, just sad. What a mess.

At least it wasn't Patrick on the phone telling me what to do. Yet, I was softening to this big soon-to-be-retired cop who wanted to take me to dinner. I wasn't making any sense, even to me, so my reactions couldn't have made sense to him either. Given my own ambivalence, he was doing pretty good hanging in there with me. But I wasn't sure I wanted him to.

Judith had been very blunt last week when she'd said, "Shep, you hate it when people complement you or attempt to take care of you, especially men."

"Well, sort of," I'd told her. "Sometimes I enjoy the attention and maybe the connection, I just can't stand feeling smothered and I always think it's coming. God forbid a guy leads me across the street by my elbow like I can't get across myself. He tries that, he's toast. TOAST." At that Judith had lost her professional cool and started laughing.

"You don't believe that. You're just missing the connections somewhere inside you that make that kind of attention feel good. Maybe you need to give your dates an instruction manual. You know, with directions like, 'When crossing the street be sure not to lead me away from traffic. I can handle it, and if I get hit by something, it's my own damn fault.'"

Surprised again by her frankness, I felt the need to defend myself. "Hey, I do appreciate help along the way, just not patronizing holier-than-thou chauvinist crap."

For some reason, I wasn't so cautious with Rupert, I thought, as I made my way downstairs to see what he wanted to show me.

"Here she comes," Rupert announced, and Max started yelling, "Surprise, Mama Shep! Happy Birthday to you. Surprise!"

The kitchen had been decorated with bunches of multi-colored balloons tied to the backs of chairs, kitchen cabinet handles and the refrigerator door. There were plates of grilled Wisconsin brats, that I knew were first boiled in beer, served on whole-wheat buns with grilled onions for the grownups, and plain hot dogs for Max. On the table there was also homemade potato salad, thick slices of watermelon and even a birthday cake.

"This is great, you guys. Thanks for the celebration but you know it's not..." At that I caught Crystal's eye as she pointed to Max. But Max didn't miss her gesture.

"It's a birthday party for you. My mom said we were going to give you a party for your birthday, so we're doing it today since you got your arm hurt."

Hugging Max with my good arm, I said, "This is the best birthday celebration ever. Thanks for helping me feel better little guy, but, honey, don't worry about my arm. It'll be fine in a few days. It just hurts, like I got hit hard with a baseball, a baseball bat, actually. Do me a favor and don't hug me on that side for a while. And pass the Dijon, would you?"

"Ow," he said in sympathy, rubbing his own shoulder. "Mama had big owies too. She fell down the stairs once when I was at school and got a black eye. Can I have another hot dog?"

I nodded as Rupert turned on the radio.

We let Max's comment about his mother slide. Nobody wanted to know what Max had seen, but at some point we'd have to get there. Soon there would be an interview with Max and DCFS. In fact, I was surprised they hadn't been here yet. Patrick said they'd call the next day. That was two days ago.

WXRT was playing Beatles songs all day, and Rupert picked up a carrot and started singing along with the radio. "I wanna hold your hand, I wanna hold your hand." Crystal and I joined in as Max put his hands over his ears. That got the three of us Beatles fans laughing until our sides hurt and tears ran down our cheeks. Max just shook his head like we were daft, but he was smiling. What a relief. My arm throbbed with pain from laughing but it was worth it.

Altogether Max polished off two hot dogs, a whole apple with peanut butter and a piece of Rupert's homemade German Chocolate cake before he said much again. "Mama Shep?"

"Yes, honey?"

"That mean guy who hurt my mommy was my dad, right?"

"I don't know, honey," I answered truthfully. "Max? Do you know the names of the men who were there that night?"

We held our breath trying to act natural as Max reached for some watermelon—he'd already eaten more in one meal than he'd eaten in total for the last two days.

"I couldn't see their faces because of the masks, but I think it was Derek and Earl. Mommy gets mad when they come over. She tells them to stay away like they said they would. They aren't very nice and there's always lots of yelling. Derek can't be my dad. He's too mean. I'm full. Can I watch TV? Is *Magic School Bus* on?"

I knew better than to ask more questions, "Sure honey, TV it is."

To hell with the rules.

CHAPTER 14

The valet had taken my Subaru Outback, and I decided to sit on the porch swing at the end of the long veranda in front of the restaurant and wait. Just as I sat down, Patrick pulled up, not in his squad car but behind the wheel of a little black RX7 that looked as spit polished as his shoes.

"Nice car, sir," I heard the valet say. Patrick nodded as he handed the valet his key.

Nodding at me, acknowledging my presence, I could hear Patrick lecture the young man about his car, "Young man, this is my baby. I expect you to be extra careful. And park it legal." The young man blushed and nodded his head. He looked pleased, to be the one to get to park the little black sports car. Patrick watched him drive away like an anxious papa, and then turned to walk the few steps to where I was sitting.

"So this is a side of you I haven't seen yet. Fancy sports car, stylish white summer linen suit. Looks good." I stood up.

"Let's start with the car," he said, as we walked toward the restaurant. "It's a 1993 Mazda RX7, only 1200 in the U.S. It goes 0-60 in 4.9 seconds. That hard-to-get-into chunk of metal is where I pour most of my spare cash. I don't drink much, don't smoke or do drugs, and I wear average clothes to work. I spend the rest of my money on books, concerts, travel and an occasional piece of art. You look surprised."

"I like surprises, but why lecture the valet?"

"That's just to forewarn him to get it right. You'd be surprised how many valets can't drive a stick, parallel park, or acknowledge 'permit only' signs."

"Got it."

This was good. I liked the idea that Patrick had more to him than the obvious cop persona. Tonight Patrick was chatty, maybe because we were talking about cars and not Marnie.

"Guess this is a date." He smiled, as he held the door for me.

Le Petite Gourmet is a beautiful place once you get into the restaurant itself. It was on the first floor of an old hotel where the upper levels have been turned into a retirement home for wealthy elderly gentlemen. Comparatively speaking, having a five star fancy restaurant on the first floor of an upscale nursing home for rich guys was kind of a disconnect, but somehow it worked.

A quiet gentleness awaited us as we walked in the door. The restaurant was small and elegant, with simple furnishings, white linen tablecloths and lots of fresh exotic flower arrangements. A few stunning watercolor paintings hung unobtrusively and were exquisitely lit.

The Maître d' brought the bottle of wine Patrick had ordered as we were seated. "I love a place that leaves you alone and still makes you feel like you're the most important person in the place!" I said to Patrick as my first glass of wine was relaxing me just a bit. "By rights I shouldn't be hungry. I had a big lunch. But what the hell, it was my birthday."

Patrick raised his eyebrows. "Your license says April. Aries, right?"

"Right. But now you're scaring me. Are you into astrology or checking up on me?"

He laughed. "A little of both, maybe."

"A cop into astrology? That can't play too well in the break room."

"You'd be surprised what plays well for cops. So, what about this birthday lunch?"

"Max decided I needed a birthday party since my arm hurt, so Rupert and Crystal obliged."

"I see. By the way, birthday girl or not, you look lovely."

"Thanks," I said, feeling a little unfocused. His look was a mixture of curiosity and surprise. "Sorry, I don't do complements well." I answered, as if he'd asked a question. "I never know quite what to say."

"*Thank you,* works just fine with me," he said.

It hadn't taken long to pick out my clothes for tonight. Having retired from ministry, I now felt I could wear clothes I hadn't dared wear for years. My close-fitting sleeveless black crepe dress and strappy high heels seemed perfect. I'd also brought my hot pink silk sweater for the air conditioning. Black is chic, but a girl has to be practical.

I felt a little bruised, but good. In the dimly lit room you couldn't see the dark purple patches on my arm from yesterday's encounter. Besides, I was looking forward to food that was touted to be some of the best in Chicago.

Patrick took a quick look around the room and seated me with my back to the bay windows and the door. This gave him the vantage point to watch who came and went in the restaurant.

"And they call *me* a control freak," I said.

"Goes with laying down my cloak so you don't get your feet muddy."

The rain earlier in the day had cooled things off, and the sunset was visible from the window behind me. I could see it from the reflection in the oval mirror, framed in an antique gold-leaf frame that hung on the wall behind Patrick. Big billowy clouds streaked with shades of color covered the horizon. The colors were an odd mix of purple and orange that reminded me of one of the haystack paintings by Monet that hung at the Art Institute of Chicago.

We talked about the weather and the beautiful restaurant as we made our way through the complex menu.

"I'm worried about Max," I finally said after we ran out of more pleasant things to say. "My gut tells me I should take him to my sisters' place."

"How many sisters do you have?" he asked with a surprised look on his face.

"Twelve. Benedictines into God, Lectio Divina and environmental good works. They have a fabulous retreat outside the city. They've taken in kids before. The day care center Max usually goes to closes for two weeks in August. Might be good for everybody if he has some fun."

"Guess it couldn't hurt." Patrick picked at his salad. "Could we leave this case alone, at least while we eat dinner? This kind of cop work is dangerous, seedy, boring as you wait for a break and, well, I confess, it makes me nervous. That's bad for a detective to be nervous."

"Sounds like you got shot."

"You don't slow down, do you?" He smiled as he took my hand for a moment and then gently let it go. "But you're right."

"So watching me walk into trouble these last few days can't make you happy. And please don't give me that damsel-in-distress business."

He wasn't drinking but instead twirling his wine in the perfectly blown goblet he held like an expert. "No, I was wrong about that part. I can see that." Pausing, he looked like he was going to make a joke, then he got serious.

"I was on a stakeout, missed a cue, got shot and my partner was killed. She was a great woman, a bit like you. That was five years ago, on Division Street near the Gold Coast, outside one of those clubs where drinks cost a fortune and the waiters are snorting cocaine in the storage room. When I got back in uniform, I gave up the Chicago checkerboard hat and moved over to a quasi-administrative job in Evanston. Now I only wear a uniform to fill in for the sick, wounded and vacationing. I'm still called detective, but it's just a courtesy, more than anything.

"Last week I was happy to give parking tickets, order supplies and count down my days to retirement. The night your friend Marnie disappeared, I was doing a double shift for a guy who had the flu. It's like a karma thing, I figure. Maybe I'm destined to make up for Gladys' death, but really I'm just not into this anymore. Worse kind of scenario is when a cop loses the itch to catch the bad guys and save the world. But here I am," He took a sip of the expensive Cabernet Sauvignon he'd ordered. "Oh, and as it goes, regardless of my looming retirement, the powers that be agreed to give me the case."

"Gotcha," I said, pleased with his openness, but I was used to folks confessing. "I do have a few things..."

"After dinner?" Patrick shifted in his chair, leaning closer towards me in a hesitant way, like he was being pulled toward me, then he sat back, looking a little more relaxed.

A young woman, maybe a Northwestern University music student ready to be discovered, started quietly playing jazz standards on the shiny black grand piano in the corner behind me, next to the windows. Patrick seemed to watch the door, the huge bay windows, me, *and* the lovely young chanteuse to his left, all at once, all without being too obvious. Even though it has been a rough few days, Patrick's attention made me feel safe and cared for, and he wasn't hovering, which I appreciated.

We chatted about little things—the fabulous menu, and bits and pieces of history from our past. Tonight there was no need for my usual food snobbery. Everything brought to our table by our well-mannered waiter was amazing, even if some of the courses were hard to recognize. It was impossible to figure out what each dish would taste like from the description on the menu, yet each course was a taste experience to savor and wonder about. The menu listed a host of small tantalizing dishes that had the ability to please both brain and senses.

All in all there were twenty-three different tastes in my dinner, including Pacific Sea Urchin with banana and parsnip milk, and Wild French Turbot served warm with ginger mussels, beer and green apple.

"Thought you didn't eat veggies and fish," I said.

"Well, not for lunch." He gave me that big smile I was beginning to fall for.

The in-between palate cleansers on the menu were Nugget of Mango and Spicy Yuzu. To finish it off there was coffee that could have come from one of those cafes along the Seine in Paris, thick and delicious with tiny chestnut-colored bubbles circling the inside of the cup. And who'd think a dessert called Chilled Moroccan Milk Soup would be stunning? But it was.

Nothing like a to-die-for-meal to take our minds off the last few days; but Marnie's case lurked in the background, no matter how relaxed we were getting.

"I'm going to the mademoiselle's room. Be right back." I could see he was a little nervous at letting me out of his sight, but he decided not to make a fuss. By now the place was almost empty, it was dark outside and the old-fashioned streetlights of Evanston were shining through the window. For some reason, we'd spent both the first and second seating leisurely eating and talking. No one disturbed us, and we still had a little time before the place closed for the night.

On the way back to the table I made a quick decision to do something I never do in public anymore. I asked the young woman at the piano for a favor, and she was happy to accommodate me. I'm sure the sizable tip I stuffed into the brandy snifter on the piano didn't hurt. I picked up the microphone and looked at Patrick, who was still concentrating his eyes on the door, and I started to sing. *I'm always chasing rainbows, watching clouds drifting by*, which was exactly how I was feeling at the moment.

I got lost in the gauzy, depressing music I loved so well and almost forgot where I was. The guy in the corner, who'd been there when we sat down, got up and headed for the door. He was leaving in the middle of the tune. How rude.

I'm always chasing rainbows, waiting to find a little bluebird, in vain.

Patrick had looked up as soon as I started to sing. But this didn't feel right. Maybe it was too soon to be singing to someone you didn't even want to like. Damn, there it was—that all-too-familiar feeling at the pit of my stomach that something could go very wrong if I even remotely tried love one more time.

Trying to shake off my foreboding I came back to the table. Patrick stood up and pulled out my chair. "Judy Garland," he whispered in my ear, giving me the chills that make one forget you ever had any good sense.

"Right," I said, with a coy smart-ass little look, trying to shrug off the conflicting emotions coming at me in a hurry. "You didn't know I could sing." I smiled. He turned to sit down. "But there are many things you—" I was interrupted by three sharp percussive pops that shattered the front window. Patrick grabbed my good arm and flung me to the floor as he drew his gun from inside his suit jacket and returned fire. Then it was quiet. Patrick clutched his chest. As fast as it started, it was over.

Two bullets looked as if they had embedded in the mahogany paneling just to the left of Patrick's ear, but the other one had hit him in the chest. Blood was spurting, but not lots of it. After those few seconds of violent noise, everything was quiet except for the strange sounds of night birds coming through the shattered window.

Patrick was conscious. People were scurrying around us, I leaned over to say something just as he whispered, "Never finished the coffee."

Shit, shit, shit. I meet a guy I could maybe like and he gets shot. I felt like I was moving in slow motion, as I ripped open his shirt. His chest was full of scars, maybe from Desert Storm or Chicago thugs—gang bangers of one ilk or another. Finding the wound, I applied as much pressure as I dared. I knew protocol was to contain the bleeding that was oozing, not spurting but my minimal training in first aid was failing me fast. I heard the Maître d' calling 911.

Our waiter and the piano player stood watching me with piles of napkins in their hands, whispering, gesturing and wanting to help somehow but not knowing what to do. Except for those two, plus the Maître d' and the busboy, we seemed to be the only ones left in the room. Then the well-dressed, bad-mannered man who'd left the restaurant when I was singing, came back, as if to see what had happened. He looked shaken, and left quickly out the front door.

"Glad it wasn't you," Patrick whispered. "That would have killed me." He managed a little pained smile as he closed his eyes. "Amateur."

PART II

CHAPTER 15

She felt like a fool. How stupid to think she could escape the inevitable. She couldn't remember what happened. Everything was hazy and she was cold.

Shackled to four corners of a bed in a windowless room, her wrists were cut and bleeding. If she moved, the pain was excruciating.

Touching her cheek to her shoulder, she could feel her clammy skin, cold like a dead body at a wake. She felt disconnected, like she was floating outside her body.

As compromised as her thinking was, she knew she was in deep trouble. Why had they stormed her house, and when was that, yesterday or three days ago? It was hard to concentrate, hard to remember what happened or why. She prided herself on having a good memory. She could usually keep most pertinent details straight in her head. This loss of memory frightened her more than the cold. She always figured if she could use her mind, think things through, use her memory to give herself the signals she needed—she'd survive. But she was never so stupid as to imagine she would thrive; that was for people who lived in the suburbs and had real parents.

~~~

After three hours of surgery to repair the damage that stubby bullet made to his insides, Patrick was hooked up to tubes and monitors in ICU, and he looked like hell. The bullet had missed his heart and lungs and exited his back without leaving a gaping hole. From the slim glass window in the door, I watched the team finish settling him in a small, efficient room in intensive care.

"There's nothing you can do here. I will stay with him, Ma'am," a young cop said as he came up behind me. Doctors, nurses and bevy of medical professionals, all with their own tasks to accomplish, arranged various tubes and machines and settled Patrick into their care for the night. And in the center of it, Rupert stood at the foot of the bed watching the face of his old friend.

"I'll call you if there are any changes," the young cop said. "We have your information."

"Thanks. I appreciate it. I'd stay, but tonight I gotta go."

I moved outside the cubicle, leaned my head against the wall and tried to think.

Rupert slipped out of Patrick's room and just about knocked me over. "Pat's in good hands, let's get out of here."
~~~

My teeth were chattering. I was cold and numb.

"Is Crystal with Max? The monitor isn't good enough, not after this."

"She's been with him all night." Rupert said.

"Reverend Murdoch, before you leave," the young cop said, holding a clipboard in his hand and his hat under his arm, "we want you to know that given the circumstances, we'll be watching your place tonight."

"Thank you, officer, I appreciate it, but I don't think anyone is coming after me. I don't lock my doors, much less set the security alarm. But thanks," I chattered.

"Besides your statement here, please be sure to call with anything you might think of." Looking at Patrick through the glass, the man said, more to himself than me, "He sure didn't deserve this. And he's so close to retirement."

"Thanks, Joe," Rupert interrupted. "I gotta get her home." He took my arm and led me down a too bright corridor, to his car parked in the emergency lot. I didn't protest.

"He didn't have a bullet proof vest on," I said, out of nowhere.

"Neither did you." Rupert opened the passenger door, and I slid in. His car smelled of greenhouse supplies—clean fresh dirt mixed with the smell of gasoline, and rotted manure. I jumped as Rupert closed the car door. All the sounds around me were loud and scratchy, echoing like fingernails scraping long and slow against a chalkboard inside my head.

Rupert started the engine of his ancient Volvo wagon, and I was assaulted by the high-pitched grinding sound of the gears, followed by the low rumbling of the engine.

"I need to do something. I have to get to those books of numbers you got from Marnie's basement. And the flowers for Presbyterian Home and the Evanston Garden Walk, they are already in bloom, aren't they? The flowers, they have to be taken care of.

"Oh Rupert, I held pressure on Patrick's chest. I tried to not panic. What is this all about? What's happening?"

Rupert nodded as I droned on.

"There are thousands of entries in those books. There has to be a book with names. I was going to talk to Patrick about this tonight but he asked me not to until..." My voice started to shake. "Until we finished our coffee." I cleared my throat, smoothed my bloody skirt and got control of my voice. "What if I'd..."

"No *what ifs* and no panic." Rupert interrupted. "Stop with the guilt. It won't help and no, you couldn't have prevented this."

"Right." I sucked in air and accepted his admonition. "The ambulance got there pretty quick. The fire station is on Greenleaf Avenue, just west of Hinman Street. Thank God. Why am I telling you all this, you know where it is. The EMT's crashed through the door, swept in like efficiency personified—took his vitals, slipped an IV butterfly into his vein, hooked up saline, antibiotics, morphine and wrapped him, in a white sheet, too tight, I think."

"Slow down, Shep," Rupert said. I nodded and concentrated on the road ahead, trying not to be unnerved by the thwapping of the car wheels on the pavement.

"One asked me, 'You want to ride in the ambulance Mrs. Kelly?' That made Patrick smile a tiny bit." I turned to look at Rupert, who was more serious than I'd seen him since Livy's funeral. Even with Marnie's disappearance he'd kept up that calm, balanced exterior he's famous for. But Patrick getting shot was unraveling even Rupert—who was usually the ultimate personification of cool.

"Shot in the chest, eyes closed, no color in his face and Patrick smiles."

Rupert continued to nod his head, as if he understood this scenario all too well.

"So, Patrick, in his best serious cop voice, says, 'She's going home.' The paramedics shrug and keep moving Patrick toward the ambulance. I knew he wouldn't want me to watch the hospital madness. Everything in Le Petite Gourmet was a blur. Glass everywhere and I had blood all over me, again. Patrick's this time.

"It got surreal when a bevy of cops and investigators arrived. I was shivering cold and somebody threw this coat around me." I looked down at a tweed men's sport coat that could have been from Patrick's detective wardrobe. "Maybe we can return it tomorrow?"

"Shock," Rupert said, as he pulled up in front of the kitchen entrance at Woodstone and parked the car. "The chattering, feeling cold, heightened auditory stimulus, feeling panicky—all shock."

"Right—shock, well that explains it. Thanks for veering me from self-pity's bottomless pit to logic. My God, what have I gotten myself into?" I looked at the dried blood under my fingernails.

"How'd you get to the hospital if you didn't go in the ambulance? Did you drive?"

"Oh," I said, embarrassed, "A minute after they wheeled Patrick out of the restaurant, the cops started asking me questions, and without thinking I ran across the lawn where the ambulance was tying up traffic. I couldn't let him go alone. That's against everything I do.

"Anyway, I got to him just as they collapsed the bottom of the gurney and loaded him into the ambulance. I jumped in, held his hand and prayed all the way to the hospital with the sirens going off. But by this time he wasn't talking."

"So your car is still in the valet lot?"

"His, too. Rupert, I know it isn't your thing, but can we pray for just a second?"

"Sure, go ahead." Rupert nodded his head and folded his hands like a young boy in Sunday School.

I closed my eyes and tried to settle myself, longing for grace to wash over me, but I felt none, none at all.

CHAPTER 16

From far away she began to hear voices. Someone was coming. Naked and tied spread-eagle to a bed, she knew there was no way to fight them off. Pretend to be asleep, she thought, like when Mother would bring a stranger home from the bar. "Good at pretending aren't you, my little liar," Mother had always said.

As a kid she didn't know what was the truth and what was a lie. But she always knew that disobeying her mother's orders had bad consequences.

"Turn that stupid thing off, you jerk." The voices were sharp and crisp now, and close.

"Hey man, what's Shana going to do, like hurt me or something?"

Kids. It sounded like they were coming downstairs. She must be in a basement. Her heart started to race. She couldn't stop the automatic panic that grasped at the inside of her belly and her throat at the same time. Awful things had happened to her in basements. Her mouth felt dry, and she tried to concentrate, pretend to be asleep but stay conscious.

"We're just supposed to check on her. And turn that off, I hate that nasty music. Nasty. Turn it off." They were close.

"Hey, I thought you liked music."

A metal grinding sound like a bolt sliding sideways to unlock the door confirmed her suspicions. "You're in for it now, you little shit. You deserve everything that's coming to you." Her mother's voice played over and over in her head. She couldn't shut her up. "Play dead, little liar."

~~~

I sent Crystal home, threw my bloodied party clothes in a pile on the floor and went zombie-like into the shower. This time I just stood in the granite double shower as the water fell all over me from all sides. I wanted each little drop of water to lick me clean. But no fancy-ass shower or even a tank of holy water blessed by Mother Teresa herself could clean off what happened tonight.

Each time I thought about Patrick lying on the floor of Le Petite Gourmet, my stomach dropped, my heart raced and I prayed my meditation words over and over: *Be still and know that I am God. Be still and...*I leaned my head against the shower wall and prayed whatever words I could think of. I prayed until the tension subsided and there were no more words, which was well after the water turned cold.
~~~

Without drying off, I grabbed the fluffy terry cloth robe off the hook next to the shower and trundled up the long staircase to my room.

It was two in the morning, but now it was my turn to make a phone call in the middle of the night. I dialed Sister Judith's private number.

"Yes, yes, yes, we'll be ready," was all she said; she didn't ask questions.

Then I called Rupert who, I supposed, had just sat down on that comfy couch in his small house just to the south of the mansion. "Rupert? I know you are tired, but I need you to do something. Will you take Max and Crystal to Judith at the monastery?

"Judith knows they're coming. They'll be safe there. Take Grandma's Bentley and wear that stupid hat. Patrick's shooter may know a lot more about me than we know about him, or her come to think about it, but very few people know about the Bentley, so take it. I suspect we're being watched by more than Evanston's finest, so wear the uniform, and hide Max and Crystal 'til you get out of the city."

"Shep, you better call the police and tell them a car will be leaving the property. This may not have anything to do with you or Marnie. Remember, Patrick was a detective for a long time. Cops in general have a boatload of enemies. We may never know who did this."

"That's a sad thought. I'll tell the cops you're leaving and I'm here. And thanks. Thanks for everything." I felt exhausted as the drop in adrenaline drained me.

"Good thing I've kept the grey beast in tip-top shape. Crystal can call the church and take off a few days. She can stay with Max. I'll be back in the morning."

"And Rupert, would you set the dreaded alarms? Shit, I hate those things, but I gotta sleep, and I can't be afraid someone's going to creep in on me."

Going into Max's room, my tiredness was replaced by waves of goodness. Max was a sound sleeper. He didn't flinch as I switched on the light and packed a bag of clothes, books and toys for him to take with him. Then I sat on the side of the bed and watched him sleep.

"We're here," Crystal whispered at the bedroom door. I jumped and gasped too loud. And this wasn't lost on Max.

"I'm tired," Max said, stirring at the noise.

"Hi honey," I said, rubbing his arm. "Rupert and Crystal are going to take you to see Sister Judith for a few days." I drew his warm little body onto my lap, rocking him back and forth.

"I'm tired...too bright," Max whined, covering his eyes.

"What are you talking about? You never like to sleep." I sat him up as Crystal dimmed the light, "Come on, buddy. Let's get going. You can even stay in your jammies."

"Sister Judith?" He squinted at me. "Really? I love Sister Judith. Did you know she has a lake in her backyard?" He was waking up now and getting excited about this adventure like only a child could in the middle of the night.

"I know, Max."

"Did you know there are frogs in that lake?" He was awake now. It was more of a pond than a lake, but for sure there were frogs and every other kind of slimy creature in the sisters' environmental refuge pond. Just the kind of ministry one might expect from this small band of calm holy women where I was sending Max for protection.

As usual both Rupert and Crystal looked unsullied in clean jeans and denim work shirts, smelling like their clothes were fresh off the line. Last summer when Marnie, Crystal and I had taken Max to the monastery for the weekend, I'd laughed when Marnie told Crystal, "I just hate you, girlfriend. You always look great whether you've partied all night or come straight from playing with kids all day. How do you bottle that fresh air perfume?" Now Crystal was pale – she too seemed afraid.

"Crystal," I said, "when you get back, let's go over everything. You have a knack for puzzles. Maybe you can help fill in some blanks." Crystal didn't respond. "You remember how to get there?" I asked. She nodded.

"We have the GPS," Crystal said, as we stood, now with our arms around each other's waist watching Max and

Rupert have a serious conversation about frogs and Teenage Mutant Ninja Turtles.

Wide awake now, Max hugged Rupert around the neck, and they were looking at each other eye-to-eye talking about Leonardo and the other turtles. Rupert was more the talking kind of friend for Max and not the hugging kind. But tonight, it was as if this detailed, huggy face-to-face deep conversation about slimy, noisy creatures, both imaginary and real, was the most normal thing in the world that these two friends would do before leaving the house in the middle of the night.

Desperate people do desperate things, and I was at least going to do my best to keep Max safe. Even if Patrick being shot had nothing to do with Marnie and Max, I wasn't going to risk anything happening to that little boy. Not again, not if I could help it.

With Patrick in the hospital, and Rupert and Crystal on their way to the sisters with Max in tow, I should have been more nervous for my own safety since I was alone but I knew the cops were keeping me on their route, so at least I was assured of some help if the proverbial shit were to hit the fan again tonight. Besides Rupert would have set the security house alarm. What I couldn't tell people is that I know, beyond a shadow of a doubt, that God has a blanket of protection around me. Religious woo-woo comes with the territory. How could it not, with a name like Shepherd? Unlike earlier, as I was trying to summon grace that didn't show up, now I somehow knew everything was going to be good for a while and I could finally get some sleep.

My bed was turned down. Crisp white cotton sheets and my small down pillow welcomed me. I needed to sleep. Again, I needed to remember to thank Crystal for all the little kindnesses she scattered my way on a regular basis.

She and I didn't talk much, but I'd be lost without Crystal. I hoped she knew that.

Much as I need sleep, I was restless. I tossed and turned until the sun crept into the room, and God's light started to replace the dark. Guess I wasn't going to get that good, long, hard sleep I'd hoped for.

The view from my window showed a bit of pale pink sprinkled where the ragged edges of sky and the lake collided against each other, announcing that once again, we were starting over. There was something about the beginning and ending of the day being punctuated by this never-the-same up-and-down sun. I could never get enough.

Coming down the stairs to make coffee, I first panicked as I heard a car creeping up the gravel driveway. A quick glance out the leaded window next to the landing told me it was Rupert in that obscenely large, well-kept Bentley. These recent fight or flight reactions were doing a number on me. Hard to look cool and collected when I'm always fighting off a potential disaster.

I deactivated the alarm, opened the doors and stepped into the crisp air and sat on the back porch waiting for Rupert. Instead of going back toward the garage, Rupert pulled up again to the very utilitarian and user-friendly kitchen entrance.

Rupert got out of the car and came up to the porch. "Let's go to the other side of the house and watch the sun," I said. We walked around the driveway as it circled from the kitchen entrance into the front of the house. There was a formal porch with white wicker furniture and rose chintz cushions. It was like going back to what my imagination thought was a gentler time.

Only from a sailboat out in the lake could one get the full effect of this amazing house I now lived in. As with all things on this property, the circle drive in front of the porch looked natural, as if it had always been there. Sitting in the great rockers on the porch, you couldn't even see the driveway as it tucked under our unobstructed view of Lake Michigan. We sat listening to the lake lap gentle waves on the beach and watched the sun come up over the horizon.

"Always the functionalist, that grandmother of mine, don't you think?" I started talking first.

"She liked things that way," Rupert nodded, rocking slightly, in a white, high backed chair. "Functional first, then aesthetically pleasing, but never the other way around. She and Leona were always patting themselves on the back for how Woodstone has such well designed and usable space, as well as being breathtaking and beautiful."

"Guess you decided to turn around and come right back? Don't you sleep?"

"Oh, it wasn't all that far, and sure, I sleep. In fact, that's what's on my mind this very moment. You?"

"I just lay there—too restless. How'd everything go with Sister Judith?"

"It went great. Max wanted to go catch frogs all the way up there. He didn't fall asleep until we were a few miles away. I'm sure Crystal and Judith talked until dawn, and they'll still make it to morning prayers. Funny how Judith can get Crystal to talk. The younger sisters will have a ball keeping up with Max. This was a good idea for both Max and Crystal, and of course for the girls. Having a kid around makes them happy."

"Novices, not girls," I corrected.

"Don't give me that feminist crap. Girls is girls," he said, smiling. Then, as if he could read my mind, Rupert said, "No one followed me, and you had great protection. I could see the cops rounding the cemetery on Sheridan as I pulled in the driveway."

"Right. Whoever shot Patrick had their fun. Now they are back to shooting Xanax or whatever crap they do that allows them to try to kill someone who is quietly eating dinner. They're undoubtedly too high now to mess with me this morning." My voice was pitching upward. I was shaking. "I will not cry. It's such a waste of energy. That's how Marnie and I are so alike," I said, more to myself than Rupert. "We hate to cry."

He didn't move to comfort me, nor did he speak. We both just stared at the sunrise.

"This beauty seems so out of sync given what's happened," I whispered as he leaned over and took my hand.

"We'll get to the bottom of this." Rupert paused for a minute, "I know she's alive. She's too tough to get killed."

"You tired?" I asked, ready to share my discovery.

"Wide awake at the moment, but you know when I crash, I crash."

"Well, before that, want to see what I found? Want coffee?"

"First, I'll put the beast back in her lair," he said as we walked back around the house and he got back into the Bentley.

"Rupert, you want breakfast too? I'll cook."

"Sure. Be right back."

I ran upstairs to get the book Rupert brought me from Marnie's basement. I threw on my most comfortable baggie Levis and scruffy old Trinity College sweatshirt, and started breakfast.

As we were being revitalized by the strong espresso coffee, I handed Rupert the book.

"What do you think?" I asked as he leafed through it.

"I saw this when I put those books up there, little missy."

"Only you can get away with that shit. *Little missy?*"

He just shook his head between bites of crispy French toast topped with fresh blueberries, as we drank more thick black espresso.

As we ate I explained my theory. "I think there's a number in that book that represents one frightened person or more. The numbers must coincide to names. As far as I can tell, we only have these ledgers. No key. No book explaining who or what the numbers represent. There are some repeat numbers and others look like they are a once off. With all this detail she has to have a key, unless it's all in her head."

Rupert, was yawning. "I don't doubt Marnie could be a sex worker of some kind. I have thought that for some time now, but by the looks of this she was more than that."

"Like what?"

"Not sure. With Patrick in the hospital, we aren't going to get help from the police. Marnie's disappearance will not be a high on their list today. Last night, on the west side, a couple gang bangers took to shooting at each other, only this time an innocent four-year-old little girl was killed in her bed—bullet went through the window. That shooting will take priority. It's just us. I know Patrick; this won't keep him resting for long. By the way, how are you?" Rupert asked with another big yawn.

"My bruises don't hurt so much, and after only a few hours sleep I am wide awake."

"Good for you, but I'm tired. That yummy French toast did me in. Tell me more after I get a little sleep."

Last night, the doctor had assured us Patrick would be out of it for at least a day or two and we should let him rest. All the more reason I had to try to find Marnie; the more hours that slipped by, the worse it could be for her. I hoped someone at the station was going over Patrick's arrests to see who might have it out for him. Had Patrick said something about letting his guard down? What did he mean?

"Rupert, I have a plan but I want you to know, right up front, you aren't going to like it."

He nodded, and took the book with him as he went out the door. "Tell me later. I'm on overload—"

"Why Rupert, it seems even you have a limit...sleep well."

"Brain cramp is all, and Shep," Rupert said as he turned back, looking me in the eye and pointing a parental finger, "don't do anything stupid."

"Who, me?" I laughed, pointing at myself. He shook his head, waved and headed home.

CHAPTER 17

"I'll change it, hold on," the voice said. The music switched from gibberish hip-hop, to what sounded like classical. "That better?" There was a slap, like a hand hitting flesh, a bang with an eerie grating, then tumbling and scattering—grunting noises as one of the kids must have hit the other, who'd fallen with a thud. Now she couldn't understand what they were saying.

As they opened the door, she was worried they could hear her thinking. She had to concentrate and not float away. The door must have been open wide now; wind blew in, and it was that sharp sweet warm air that comes before a storm. She could feel them in the room.

"Shit. She don't look so good." The hip-hop-lover voice said.

"SHUT UP, I knew I should've come by myself."

Not moving she could feel sweaty fingers touching her breasts, pinching her nipples.

"Wanna do her?"

"Shit. I don't want to do no corpse."

"I think she's breathing. That's all we had to do, see if she was breathing."

"This is creepy. I'm getting out of here."

"I'll be right behind you, Toadie." The voices were familiar —she recognized their voices now. They were the same guys with Derek the night they took her from her house. She wanted to ask about what was going on, about Max, but she knew better

~~~

The cab dropped me off at the parking garage near Le Petite Gourmet all covered with more of that damn yellow and black crime scene tape. My heart sank when I saw Patrick's little RX7 parked next to my Subaru. Even as I did my best to shake off what had happened, my eyes filled with tears. Most days I'd meditate at a time like this, but I had to go.

I pulled out of the lot, paid what seemed to be a small fortune for all-night parking and headed toward Goodwill down the street to buy some items I wouldn't find in my own closet.

I threw the bag in the car, grabbed a coffee from the fast-food drive through and made a plan. I knew that going home to change into my purchases wasn't a good idea. So, I drove south for a couple hours, past the city of Chicago
~~~

to where the scenery gets simpler and the big buildings start to thin out and it gets grittier by the mile. I stopped at one of those hotels that say they leave the light on.

Sleep was the first order of business. Then I would get ready for an evening that could very well get me killed.

Of course, I couldn't tell Rupert this part of my plan because he'd do everything he could think of to stop me but it was the mention of looking up Gentlemen's clubs that gave me my next idea.

After a few hours, I again gave up trying to sleep. This nondescript room that was identical to any other room in this hotel, even down to the paintings, is where I would prepare for what I'd hoped would be a believable transformation.

I put on the new-to-me platinum wig and tucked in my hair. This wig was too small, but it would have to do. I'd never liked my hair blond. I look washed out and one-dimensional. I teased out the fake hair, then smoothed it down, sprayed it with hair spray and did it again. I applied thick eyeliner and mascara and watched my appearance in the bathroom mirror turn into one that belonged to someone else.

"Well," I said, to the face staring back at me, "a girl's gotta do what a girl's gotta do."

After daubing more cake make-up over my well-earned wisdom lines, I was done. I knew I had to stop looking in the mirror, because soon the reasonable side of me would take over, and talk me out of what I was planning to do. And rightfully so.

After I'd found that picture of Marnie in the back of one of those books, I did a little unpleasant digging on nasty adult sites. Only one had the word "dream" in the name, so I was hoping this place I was headed might be where the picture was taken. I also know enough to know that I couldn't just waltz in asking questions with my clergy collar on.

This would be the kind of seedy place where men watched women dance evocatively around a pole and then, they would, presumably, purchase sexual favors. I knew I was grasping at straws, but doing something was better than waiting around for more bad news. If I was wrong about this, I was back to square one.

I was pretty sure that my Goodwill purchases, a skin-tight black mini-skirt and low-cut red sequin top, were required attire if I was to walk into the Dream Palace and not be kicked out right away. The outfit was very much like the one Marnie wore when I'd first met her.

I pulled on black fishnet stockings to finish the look, but it all was a little off because of the shoes. I'd decided against four-inch heels and wore simple black flats in case I had to run.

The inside of my legs were already uncomfortable and sticky as they were being held together by this tight skirt.

I punched in the address into my phone, and according to Google Maps, the Dream Palace was only an hour south from this motel. I'd been this way only once before; it was not a pretty part of Illinois.

For about thirty-five more miles I stayed on the same nondescript highway and found the place right away. It would have been impossible to miss, with the larger-than-life sign on top of the building announcing the *Dream Palace.* The grimy one-story building was part of a compound that seemed to be a huge junkyard. The whole area was surrounded by a tall chain-link fence topped off with razor wire, and in an area cluttered with similar industrial buildings. Some looked like small manufacturing facilities, others storage lockers or chop shops..

I pulled in around eleven o'clock as the parking lot was filling up for the evening. There were no windows, menus or placards near the entrance. There was nothing that would identify what went on inside here, just an outrageous pink and purple flashing neon sign.

I hoped I could get away with asking a few questions before they threw me out as an impostor. Spurred on by the hope that maybe I'd meet someone who knew Marnie, I sucked in my breath, opened the heavy wooden door, and was immediately assaulted by noise and darkness. Ear-splitting heavy metal music was blaring, but this was not Led Zeppelin or AC/DC or anything to hum along with. This noise was so loud and awful you quickly got disconnected from yourself and couldn't think about what you were doing. But, of course, that was the point.

If anyone was watching the door, like Patrick had tried to do at Le Petite Gourmet, they had the advantage. They could see me in the dim light, but I couldn't see them. If the thugs who'd shot Patrick were here, I was screwed. My disguise wasn't all that good. I still looked like me. Too late to think of that now. Waiting by the door until my eyes adjusted, I headed toward a short bar that faced a long stage with a runway. Tables with one or two chairs were scattered everywhere in the large room. At every other table was a solitary man looking at the stage with a blank stare, waiting for something to happen.

I sauntered the best I could without high heels to the bar where a hard-looking woman was already studying me.

"Scotch on the rocks." I did my best to be gruff and impolite.

"You lost. girlie? Only soda-pop at this bar."

"I'll have a Coke," I shot back, surprised there was no alcohol to soothe what went on here. What kind of a creepy place was this? The bartender took what I hoped was a clean glass from a stack behind the bar and filled it to the top with ice.

"You look kind of familiar," she said. My heart sank and pounded harder.

"Why, you got my mug shot taped up somewhere?" I tried my best to play along.

"Worse than that, girlie. You look like everybody else down on their luck needing to make a few bills. Ever rode the pole?" The half dozen metal poles along the stage stood fixed at different intervals from the front of the platform to the back. These poles were not there to hold up the ceiling.

"No, but I can use one of those things." I pointed to the pressurized hose she had in her hand. I'd learned to use one of those soft drink contraptions at the church bazaar several summers ago.

The woman threw back her head and laughed. Tucking a wisp of brittle, over-dyed red hair under a hairpin, she rubbed her neck before going back to the task at hand. She squirted brown liquid into the glass she'd been holding—she must have been deciding whether to kick me out or say more.

"Ten bucks," she snapped, holding out her hand. I must have flinched. All I had on me was a fifty-dollar bill that I'd tucked in my bra at the last minute. Catching my hesitation, she said, "How do you think we pay bills? Business is business."

I handed her the fifty, realizing right away how stupid that was.

"What's this, Goldilocks? Rent money? Forget it, first Coke's on me. And if you're looking for a job, like I said before, we only have pole riding, and we always have openings. Wanna try that?"

I must have flinched again.

"No, didn't think so. They never do, at least not right away."

As she walked to the other end of the bar, I sat on a stool and watched the room fill up with men. Old and young, dressed in suits or jeans, some almost in rags—Black, white, Asian, brown – all nervous. This was not a boisterous strip club where guys went for bachelor parties. This was something altogether more sinister.

As the men came in the door, each undressed me with their eyes and moved on. They had that same identical blank creepy look as the men already seated at the tables. Nobody talked but just found their way to a table and sat down. I was at the bar and not in the back waiting to go on, so maybe I didn't interest them. Each man sat down, ordered his Coke and kept his hands under the table. Except for the over-dyed red bombshell slinging ten-buck Cokes, I was the only other woman in the place. So far.

Then, one at a time, six women came from the sides of the stage and took their places at a pole and started gyrating to the hard, pounding music. For the most part, the women made no eye contact and had the same blank faces as the men watching them.

As still as the men were, these women were constantly moving, wrapping themselves around the poles, trying to entice one of the men to make a purchase. None of these women smiled or showed any emotion. A young woman with long blond hair and a few inches of dark roots stood in the middle, looked about fifteen while the others had been around for a while. On the end was a woman dressed in a black bra and underpants. She looked at least fifty, with a body that was lumpy all over. Her eyes locked on mine with hatred. I looked away.

"That's Brenda," the bartender said, noticing the interchange. "She's been here for years, and she hates women like you—the women who come in here are cops or wives up to no good."

"I am not a wife or a cop." I said, telling the truth. "Just looking for a job for a few days." I could tell she didn't believe me, but she didn't show me the door either.

"What do they call you?"

"Max," I said, lying easily this time. The name just came out of my mouth. But if any one knew about Max, it might start someone talking.

"They call me Irma," she said, in a long, drawn-out way as if to make sure I heard her. Her mouth smiled, but her eyes were like cold black holes.

The women on stage kept dancing, trying to look sexy in an unengaged sort of way. One at a time they would come off the stage and sit with one of the men. After a minute or two, of what I presumed to be negotiating the terms of the agreement, both would disappear to the side of the stage behind another curtain.

When her turn came, Brenda came down to talk to a prospective client, but nobody seemed interested in buying what she had to sell. After a few minutes of rejection, Brenda was back up on the pole with her hateful look continuing to spiral in my direction. It was as if somehow her misfortune was my fault. It was obvious that Brenda was the hardest working woman there, but she was a terrible dancer.

Later, when two new men walked in, Irma rolled her eyes and shrugged her shoulders as they made their way to an empty table. They didn't fit in with the others—they couldn't wipe the pity from their faces. I recognized a bleeding heart when I saw one.

"Irma," I hollered over the music, "I'll get those two." She nodded and went on washing glasses, while she kept her eagle eye on me and how things were going in the room. Once in a while Irma would dry her hands and jot something down on a pad of paper next to the cash register. I had the feeling she didn't miss much.

"Evening, Father," I said to the older of the two men.

"You new here?" he said, not denying my guess, but not confirming it either.

"Temporary, actually," I said.

"Aren't we all," said the younger one. I'd guess him to maybe be a seminarian—or at least a bleeding heart in training.

"Two Cokes?"

"Right," said the older one, who sat with his back to the stage.

When I returned with the Cokes, the older one seemed to be explaining to his friend what was going on. I went back to my spot by the bar and waited for something to change.

As the evening wore on, I tried to think of a way to get backstage to talk to the girls, and equally worried about what I'd find. I imagined men lined up against the wall with women on their knees trying to pay off their pimp, one blow job at a time. Sneaking around would make me vulnerable under Irma's eagle eye, so I waited by the bar without trying to appear too nosy or nervous. My fear of being found out in this dark hole of a place, kept me ever vigilant and my stomach in knots.

When Irma's hands were full she nodded at a table, indicating I was to share the menu, "Coke and Coke." By the looks of things it seemed I was being accepted for training as a waitress wannabe hooker at this end-of-the-line Gentleman's Club, where the men looked anything but gentle.

With a temporary break in the action, Irma sat next to me at the bar. I could see that she was beginning to take an interest in me.

"Got any college? You act like you got some."

"How's that?" I hollered over the noise.

She shrugged. "You just don't look the type. Lots of women down on their luck consider this work." She hooked her thumb hitchhiker style toward the stage, "but not everyone gives it a try." When I didn't say anything, she went on.

"Me, I was born into it. Dad was a cop, mom worked the street. Perfect combination. Sex, guns, drugs and rock and roll." She pointed to the jukebox, programmed to never stop playing that god-awful noise. "Shit, why am I telling you this?"

"Don't feel bad. Everybody does." I said, instantly regretting saying anything true.

"Looks like they want more," Irma said, ignoring my faux pas. Following her gaze I saw she was indicating the ones I'd guessed were priests. The old one was pointing a long finger at his empty glass.

Irma stood up. "You go over. I don't like the old one. He's a regular but not like the others. I don't trust him. He pays so good I let him and his sidekicks in. Go see what they want. Better yet, get rid of 'em."

The two men sat across from each other, the young one facing the stage and the old one still with his eyes on the door. I brought their next round of watered-down Cokes and sat down next to the old man.

"How'd you know who we were?" he asked, with a tentative smile.

I smiled, enjoying the question. "You just have that look. Are you from CTU by any chance?" I took a wild guess at a pretty large Catholic seminary in the city.

They both nodded, looking a little surprised, but then the younger one leaned over and asked, "What's your name?"

Before I could answer, the dancer who had looked like a teenager from a distance slipped her skinny body into the chair next to the young priest and said, "Pammy Jo, my name is Pammy Jo. I saw you come in." She looked right at him.

Pammy Jo had looked almost pretty on stage. The bright colored lights had caught her face and long blond hair in a gauzy, kind of ethereal way as she danced into what seemed like a frenzy. Up close Pammy Jo was an over-bleached, anorexic woman with bad teeth who was sitting in cheap underwear at a table of ministers masquerading as regular guys.

"I'm new here," she volunteered. "I gotta job so now I can tell the welfare lady to give me my kids back."

"Honey, everybody loves their kids," I touched her hand without thinking.

Pammy Jo pulled her hand away from mine, "Hey, wait a minute, I don't do nothin' wrong." She straightened her cheap white camisole as she tried to collect herself. "You like my outfit? Target." She smiled, changing the subject. You could see she would be toothless in a few years.

"Every day, first thing, I look in the mirror and start talking," she volunteered, out of the blue.

"Who do you talk to?" the young man asked.

Pammy Jo looked confused. "Who do I talk to? To me! Who else would I be talking to in the mirror? That's a crazy question."

"Not necessarily." He paused.

"What?" She said, looking at him like he was round the bend. He paused again. "God?"

"What?"

"Well, sure, why not God?"

Pammy Jo whipped her body sideways to face him head on. He looked taken aback by this visceral, intimate response to his dangerous line of theological psychologizing. He glanced at his mentor, who nodded for him to continue.

Pammy Jo stared at him for a minute, "God?" Her face was full of excitement, "Did God send you here to take care of me?"

Before he could answer, Irma was at the table, gripping Pammy Jo's shoulders with both hands, "Time's up. You guys've had enough. Girls back to work." Irma held her hand out, palm up, to the old priest who gave her a wad of cash.

"Maybe next time around you'll get lucky, old man," she cackled.

It was clear not much got past Irma. She knew they were not her usual guests, but I doubt she realized it was more redemption they were interested in, not sex. The old guy never turned toward the stage. I had the strange feeling he hadn't always faced the door, but the younger one? It wasn't all that obvious he was ordained, but he did have that priest-in-training aura I recognized from my Catholic classmates in seminary.

Pammy Jo calling this viable employment, well, the idea was ludicrous, but I'm sure she believed it with all her heart. After Pammy Jo got back on the pole, you could see all the energy had gone out of her performance. She kept staring out into the sea of blank faces. My heart went out to her as she wrapped her skinny legs around the pole and moved up and down, but she couldn't quite get the bump-and-grind thing going like she had earlier.

I returned to the bar as a group of three men came in the door and, without looking around walked toward the bar. I started to panic as I recognized the well dressed heavy-set man from the night before at Le Petite Gourmet. I stayed where I was and leaned down to pick up a napkin that was on the floor. The men didn't stop to talk to me or Irma but they proceeded to go through a door on the opposite side of the room.

"Washroom?" I asked Irma, trying to look bored even though everything inside me was racing with a combination of fear and excitement.

"Little girls' room at the end of the hall, go right, not left," Irma pointed to the curtains at the side of the stage where I'd seen men going in and out all night with the dancers—this was on the opposite side from where the fat man disappeared. Taking a deep breath, I walked through the curtain.

Here was a spic and span hallway, painted hospital-shit green and lit by naked light bulbs hanging from the ceiling. At the end of the main hall was another hall lined with rooms, each with garbage can just outside the door. Glancing in the can I could see the cans were for used condoms. I thought this hallway might curve around behind the stage and make a big U but I wasn't ready to find that out. Not yet.

Half way down the hall was a black-and-gold sign glued to the door that said, 'Women.' Inside this looked like any other public restroom, except cleaner. It was spotless actually—maybe to give the illusion this wasn't the last bathroom on the road to hell. Here, at the Dream Palace, where privacy was nonexistent, the stalls had doors. It was a relief to go in, lock the door and be alone for just a minute, but I stood up to pee, I wasn't taking any chances. Now I was pretty sure I needed an escape plan. The fat man could recognize me and I'd be no closer to finding Marnie. But now I knew I was getting closer to something. What I didn't know.

To be on the safe side I thought I'd just leave the *Dream Palace* now, tell Irma I'd see her again. I washed my hands at the sink and thought about Pammy Jo's question, "Did God send you?" Isn't that what we all want? We want God to rescue us from whatever mess we're in.

The whole thing made me want to turn on the lights in the bar, do a group counseling session, fix everyone and go home. I shook my head. Like that would help? No, more than likely even the stupidity of that thought could get me killed. Instead of imagining I could fix what was broken with these people, I first need to concentrate on getting out of here.

Now, more than ever, I wanted to know Marnie's story. I wanted to know how she'd found me in the first place. How had she escaped all this, and where was she now? I reached for the handle as the door opened hard, pushing me backwards against the wall with great force. Brenda.

Her anger appeared already at a dangerous level. She leaned back against the door, blocking me from leaving, and lit a cigarette.

"Hope you don't mind the smoke?" she said, blowing smoke rings in my face.

"Hey cut me some slack, will ya? I'm just looking for a job." It was a weak comeback.

"Cut the shit sister. We all know you aren't here about a job."

I sucked in my breath. Cutting to the chase, I said, "Shana Smith." One of Marnie's aliases Patrick had given me a few days ago.

"You a cop?"

"Friend."

"Friend," she cackled, taking a long drag off her Salem Light. "Well, 'friend,' you are stupider than you look. Shana's dead." Brenda looked away, then she turned right back and glared at me with piercing almost black eyes, her body tensed as if she was ready to spring toward me.

"Did you tell Irma you were looking for Shana?"

"No."

"Well, that was kinda smart—or you'd be dead too." She took a long drag off her cigarette, "Shana was nothing but trouble when she was alive. Trouble like you." Brenda was still pissed as hell at me for what I must have represented to her, but her shoulders had softened a bit. She was talking but seemed confused.

"Can you help me find her? I don't think she's dead," I whispered.

"You must be shitting me, you stupid bitch. Who the fuck do you think you are?" Brenda slapped my face full force. I fell against the stall door, slipped on the polished linoleum and hit my head on the toilet.

There was a push on the women's room door, as the ever-present Irma interrupted, "What the HELL?" Brenda jumped away from the door as all color drained from her face. "Smoking isn't what we do in here, Brenda, and you know it." Irma saw me on the floor and said nothing.

Brenda started to talk, "She slipped and I—"

"Shut up."

"Right, no smoking, sorry," Brenda said. Now her demeanor was subservient as she flushed her cigarette down the toilet. Irma ignored me and was gone as fast as she had appeared.

"Later," Brenda said to me with a phony lilt in her voice and a tiny smile as she walked out after Irma.

Following them out the door, it seemed as if I was getting a little closer to something. One thing was obviously clear—I was way over my head.

Just as we emerged from the Women's room I saw the back of fat man and the three others leave the *Dream Palace*. With him gone, I decided to wait it out.

For the rest of the night I pretended nothing had happened between me and Brenda. I continued to serve Cokes to the derelicts in the room, and I prepared to leave when the place emptied out. I might be in new territory but I was learning. I could be as tough as they were. My head throbbed. I was pretty sure I had a second concussion from my head hitting the porcelain toilet. This was re-injuring my head bang from that rock in Marnie's driveway. I knew that if I wasn't super careful, I still could get more than a slight concussion and a bruised arm before the night was over.

CHAPTER 18

The boy touched her shoulder, then her cheek. Involuntarily she shuddered. He gasped and seemed to jump back. He didn't move for a minute or so, then he poked her. She didn't move this time. Then there was a rummaging noise like he was searching for something. After a few minutes, he covered her with what felt like an old burlap feed bag.

Sighing out loud, the boy began to untie her wrists. She wanted to open her eyes, but wouldn't risk it. Who was this boy-captor who would tweak her nipples one moment and untie her wrists the next?

He tugged and pulled at the rough rope cords around her wrists, and it was all she could do to not scream from the pain. Each time he pulled, the rope went deeper into her skin. But she'd felt worse. So she concentrated—kept her mouth shut, and played her best dead girl.

"Always said you'd be good in movies, little shit, you and all that drama."

As her rescuer pulled and struggled to untie knots around her wrists, she focused on her breathing, but she was getting woozy. The pain was getting unbearable. She concentrated on trying to stay conscious. But now she drifted to that place where her dreams tortured her spirit—tortured her as much as any man who had ever abused her body.

In the surreal world she had created, meditation was critical to help keep her focused. If she didn't meditate an hour before falling asleep she was at the mercy of her dreams. And that was worse than not sleeping at all. She'd learned a long time ago that staying awake gave her the extra advantage of being able to keep her eye on the door. But now, physically and spiritually wounded, she faded again into that painful unconscious world she knew all too well. She'd gotten sloppy, she'd failed to protect herself. She felt like she was falling over a cliff and could do nothing to stop it and this was leaving her at both the mercy of both her captors and her demons.

Waking up again, she was colder. The boy was gone and her wrists were untied. The burlap itched – but she was grateful for a cover that kept some of the chill off. The room was pitch black – there was no light, but this time she could smell fresh air. The door must be in that direction, and maybe they'd left it open.

Untying her feet she gritted her teeth against the shooting pains. Slowly she worked on untying her ankles. She could feel her oozing flesh sticking to the rope. Finally finished she unsuccessfully tried to stand, but falling hard she collapsed against the bed.

Slower this time, she tried again to stand up and this time she succeeded.

Even in the dark, this place seemed familiar. Evanston City code would have had folks get rid of this dirt floor long ago, so she knew she wasn't near home.

Bile crept into her throat as she became more conscious of her surroundings and fear was again attempting to sabotage her need to stay alive. Her phobia of basements often got in her way. Shaking off fear the best she could, she wrapped the scratchy burlap around her shivering body and inched toward the smell of the fresh air. Moving helped get her mind and body back in gear, she had to let the pain go. She had to get out of here. She had to face what ever was outside that door.

Reaching down it seemed she had bumped into a box of sand. This is a cold-cellar for sure, she thought, a storage place for vegetables like the monks did at the monastery she'd visited many times as a teenager. The same place where she'd met Father Sawyer and Father Alphonso. Their faces appeared to her in her mind. She could not prevent thoughts from coming now. She had no filters now, so the thoughts were coming at will.

There was no doubt that these two men, along with her mother, had been responsible for most of the best and the worst experiences in her entire life. Again she was starting to panic.

Fingering the sand in the box, she found a few soft leftover carrots. Brushing them off, she tasted one and realized that she must not have eaten for days. And she was so thirsty. The carrots were mushy but still flavorful and sweet. Her stomach lurched as bile crept again into her throat and she threw up the carrots on the dirt floor.

She couldn't let her fear of basements continue to distract her. It was too dangerous to not do everything she could to get free. Shep had been teaching her meditation and breathing exercises not just to sleep but to help keep the old memories at bay. But nothing was working now, and she was at the mercy of the craziness she'd worked so hard to stop.

Think about Max, she told herself, do what you have to.

She wasn't hungry or feeling much of anything anymore. Her wrists and ankles had gone numb. Her need to survive for Max helped her ignore the pain, the fear and the cold.

How long would Derek stay away? He must've already heard that the boys thought she was dead, but when would he find out she was free, and come after her again?

If she was lucky they'd be gone and her car would be close by. The memory of what happened was starting to come back.

There had been the yelling, the blood all over the kitchen – she'd cut someone with the knife she'd pulled from the dish drainer, then someone took it and cut her. She felt her stomach and felt a 3-inch, hot, crusted cut on her stomach. The men had stormed into her house. They came in through the kitchen, up the back stairs and wore black ski masks. One, whose voice she didn't recognize, had been asking questions about documents she knew nothing about. Derek was there, she remembered his voice...but had he shown up later or was he one of the three? She couldn't remember. Probably he was screaming and threatening to kill her...as usual. They'd left in her car.

~~~
~~~

Sergeant Kelly hunched over the old Smith Corona typewriter that he still preferred over a computer.

"Kelly, don't you ever give yourself a break?"

Patrick smiled at his friend. Harry Long's name was all wrong since this man was short and didn't have a hair on his head. Patrick called him NVH, for not-very-hairy.

"Here I am, NVH, typing this report from my shooting incident when I should be out there tracking a kidnapper."

"Ah, no, man, you should be in bed with a harem coolin' your fevered brow. But *oh no, not Patrick,* three days out of the hospital and you're at work. You're a tough act to follow or even be near for us lazy types."

"Never good to lie in bed—there is pain in bed or the office. Keeps me young. Besides, a boy's without his mother, and now a friend is missing and playing detective without me."

"I heard. But you know the rules Patrick: *When shot, no beat for even the most zealous cop until the captain signs off,* which I doubt he has—so it's paperwork my friend, *until further notice, following the review of the incident.*"

"I'm ignoring that at the moment."

"So, hard ass, how you feeling, really?"

"Sore, lucky, worried, packed full of antibiotics, and, aside from that, the damage is minimal. As they say, I've had worse. Forensics will be back tomorrow, and we'll see what the gun was. This was a premeditated hit, so maybe this was somebody I pissed off who just got out of jail."

"Or maybe pissing off?"

"Not sure. I have to think that Marnie's disappearance is a personal vendetta—you know, the usual pimp-looking-for-his-cash routine. Shooting me at Le Petite Gourmet is pretty extreme even for a pimp. I'd guess this is pay back from an old case. Captain wants my list of folks who hate me."

"What's-an-ever, as the kids say. I'm going out back for a smoke. See ya, Superman. Oh, and I heard that missing hooker is a friend of Rupert. "

"In a way."

At his colleague's raised eyebrows, Patrick reiterated, "In a good way. Rupert's good people, NV. For God's sake, just 'cause you don't like him since he got himself arrested protesting that war you and I had the bad fortune to get shot up in, is stupid. He was just out of Vietnam too and pissed off. That was a long time ago. And looking back I wish I had been protesting too. That was a bad war. So, give Rupert a break."

Harry smiled and saluted, "Aye, aye sir."

Patrick had been standing up for Rupert for years. Lots of folks hated him for being smart, aloof and marching to his own drummer. You either loved Rupert or hated him, but you'd never forget him.

In fact, since he couldn't officially get back to work until he was cleared for duty, Patrick thought Rupert might be the perfect person to talk to.

NVH was a longtime colleague, but he was uninspired and maybe a little dirty, just like some cops get when they are tired of all the perps getting away with murder. These cops get sluggish and worse. Patrick knew there would be minimal help from Harry.

"Hey, I got a question for you," Patrick hollered just after his colleague had shut the door.

Coming back in, Harry said, "Yo."

"Any rumors about the disappearance of Marnie Cooper? I've been laid up a few days."

"Pretty quiet, Pat. Kidnapped hookers aren't exactly Wall Street execs being extorted for millions, as you well know." Harry Long turned to leave, showing his distaste for the conversation.

Leaning back in his chair, Patrick felt that this old cop he'd known for years was acting out of character. Even though he didn't trust Harry, Patrick would often listen to him. NVH had good instincts, and he'd sit on the corner of Patrick's desk talk for hours about a case. Patrick decided to let it drop and dialed Rupert's cell phone.

Patrick jumped when he heard Shep's voice on the phone. "Shep, I forgot Rupert had given you his extra phone. Where the hell are you?"

"Hey, right, hi. I'm busy, can't talk, gotta go." And she hung up before Patrick could threaten to send out an APB, which he knew he should have done already. Redialing the number, Patrick heard Rupert's cryptic message— "You know what to do." Shepherd had turned off the phone.

CHAPTER 19

She stubbed her toe on something hard next to the bed and wanted to holler but she bit down hard on the inside of her cheek to stifle any noise that might give her away. She could taste blood.

She rubbed her toe.The thought of Max made her lose her balance. 'Shut up, you stupid girl.' Shutting off the voices, as she'd trained herself to do for many years, she was even more determined to get out.

'Don't forget, little liar, somebody knows you're untied,' her mother's ghost added to her internal conversation.

In the dark, windowless cave-like room, she got down on all fours and crawled on her hands and knees toward the smell of fresh air. Time seemed to stop as she inched her way in the darkness until she found the door.

'Be glad it's not November, little liar, or you'd be frozen to that bed.'

"Shut up, mother," she said, then sorry she'd spoken out loud. Shit, they could be out there.

Whoever he was, he'd not only untied her, but he'd left the door unlocked. Adrenalin started pumping even more as she inched the door open. What if this was on purpose? What if they wanted to chase her, to have a little fun raping this crazy wildcat who thought she could change? Maybe they'd tackle her as she ran naked through the trees. That would be more titillating than doing a cold creepy body lashed, spread eagle to a bed.

The door creaked, each half-inch of movement sounded too loud.

Slipping through what seemed to be an inside door she could see a little better. The night sky peeked through the slit of two more doors closed above her. She did see that four narrow steps and the big storm door above her was all that was between her and freedom.

Bent over at the top stair she was ready too push the metal door open with her shoulder, but she heard voices. They were soft and gentle, almost with a lilting quality but far away. As the words registered, she almost laughed out loud.

"This is your classical music station," said a barely audible voice. "We play classical music 24 hours a day." It was the kid's radio that must have gotten stuck in the corner of one of these stairs when the other guy knocked it out of his hands. Feeling around she found a small object. It was not a radio but some kind of phone. She must have kicked it and turned up the volume as she'd made her way up the stairs.

That kid might be looking for this. Fiddling with the phone she turned it off, stuck the cigarette-sized contraption under her armpit, to leave her arms free for whatever she might encounter outside.

She put her ear to the cold metal storm door again and all she heard this time was the chirping of birds announcing that morning was on its way. Bit by bit she pushed up the metal door with her shoulder.

The pain in her wrists and ankles pulsed, as did a new awareness of a dull throbbing pain on the insides of her thighs. Pain that comes from rough sex. She must have been drugged and raped, she thought. Now she was back in her body, no longer floating, but colder than ever.

The door was heavy. There might be a loud thud when it crashed to the ground, giving her away for sure, but there was no other way. No going back now!

~~~

The night had dragged on at the Dream Palace after the incident in the bathroom with Brenda. She kept giving me if-looks-could-kill messages but I was ready to lick my wounds and get out of there.

At dawn, Irma waved at me and I started for the door. Brenda stood in front of me, and I shocked myself.

“Hey Brenda, I know you’re truck’s broken. You want a ride?”

She nodded, shocking us both.
~~~

"I'll wait outside," I pushed out the door into the huge gravel patch that was a poor replica of a parking lot.

As the minutes ticked by, I began to wonder if Brenda was telling Irma about our conversation in the bathroom. Was Irma putting two and two together? Irma struck me as a shrewd woman but maybe not the deepest thinker. Brenda appeared to be afraid of Irma, so taking a ride from me seemed out of character. With the memory of Marnie between us, she must have realized we weren't each other's enemy.

"Shepherd," I said to myself out loud as I sat in the car, watching the sun come up yet again. "I hope you are up for this. The only detective work you have ever done was in a library trying to discover the genus of a plant."

Brenda emerged from the door, not with Irma, as I'd feared, but with Pammy Jo. In the light of day they both looked tired and pale, their eyes smudged dark from black liner and mascara. The two had covered their cheap pole dancing underwear with jeans and sweatshirts. This was now another uniform, the uniform of American anonymity.

Without talking, the women got in my Subaru. Pammy Jo got in back with Max's car seat fixed and snug in the center of the bench seat, and Brenda got in front, sitting rigid and staring straight ahead.

"Anybody up for breakfast?" I said, a bit too upbeat.

"If you're buying," Brenda said, in a quick burst, surprising me again. "There's a place a few miles from here, Rosti's

Cafe, down on the left. My shower can wait." Brenda almost spat as she talked.

Pulling my out-of-sync suburban wagon out of the parking lot, I hoped neither of them would notice the clergy sticker in the back window. The two other vehicles in the lot were the same Dodge Durango pick-up trucks that had been there when I came in last night. One was old and battered, and now I could see all jacked up and going nowhere. The other was the same model Dodge only shiny and new. I figure the new one must be Irma's truck since she was the only one who hadn't left yet. If that *was* her truck, Irma must be doing pretty well for herself.

Pammy Jo leaned her head against Max's car seat and closed her eyes. I wondered if she was still thinking about God? Or was she thinking about her kids, or maybe she was just trying to erase the night from her mind. Pammy Jo wasn't as tough as Brenda, nor as smart, but she wasn't as stupid as she would like others to believe either. I would guess acting stupid was Pammy Jo's cover. Not much could be asked of you if everybody thought you were stupid.

The Rosti Cafe was a cutesy diner with blue and white checked curtains, located off the side of the highway. From the number of cars in the parking lot, it looked crowded for five o'clock in the morning. Inside were display cases with more pies than I could count, all with enticing names like French Silk, Chocolate Cherry and Key West Lime. Brenda guided Pammy Jo to sit inside the booth bench and she sat next to her. I was across the table looking at two haggard, tired, hard-working women who looked exhausted.

“Those pies will all be gone by tonight,” Pammy Jo said, as we sat down in the back of the restaurant at the only empty booth. Brenda glared at her, “Pammy Jo, cut the small talk.” Then, turning that same impatient and indignant look on me, she said, “How do you know Shana?”

Pammy Jo gasped, and Brenda silenced her with a hard-ass look just as the waitress walked up to the table.

“Coffee, girls?”

“Sure, thanks.” I wanted herbal tea but I definitely needed the caffeine instead.

Brenda nodded her head, and with uncharacteristic gentleness took Pammy Jo’s hand off her mouth. She seemed to understand what Pammy Jo was going through.

As the waitress poured three cups of coffee in silence, Pammy Jo looked at Brenda, who again nodded her head at her sister.

“Know what you want, girls?”

Without opening the menu, Brenda said, “Fried eggs, pancakes, bacon and hash browns. White toast buttered.”

“Times three?”

I nodded as Pammy Jo continued to stare at me in disbelief.

For no good reason at all, I decided to trust these women and I told the truth. In short clipped sentences I went over my friendship with Marnie from the day I met her right up to her disappearance. I left out the part about me being a minister.

“Isn't this something the cops might be good at?” Pammy Jo asked in earnest as she poured a long stream of sugar in her coffee.

“That's how you got those bad teeth, stupid,” Brenda snapped, moving the sugar shaker to the other side of the table, like you would with a child. Brenda had returned to her hard edge persona, leaving any momentary tenderness for Pammy Jo aside.

Pammy Jo blinked at Brenda's insult and continued talking as she reached across the table for the sugar. “Cops are supposed to look for missing persons aren't they? That's their job.”

“Right, Pammy Jo,” I said, “but since a body hasn't been found, it's just a crime scene with a disappeared mother who has abandoned her child.”

Brenda's shoulders started to relax, “So she *was* pregnant?” Brenda said in a whisper, almost to herself. “Last time I saw her she said she was gonna get out of this mess. ‘For the kid’ she'd said. I already thought she'd gotten out *before* she said she was pregnant. Shana had left dancing the pole at the Dream Palace a long time ago. She was tricking in fancy Chicago hotels, making real money.” Brenda's face had softened as she talked about Marnie.

"She didn't live with us then, but she'd come back every once and a while to say hi."

"Shana would give me money for the kids every time I saw her," Pammy Jo said.

I must have looked a bit puzzled at the reference of them living together. Brenda interpreted without being asked, "Pammy Jo's my half sister—she had the dumb father," Brenda explained. For the first time since I'd met them, they smiled at the inside joke. Not at each other or me, but at what was family-accepted truth. "And Shana, well, when Irma brought her to live with us...well, then she was family too, at least that's what Irma said." Brenda stared at her hands as she talked, as if she were concentrating on the consequences of what she was saying.

At an empty spot in the conversation Pammy Jo started talking again. "After Shana left for good, Irma said if she wasn't dead, she better be. We won't go in Shana's room at the house. Irma says it's bad luck to be in someone's room after they're dead." Pammy Jo shivered as if a cold wind had blown in the room. "Marnie's ghost could be hanging around. Ghosts scare me."

"Pammy Jo," Brenda interrupted with a sigh, "cut it with the ghost stuff. You make me crazy with that nutsy crap. You know better." Brenda again talked to Pammy Jo like she was a little kid without a brain in her head.

The waitress appeared, placed the plates of food on the table, and turned away without a word. We ate fast, inhaling our huge breakfast without talking.

"More food? How about some pie?" I asked, trying to buy more time.

"Sure, why not?" Brenda seemed as if she wanted to learn more from me too. But I had to pee.

"I gotta go to the little girls' room," I said, grabbing my jacket in an effort to cover the skimpy clothes I was still wearing. Brenda half smiled and nodded, seeming to appreciate how uncomfortable I was, parading like a hooker in broad daylight.

Avoiding my reflection in the mirror, I washed my hands. I was shaking. I was getting in deeper and deeper and I didn't have the good sense to turn around and leave. If I had a brain cell left, I would at least call Patrick back, but I didn't. If he came too soon the girls would never talk. I copied Brenda and stood straight, looked in the mirror and was surprised at my bleached blond wig, over dark eyes and super white skin. I didn't even look like me.

My experiences of the last few days were causing my face to look more cautious. Most of the time I liked my open, almost naive demeanor, but now I hoped I could keep up this hard-ass façade for Marnie. These women, Marnie's "family," as Brenda had said, were the only trail I had. I pinched my cheeks for a little color, and headed back to the table.

As I slipped back into the booth, Brenda had ordered her pie and already finished it. Pammy Jo was picking at hers one tiny bite at a time. She turned to her sister and asked, "Should we show her the letters?"

"The ones you can't read?" Brenda sighed, but didn't disagree with the initial question.

"Hey, we weren't supposed to read them. Besides even I know they aren't in English."

Brenda sighed, leveling her gaze straight toward me, looking resigned. "Does Shana have any marks you could identify her by? I mean how do we know it's her we are talking about? She told us last time that as far as we were concerned she was dead. We weren't to know anything about her or see her, ever again. That was over six years ago."

"Mar...Shana," I stumbled, "has one long scar on the palm of her right hand, maybe two or three inches long, a tiny little angel tattoo on her left shoulder in the back, and some little scars along the inside of her arms."

Pammy Jo gasped again and pressed her hand hard up against her mouth to stifle a sob. Brenda's look got harder as she squinted and concentrated on my eyes, this time ignoring Pammy Jo.

"That's her," Brenda affirmed, "What's your real name? You a cop?"

"Shepherd Murdoch, and no, not a cop." I said. I hadn't stuck to my lame alias of hours earlier. Lying just wasn't something I did well, at least not for long. I just couldn't keep it up.

"You can see the letters, but you can't keep them.

"Who are the letters from?" I asked.

"I'm not sure exactly. Some Italian guy. Not sure how she met him, but I do know that the letters are not written in English."

At the moment, I wasn't sure who was more lost, these half-sisters or me. I could see agreeing to show me these letters was making them both agitated and nervous. It was a big step. Before they could change their mind, I took the check to the front and ordered a strawberry rhubarb pie to go. It was Marnie's favorite.

The greasy eggs and hash browns sat in my stomach like a lump. I was tired but I was getting somewhere. The thought of finding out anything personal that could help me find Marnie made my adrenalin start to rush again.

Brenda snapped out directions for me as I drove them home. The day was sunny and bright, not chilly like the night before. It was one of those glorious late summer days that make you glad to be alive, but what about Marnie? She'd been missing for days, and this was the closest I'd gotten so far to finding her, and I was still nowhere.

Brenda's house wasn't anything like I would think a pole dancer's house would be. A house that was paid for, I presumed, with blood sweat, tears and a minimum of twenty-five blow jobs a night. I'd pictured a messy place with garbage piled up all around it. Instead this was a well-kept, if dilapidated, house with a small front yard, that was full of bright flowers in all kinds and shapes of containers, cheering up the otherwise drab surroundings.

Beyond the house was a long drive that led through what looked like wheat fields stuck in this industrial area. There was an old weathered barn on the right, tilting to the side. Farther back was a nondescript, sun-bleached tan house trailer propped up on cinder blocks. Then the road turned to the left and disappeared. Way in the back was a stand of trees lining the property that seemed like they might end at a distant creek or a river.

I was still in my bar clothes, a sight to behold at the Rosti Café, but as uncomfortable as I'd felt nobody had seemed to pay much attention. They must be used to it.

"Ah, Brenda, can you get me some clothes?" I asked, as I parked in front of the house. "No, wait, I think I have some jeans in the back of my car. Give me a second."

The emergency bag I keep in the back of my car had an old pair of jeans and a torn *Reimagining* sweatshirt that I pulled over my red V-neck skimpy top. Slipping off the spandex black skirt and fishnet stockings, I rubbed my legs. Fishnets are like self flagellation. With all those little diamond shaped dents etched in my skin, the rubbing only made it worse. I pulled on my paint-spattered baggy jeans. Now my clothes sort of matched the uniform of the other two, and I was finally beginning to warm up.

This ramshackle house was down an unpaved road, not too far from the Rosti Cafe and just past what looked like the local dump. The porch was disintegrating and sagged sideways. On the porch was an old wooden rocking chair and two cheap plastic white chairs. Most of the windows had plastic over them and paint had chipped off in places exposing weather-worn gray wood. The incongruity was the potted plants that rimmed the porch and the flower garden on either side of the stairs heading up toward the door.

"These flowers are amazing," I said to Brenda, presuming it was she who had the horticulture prowess. "You have a green thumb. I love flowers."

"Stay here," Brenda barked at me.

"Oh come on Brenda, let her come in. We never have company," Pammy Jo whined.

"You see here, missy, this is my house. You just crash here. And this woman isn't company. She's using us just like everyone else." Brenda looked hard at her sister, then she seemed to be having second thoughts.

Pammy Jo persisted, "Why are you being such a ..."

"Shut it, Pammy Jo," Brenda said, then with tired resignation she said to me, "Oh, shit, you might as well come in."

Inside the house it was like a child had done the decorating. All the dilapidated walls of the first room had been covered with what seemed to be scraps of wrapping paper. All different kinds and colors all over the walls. It gave a feeling of a circus or a kid's playhouse. It was pleasant enough, if a little weird. And everywhere were little rhinoceroses bunched up on shelves or on the windowsills. Glass, cloth, paper ones and even one made out of straw. But the most amazing part of the room were the butterflies. It seemed like hundreds of them hung on different lengths of thread from the ceiling. Some were made of paper and colored with pencil, crayon or markers, but most of them were fragile real dried-out monarchs.

There was no place to sit except for mounds of old cushions piled up in the corner. It was like a museum display of folk art, a place for reflection, not a place for idle living room chatter.

Looking through to the other side of the room, past an old-fashioned double doorway, was a huge kitchen with an old wood-burning cook stove and a long white metal table that was surrounded by five scratched mismatched oak chairs. The giant double sink had old-fashioned faucets, and there was an ancient hand water pump to the right of the sink, painted red.

Like the front yard, the porch and the rhino-butterfly room, the kitchen was spotless.

The furniture in the kitchen was old. The wood stove looked like it might have provided heat as well as being the cook stove. It was dinged here and there, so the cast iron shown through past the cream and light green enamel of the stove. Maybe it was from the 1930s or

40s. If there was any idle talk about mundane things like the news or the weather, this is where it must happen, not the sanctuary-like front room. The couch in the kitchen was huge and lumpy, taking up the rest of the wall space next to the sink. The couch had been covered with a handmade slipcover of bright colored fabric, also of all different patterns pieced together in a delightful way. I guess if Brenda was going to live a poor, drab existence on the outside of her life, she would do everything possible to make it bright and comforting on the inside. The first floor was just these two big rooms and a staircase going up.

"What is it with the rhinos and butterflies?" I asked.

"You can blame Shana for that," Pammy Jo started, "she got us collecting these things. She said that there was mayor of England—"

"New York, Pammy Jo, New York. England is country with *a Queen,* you know," Brenda interrupted, and sighed.

"Ya, New York. What was his name?"

"LaGuardia, and if you don't hurry up we are all going to fall asleep with boredom. Shit, never mind, you keep talking, I'll get the letters."

"I'll come with—" I said, getting up from the chair. "No you won't." Brenda slammed the kitchen door, as she went outside toward the back of the house.

"What were you saying, Pammy Jo, about the rhinos and La Guardia?"

"Oh ya, Shana told me that the mayor had said that to survive we had to have the skin of a rhinoceros and," Pammy Jo touched one of the butterflies hanging from the tall ceiling, "and the antenna of a butterfly."

"Are these everywhere in the house?"

"Except for Shana's room."

We sat for a minute or two. It was the first quiet moment since this whole night has begun. Before I could ask Pammy Jo if I could see Marnie's room, Brenda was standing at the door looking flushed and scared.

"Something's not right. Shana's been here, or they took someone else to the cellar. Like the old days."

This time Pammy Jo was serious, no crazy hand-to-the-mouth business like earlier. She was frozen in place, and alert.

"She's been here. I know it was her. She was tied to the bed in the root cellar. But she got away and the letters are gone. Only Shana and I knew—" She stared at me, breathless and shaking. This was a different Brenda from the angry, distrusting woman who had accosted me only hours earlier in the women's room at the *Dream Palace*.

"Brenda," I said, in an authoritative voice, "sit down and breathe. How do you know it was Shana?" Brenda just paced back and forth and ignored me.

"We haven't been home for what, three days? We were in town with Irma, waiting 'til I made some money to fix my car, and no one was buying last night. I did get something thanks to that weird old guy you were talking to, Pammy Jo. I still don't have enough to fix the car." Brenda was talking to herself. My heart ached for her. I wanted to reach out and say something stupid like, "I'll take care of it, I'll give you money to fix your car." But I kept my mouth shut. I knew Brenda wasn't talking to me or Pammy Jo; she was trying to put things in order.

"Brenda," Pammy Jo yelled, interrupting Brenda's stream of consciousness. "What are you talking about? Who was here? Will you sit down? You're making me nervous," Pammy Jo wrapped her arms around herself and started to rock back and forth in slow motion as if to sooth and protect herself at the same time.

Turning on her heels, Brenda hooked her finger at us. We all went outside through the kitchen and the two sisters started jogging down the long rutted driveway.

First, we passed the dilapidated barn that looked like it could fall down with the next big storm. Farther down, kitty-corner from the barn, there was that small dingy boarded up house trailer up on cinder blocks that I'd seen when we'd pulled in the driveway. Now I could see there'd been a significant fire at the trailer. It was left to stand there, as if a reminder of someone or something that had happened. A clarion, warning of danger ahead. As we jogged I told myself that I needed to not sponge up Brenda's panic—so I slowed to a fast walk as I followed the sisters down the dirt drive.

At the curve in the path, with no sight lines to the other buildings and low to the ground, partly hidden in the weeds, were two metal doors that appeared to go down to an old fashioned storm shelter.

Almost catching up to Brenda, it didn't take a trained detective to notice the fresh tire tracks and the remains of a campfire near the entrance of this storm cellar. Brenda stood at the wide open the storm doors and was hollering, "Hurry Pammy Jo, hurry up." Brenda yelled.

I'd almost forgotten about Pammy Jo, and turning around I could see she was holding back about twenty-five feet, her face looking terrified.

I started running again to respond to Brenda's urgency. By the time I caught up with her she was inside. It was dark and smelled like human waste. Holding my nose and wishing my eyes would adjust faster to the dim light, I started to gag. What if this was a trap and they were going to tie *me* up? Or what if Marnie was dead in here?

As far as I could see from the small amount of light that came through the door, this was a one room cave like space that held an old iron bed. The room looked like it was originally dug as a place to go in the event of one of those tornados that plague the Midwest in the summer.

"Let's get out of here," Brenda said. "Gives me the creeps. I checked under the bed where she told me she hid them letters. But she's been here, and the guys are long gone." Brenda pointed at the bed.

"How do you know that, Brenda?" I asked.

"Are you an idiot? Blood on the bed, cut rope on the floor, it smells like shit, fire outside is cold, and, let's just say I know." Brenda ran out the door throwing up her breakfast and pie on the stairs before she made it outside.

As we sat outside on the grass, waiting for Brenda to recover, I tried again, "Brenda, you've been in there before, tied up, like that?"

She shuddered, wiped her mouth with the back of her hand, and stood up. Standing tall, she moved her shoulders up and down, rolled her head from side to side and kicked the heavy storm doors closed with her foot.

"Can't leave the doors open, bad luck, the evil could come out." Brenda's eyes were glazed over. Ignoring me, Brenda walked back toward the house, kicking at the dust and staring at the road ahead of her.

Instead of following Brenda or going to look in the cellar again, I decided to walk the path in the opposite direction, toward the trees, to see what was on the other side. Maybe Marnie had gotten away.

With a quick turn, the path went into a tangle of small trees that led down to a beautiful stream. I stood there thinking of the ugliness of what was behind me and the beauty around me now, when I heard a noise, like a person walking close by. I turned to duck behind a large tree as I saw Irma standing over a lifeless man laying face up in the water. She shot him twice, and not missing a beat, she moved a bit and had a perfect view of me. I jumped sideways just as she shot her gun again, this time towards me and then she ran in the opposite direction—she was on the other side of the stream. The hot singe of pain hit the side my calf, and my leg screamed with a pain as I fell backwards into a brackish ditch. I heard a truck or car start up, and engine revved as Irma left in a big hurry.

I was woozy but not unconscious. Then there was the sound of someone running in my direction.

"Brenda," I whispered, the pain was so profound, it was hard to talk.

"Shh," she said, again in a very tender voice, "I heard the shots. When you weren't behind me, I came to find you." She glanced at the body in the stream as she helped me up.

"It was Irma, it only took seconds....Who's that in the water?"

"Best not to look. Can you walk?"

CHAPTER 20

Standing naked in the cold, she knew where she was. Maybe she had known all along but the fear of what happened to her in that same place long ago had kept her from remembering – and kept her from giving up. There was no Toyota Camry waiting for her, her car was gone. That would have been too good to be true. Now she had to do what she'd done before when she was little and been locked in that cold cellar. Run to the barn and hide. Run and hope everyone who knew she was there had left her to die. If no one was around, she could go to the house, find some clothes and escape—again.

The distance from the cellar to the barn was a good quarter of a mile. Neither her body, nor her lungs had been ready for the sudden burst of energy necessary to get to the barn but she ran like her life depended on it.

There was an old work shirt and overalls hanging on a peg leftover from when they worked the farm. The clothes smelled like dust, and almost gave way at the seams from rot but she was grateful for something to put on.

Sitting in the corner of the barn, facing the broken door, she needed to get her bearings. This was a place she'd promised never to come back to. But she was too tired and hurt to think. She crawled up the rickety steps to hay loft. Once in the corner she closed her eyes and slept for the first time in days.

The sound of gunshots woke her, two together, then a third—woozy from no food, with her wounds competing with each other for attention, she wondered if she was hearing things. Gunshots, now voices.

Peeking from the wood slats in the barn seeing Shep, she wanted to scream, "Here I am, I am here, thank God." She wanted to fly down the stairs and to come out when she saw Shep. But this was all wrong. Shep was with Brenda, they were passing the barn right in front of her hiding place and Shep was limping.

Just as she started to open her mouth and reveal herself, she heard a vehicle come screeching into the driveway in front of the house. Coming on the wind, she could hear Pammy Jo's thin high voice, "Hey, Irma, over here."

Peering out the slats on the other side of the barn she could see Pammy Jo squatting in the vegetable garden next to the kitchen, maybe picking at the late over ripe peas and second round of green beans.

The voices wandered away from her, wandered away like another bad dream. She couldn't go out now. Too dangerous.

Until a few days ago, her escape into semi-normal society had been working great—but then when Derek got out of prison and come looking for her everything changed.

Sitting back in the corner of the barn she couldn't see them any more, but she was sure Irma would have her 'Miss Kitty' opal covered Simmerling four-shot pocket-pistol and she was sure Irma had one more bullet. Calling out now would only get someone killed. She knew she couldn't risk showing herself. But wait, she thought, where was that kid's phone she brought with her from the cellar? Retracing her steps on her hands and knees she found the phone on the barn floor where she'd dropped it and without thinking she dialed 911.

~~~

Brenda gasped as she saw Irma's pick up barrel into the dusty driveway.

"Shit!" Brenda cursed loud enough to wake the dead and slowed her pace to a walk, and looked down at my bloody leg.

"Irma shot—" I said.

"You shut up. Not a word or I'll kill you myself. You got lucky. Irma doesn't miss. But you are pretty stupid, aren't you? Crap, join the fucking club – stupid is as fucking, stupid does. There are lots of hiding places." Brenda waved her arms in a circular motion. "If Shana's here she won't come out with Irma close by. You can see part of
~~~

the house from the top corner of the barn. Maybe we can look for her later if Irma leaves us alone."

"How about I go in the barn now? Irma couldn't hurt all of us."

Brenda stopped walking and grabbed my shoulders with a firm grip, "You don't get it. If Irma was in on this plan to get rid of Shana, what would she have to lose by killing us all? Besides, they may have taken Shana somewhere else. You're in my world now, so keep going and shut up."

"You're not protecting me are you?" I stared into Brenda's hardened eyes. "You're protecting Shana. You think she's in the barn because you two have an emergency plan. Isn't that right?"

I'd seen one set of bare footprints leading away from the shelter. I couldn't be sure if Brenda noticed them or not, but Marnie had always told Max that there had to always be an emergency escape plan.

"I don't know anything except we are in for real trouble. Unless she reloaded Irma has one shot left. That pistol is accurate only at short range. She must have shot at you from too far away. That's why you got that little scratch." Brenda's lips curled under like a dog ready to strike. She showed her teeth and spat when she talked, like she did when she spoke to me in the women's room at the Dream Palace. She gripped my good arm hard and led me to the house.

"If this is so dangerous, why are we walking right into Irma's hands?" I asked.

"She could hurt Pammy Jo. Like I said, Irma's got nothing to lose."

Irma was waiting for us on the front porch, combing Pammy Jo's long, bleached, thin, tangled hair with her fingers. "Well, Pammy Jo, look who we got here? Brenda, I am very disappointed you. Haven't I always told you to never take rides from strangers? We don't even know this woman, and you're giving her a tour of the place."

Irma looked too calm considering she's just shot that poor schlep in the creek and tried to scare me off. She, too, had changed into old jeans and T shirt but her harsh, black-penciled eyebrows and ratted, over-dyed red hair was the same. Irma was going on no sleep like the rest of us and, dangerous and irrational as she might have been, Irma looked a little scared herself. Like people get when they're doing something stupid and there is no way back from it.

Irma stood up and walked toward Brenda with a flourish. Brenda let go of my arm and met Irma in the middle of the porch. It was as if these were stage directions in some play they'd rehearsed before. I needed to get to my car. The keys were in it, everything in me said run, but I didn't want to be the reason any of us got shot, so I stood very still.

"You stupid, stupid idiot, why'd you bring her here?" Irma spit in Brenda's face like a military drill instructor. Brenda shrugged and turned just in time to avoid Irma's fist.

In my estimation, none of these women were stupid. It looked as if they'd each learned enough creative defense mechanisms to survive, and it had gotten them this far.

Brenda seemed to be on super high alert after seeing evidence of Marnie in the storm cellar. She glanced, now and then, at the blood crusting over on my jeans, but she never looked right at me. In contrast to the dim fear in Irma's eyes, Brenda's looked brighter and sparklier, like she knew a secret and wasn't telling.

"So what's with that look, Brenda? Cat ate the canary?" Irma asked. "Since you are so fond of your nosy friend here, you tie her up," Irma threw a length of clothesline that had been lying on the porch. "To that post there, hands behind your back." Brenda did what she was told, but the rope was loose and she laid the end of the rope in my hand. This wasn't a new trick.

"So chickie, guess I just grazed that leg of yours." Irma got close to my face and put the muzzle of her Simmerling under my chin. "I'll finish the job in a just a little minute when I figure out exactly what to do with you."

Irma backed away, shoved her gun down her shirt and focused her attention again on Brenda. Pammy Jo looked catatonic now, standing very still, frozen in place.

"You know how it goes, Brenda."

"Hey, Irma, wait a second." I wanted to stop whatever was happening on my account. Without warning, Brenda put her hand in my face and pushed me backwards against the rotten slats of the porch. Still tied, my head hit against the post, and I watched horrified as Brenda unzipped her jeans and bent over—just like a little kid getting ready for the whipping she knew was coming.

This was all too quick for Irma. She wasn't ready and looked a little confused. I untied the loose knot in my hand, so I'd be prepared the next time.

"Pammy Jo, get me the switch." Irma reached her hand out toward Pammy Jo who didn't move. "You stupid girl, I said, get me the switch."

Then we heard it, sirens coming down the dirt road. The women stopped moving for a brief second. Irma had a look of utter surprise on her face, but Brenda stood up, and almost smiled as she pulled up her jeans and buttoned them.

As the siren screamed closer, Irma backed off and smoothed her hair as if she was expecting company. Pammy Jo stared at Brenda, now beginning to show some affect on her face.

Irma started to laugh. She took the tiny little pistol with a mother-of-pearl handle out of her bra. I gasped.

"Oh, I should shoot you," she said, glaring at me. "But under the circumstances we'll save your punishment for another day." At that Irma pulled a chair away from the far side of the porch, where there was a hole in the floor about the size of a grapefruit. She dropped the gun then covered the hole with the chair. Brenda was acting as if she was untying my wrists, which I'd already managed to do. Again this seemed like stage directions, or a game they played when required.

"All this has something to do with you, doesn't it chickie?" Irma pointed at me. "I guess you call tell us who you are in the clink because that's for sure where we are headed. I can't wait to hear all about it. The suspense is killing me." She gave a wicked cackle of a laugh. "And remember this: I may not know your real name, but I never forget a face."

As the four of us got into the police van, it was clear that these women were accustomed to the routine. I'd been somewhat honest with Brenda and Pammy Jo about who I was and, to their credit, they didn't say a word to Irma. Now my leg was throbbing, the pain worse now that the adrenalin was wearing off, but I couldn't think about that at the moment. Survival was the name of the game. My survival.

"Ever been in one of these here paddy wagons before, cutie?" Irma sneered at me, baiting me with her voice.

"Yes. I have." I didn't say it was a peace rally and we never were actually locked up. Pammy Jo stared open-mouthed at me, but Brenda sat with her head back staring at the ceiling of the old van, lost in thought. Pammy Jo closed her mouth and copied her sister. Pammy Jo now followed her older sister's every move—another survival skill.

"I'd just like to know," Irma continued, throwing out the bait, "who tipped em? How'd they know there'd be four, so they'd send the wagon and not a cruiser? And what was the point? No johns, no drugs, not even a gun. Too bad, little chickie, you fell on that metal fence post and got that nasty cut on your leg there." Irma's words sounded mad and tough, but wobbled a bit."

"No matter," she said, reassuring Pammy Jo in a weird, even maternal, way, "no crime here—they have to let us go in 24 hours. Then I'll finish what I started, when I get you home."

CHAPTER 21

After all the commotion stopped and the cops had been gone for a while, she left her hiding place in the barn and stood outside. There was no wind. The August sun was blazing but it was better than the barn. Slowly she maneuvered her beat up body toward the house.

After seeing Shep through the slats in the barn she had some hope. But now Shep knew her past, and she felt hotter with shame—it wasn't the past that made her feel so guilty, it was her dishonesty. Looking at the dust on her feet she remembered what Shep told her about Jesus. What was it he said? Maybe it was when you mess up, shake off the dust and go sin no more. And that she was going to try doing, if she got the chance.

She slipped into the back door of the house. There wasn't much in the fridge but an old apple and some peanut butter which she ate like a gourmet appetizer. The pie from Rosti's was on the table. Shep knew she loved strawberry-rhubarb pie, but not

Brenda and Pammy Jo, "not enough sugar in that one," Pammy Jo would say. She took off the scratchy clothes she'd gotten from the barn and gobbled some of the pie, using her fingers.

I've got to get out of here, she thought, again as she walked through the kitchen into the living room. It was an eerie place. She'd almost forgotten about the well preserved butterflies that she'd hung from the ceiling. Now they brushed against her face. For a minute it felt like they were alive. The day she'd found these monarchs she'd been walking through the field, near the house, wanting to run away but not knowing how.

As she began to slowly move towards the stairs she felt like she was in a dream and was losing touch with reality. It was a mystery why so many monarchs died in the same place that day. She remembered thinking it was her fault for being bad. She didn't want that to be true. She had gone back to the house to get a box. Carefully she'd picked up each one from the huge field of dead butterflies. More than likely, she thought now, they'd died from pesticide spray the farmer's crop dusted over their fields.

But she remembered how carefully she had attached thread to each lovely creature with a dab of super-glue. Then she plastered them with hair spray to keep their shape, and hung them all over the living room.

"Shit, you are loosing it. You aren't Shana anymore." She said out loud, trying to keep the bad thoughts from coming. Just walking into this house was scary. On the outside with Max, she'd done a good job talking her crazy thoughts away. But here, back at this awful house with dried blood all over her naked body, she couldn't keep clear.

The butterfly wings on her cheek began to feel like soft little fingers that gave her energy. For a moment it felt like the butterflies were coming alive, released from their strings and flying around to love her. Love in a place like this had to be a secret. Love wasn't something that happened to people like her. That was true until Max was born.

The thought of Max was like a hard slap in the face. "I have to get out of here," she said again, this time even louder. Then over and over again like a mantra, I have to get out of here, I have to get...

Four days ago after being violently taken from her kitchen, she'd tried not to think about Max. When thoughts of him entered her mind, she'd push them away, like she would push Max if a car was coming and she needed to save him from danger.

Well, she hadn't done a very good job of saving Max, had she? She was actually worse than her own mother. She let Max think everything was going to be ok. At least her mother had told her the dirty truth from the beginning.

Her body started to heave with great sadness and she couldn't keep the tears away any longer. She sat on the stairs she sobbed. But crying wasn't her friend, crying released all her demons. Shep would say, "Go ahead and cry. It'll make you feel better." That was hardly true for her. If she cried as a kid her mother would beat her with a hairbrush, screaming, "You little shit, you have ruined my life and you have nothing to cry about. You are just a piece of crap, and crap doesn't cry."

Terrible things happened when you cried, she knew that. You felt your insides, you stopped watching your back and more could happen than getting beat with a hair brush.

But she was crying hard now. Max had opened up places in her that let her feel love and that was dangerous. Crying was like an entity all in itself. Like a bad dream monster you can't shake. "It's the way it is for you," Shep had said, "Your fear of crying might not ever go away." But she hated crying. She was afraid she'd get lost in the past and in that place it was hard to sort out what was real and what wasn't.

She looked out the front window and saw Shep's Outback and Bell's Durango and started to panic. Of course, they left the cars because the cops carted them off. Reason returned and just like it had started, the crying stopped. Like a quick summer storm that threatened to kill you one minute, and was sunny the next.

She knew the women would be back tomorrow after Bell got somebody to pay their bail. Shep would not stay overnight in the lock-up. But where were the boys who untied her and had taken her car? They'd be back to check on her. Before she could leave the house she had a few things to do and now she figured she had enough time.

As the sun shown in on the butterflies, she noticed now that they were old and cracking, not sparkling like she'd seen them a few minutes ago. In this house the past was holding her hostage. The demons wanted her back. She shivered.

"I have time for a bath," she said out loud, surprising herself with the strength in her voice. She climbed the stairs gently touching each decrepit butterfly. "You will never make it to that

place in Mexico, down that valley, to Piedra Herrada," she said as she passed them by. "One day I will go for you." As she slowly climbed, one stair at a time, she was sobered by the pain in her body and what she needed to do.

~~~

The ride to the police station in this seedy industrial district wasn't far.

"All right, ladies," snarled the craggy, cop. "Out of the truck. We don't need cuffs do we, girls? Nobody's planning on a quick escape, are you?" This cop looked as if his uniform had been sprayed on—you could see every muscle in his arms and every roll of fat around his belly. He looked mean. Inside the station he barked orders.

"You." He pointed to me, "New Girl. Over here. The rest of you old-timers go with Officer Stitt." He pointed to a grizzled, older woman officer who seemed unhappy to leave her crossword puzzle to take Brenda, Pammy Jo and Irma to be processed before they went to the lockup.

As I watched them walk off, Irma threw her left hand up over her right shoulder with her middle finger up, flippin' me off as the kids in confirmation class would say. But no one noticed Irma's gesture except me, or they ignored it. It made no difference to them.

Walking down another corridor of doors with frosted glass hiding their contents and marked by numbers, the
~~~

cop had me by the elbow and wiggled his fingers under my breast, pinching me hard. I gasped and flinched.

"Cut it out!" I yelled.

"Oh, don't give me the high and mighty attitude, you piece of crap," he said, and tried again. As I moved my shoulder to dodge his fingers, he crunched my elbow in his grip and shoved me through a doorway that opened into a large utilitarian room with a half-dozen old government-issue desks, heaped with official looking forms, and an ancient looking black telephone on each desk. Not a computer among them. This paperwork was still done by hand, real Dark Ages stuff.

I was grateful that there were other cops and offenders in the room, relieved I wouldn't be accosted by Mr. Wonderful again, at least not yet.

"Name, address, social?" I saw no reason to be cagey so I gave my correct information to the cop. I figure the arresting officers had already run my license plates.

"You want to give your side of this?"

"I want to make a phone call." This guy scared me more than Irma and her gun.

"Oh, for shit's sake, another idiot here who wants to make a *phone call*," he said in a loud, sarcastic, singsong voice. "And who might you like to call, little missy? You can't have a lawyer. Sluts like you can't pay the rent, much less a lawyer. That costs a lot more than what you got under those jeans. But Ok, just to keep it on the up and up, I'll make your call for you."

"Isn't this supposed to be a private call?" I asked, but was not in a position to argue.

"You want to make a call or not?"

"Patrick Kelly, Sergeant Patrick Kelly, Police Department, Evanston, Illinois," I said, measuring my voice in a desperate effort to stay calm. My inquisitor wrote the number down.

"You want to call a cop? That's funny, *really* funny," he said.

I looked for his name tag but the flap of his shirt pocket covered it.

"That doesn't work down here, little lady. You think you have a cop friend in another county who traded a DUI for a blowjob and you think he's gonna come down and save your ass? You watch too much TV. You whores are so stupid. You must be pretty green to want to call a cop. But let's do it *by the book*." He laughed loudly, glancing at his colleagues as he dialed the number.

"Sergeant Kelly in? Sure, gimme his voice mail." He said, and winked at me. Covering the mouthpiece, he said, "Guess it'll be a while before your prince gets this."

The nasty cop, whose breath smelled as if he was in serious need of a dentist, changed his voice from baiting singsong to more professional as he left a message for Patrick.

"Ya, Sergeant we have a hooker here who says her name is Shepherd Murdoch. For some strange reason she thinks you might like to come pay her bail. She'll be waiting for you in the lockup." He winked again, and left the address and phone number on the message.

He laughed. "So, you'll sit in holding, and we'll see how cold you have to get before you tell me what the hell this is all about. Won't take you long. The AC runs pretty cold in there. Just ring the bell next to the door if you want to talk. And if you decide to throw in one of your little tricks, everything might go faster." Was this quasi-psychopath paid to tweak nipples and verbally abuse newcomers in an effort to short-circuit the process, or was he just rogue? I'd believe anything at this point. This time, as we walked toward the holding area, he didn't try to fondle me, maybe concerned that, on the off chance a Sergeant Patrick Kelly would come to get me, he'd better back off.

Sitting in a large, cold room lined with metal benches screwed into a concrete floor, with bright lights and blowing air conditioning, I couldn't stop shivering. I could kick myself. Patrick had to be at home sleeping off his injuries. Why'd I think he'd be at work? That was stupid.

The other choice would have been Rupert, and he could have made things worse. He'd be mad and piss off this ready-to-pop cop. Then we'd both be in this holding tank. I had to wait. I still had enough faith in the system to know I'd get out sooner or later, but even so, this is a scary place. Tired as I was, it was too cold to sleep. They hadn't noticed my leg. The blood was dark against my jeans. I was just as glad it didn't hurt too much now; maybe Irma was right about this being a scratch.

I'd heard from my street ministry colleagues that cops in the poor districts were stuck with more crap than most precincts. As a rule, I stayed away from jail ministry. Once I'd done Bible study at a local county jail, and it was creepy. I couldn't decide who was crazier, the inmates or the jailers. They both looked about the same, different color uniforms and one had keys, the other didn't. Things weren't much different here as far as I could see.

But who'd called the cops at Brenda's? Had they been heading out that way already? The police had to have known Irma and the girls, so even at the slightest provocation they were brought in, unless, of course, they'd struck some deal with these cops, which wasn't hard to imagine. And there was the dead guy in the stream.

At first, I was alone in the huge cheerless room. As the morning wore on more women joined me. My new roommates looked hung over and beat up—like they'd been in a fight with some cop, pimp, husband or jealous wife. Except for one teenager who sat in the corner crying, the rest of us looked over forty and we weren't crying. It had become obvious to all of us that tears wouldn't help. Each new woman to arrive looked like a clone of the next. Like me, she sat on the bench and pulled her knees up to her chin—staring at a spot on the wall or rested her head on her knees. No one talked. We all just shivered and sighed from time to time.

Irma and the girls would know the routine. Maybe they had connections that got them a get-out-of-jail-free card. I had to wait for Patrick. I had to hope he'd gotten back to work. There was nothing left to do in this freezing room but hope, and even for a minister this wasn't a very satisfying thought. Time dragged, and I was cold to the bone.

"Shepherd Murdoch," The craggy looking woman from the front desk unlocked the door. "This way." I followed her down the hall. After a few twists and turns, we came through another door and I saw Patrick, his arm in a sling and a serious expression on his face. My eyes welled with tears. He leaned over and whispered in my ear, "Say nothing."

Patrick had already paid my bail. The woman officer who'd taken Irma, Brenda and Pammy Jo to be processed was now handing me paperwork to sign.

"Court date in six weeks. You can bring a lawyer."

"Thanks," Patrick glanced at her signature, "Officer Stiff."

"That's Stitt, Sergeant."

"Right, Stitt. Ok, *Reverend* Murdoch let's go."

Stitt raised her eyebrows in surprise. I was sure this would make for good water cooler talk at the police station. As we headed toward the door, Patrick bought me a cup of coffee out of the vending machine in the lobby.

As we walked to what looked to be a rental car, I could tell Patrick was angry, but at the moment I didn't care. I was freezing from the holding cell, and neither the hot summer sun nor the cup of coffee was helping. My brain wasn't working.

"I'm freezing."

"Just a second." He grabbed his sports jacket from behind the seat. He laid the tweed over me like a blanket. "That should help. I'll turn the heat up."

I leaned back and smelled the cologne from his coat as I tucked myself into a ball and pulled the jacket around me.

Patrick folded himself into the driver's seat and just stared out the windshield for a moment.

"Where's your car?" He asked, as he was about to close the door.

"Back at the house where they arrested us."

"Of course." His crumpled forehead looking angry and serious. Now he'd lost that detached "I'm a cop look" he'd had when I'd met him—was it just a few days ago?

"Someone called 911. It could have been Marnie. We think she was there or had been there."

"We?"

"The two women arrested with me said Marnie used to live there. They called her Shana Smith. They worked for the Irma at the Dream Palace. Irma was also arrested. Irma could be their mother or foster mother or something, and Irma—"

"Shepherd, you are lucky to be alive!" Patrick slammed the door hard. I jumped with surprise. We just sat quiet for a minute before Patrick spoke again, "By the way, this morning I got a courtesy call from an Illinois State Trooper friend of mine about a body that turned up about five miles out of town here. We won't know much more for a few days until the DNA comes back. But if we are lucky it's one of our kidnappers. Nice hair, by the way."

"What?"

"Body fits the description of what we're looking for. Recent, superficial knife wounds on the arms. But that didn't kill him. He was found naked in a stream, bullet in the head and groin. Could be one of the guys who got cut in Marnie's kitchen." Patrick started the car.

"Irma did it." I said, pulling off the hideous wig and rubbing my head.

"What? And you were going to mention this when?"

"You didn't give me a chance—and she shot my leg," I said, chattering with cold.

"Really, really, Shepherd?"

Even at that I didn't have the energy to tell him the rest. "I can't blame you for being angry at me," I said, leaning a little forward, "But it's a good thing I went to the Dream Palace. I got information."

"It isn't your job to go poking around and getting arrested with dangerous felons. What information made all that shit worth it?" Patrick leaned back in his chair and winced.

"Your shoulder still hurt?" I said, changing the subject.

"I'm fine," he said, shaking his head a little back and forth. "Doc says I don't have to wear the sling, but man, this is taking longer to heal than the others. But enough about me.

"Shep, you make me crazy. I sort of follow your flawed logic, since we professionals aren't moving fast enough for you. And it makes all the sense in the world to put yourself in harms way and get arrested, but it isn't very smart."

I wanted to talk to Brenda to put more pieces together, but I couldn't imagine her being willing to talk to me now. And who was the dead guy, Derek maybe, or one of the others? I leaned my head against the car window.

"Don't get too cozy. We are stopping at the first emergency clinic that comes up on the GPS and get that looked at."

CHAPTER 22

The door to her room was locked. Reaching over the door she found the key where she'd left it. Everything was the same. Her old room was harsh and grim, painted black. She'd refused to paint it with comfortable colors or hang bright curtains, like the other girls. She'd not wanted any illusion of coziness to tempt her into thinking any part of this was real life.

This was Shana's room, that's who she was back then. It was a fake home for a fake person. She'd left the dingy sheets and comforter on the bed. There were no mirrors in her room, no pictures on the walls and nothing personal or sentimental.

Before Max, she was sure she'd sold her soul to the devil – that there was no hope of redemption. Now she didn't believe that.

Living as Shana had been the blackest time of her life, so she'd lived in that place like she was a ghost. The other girls thought all that was bad luck. But she didn't believe in luck, because she'd never had any.

She took three clean but stale towels out of the old dresser and headed down the hall. The bathroom, unlike her room, was cheery and painted pink with little stickers of ducks and lambs put every which way above the bathtub. These must have been for Pammy Jo's kids when they'd visit. She'd heard from Father Al that DCFS had taken the kids away after Pammy Jo was arrested last year. Why Pammy Jo hadn't tried to get away too, at least for her kids, made no sense to her.

Next to the bathtub was a bucket of salt. The girls believed that salt would clean them up if they'd run into anything contagious. They also thought it would clean off any evil spirits that might have glommed on to their skin. She wasn't sure about all that but she knew the salt would hurt and she hoped it would clean out her wounds—she poured several cups of salt in the tub, ran hot water and sat in the tub waiting for it to fill up.

She could feel increased pain in her wounds as the salt water sank into them. Her wrists and ankles were still raw, but even in these last few hours of freedom they were starting to scab over.

As the blood from the knife fight in her kitchen days ago, washed dried old blood off her body. She thought that some of the blood could have belonged to one of her attackers. That made her queasy.

Maybe instead of a bath, she should have gone to the hospital and asked for a rape kit. But she'd have been asked too many questions, and who was she kidding? There would be no well-turned investigation here, no DNA samples studied. No one cared about a woman like me, she thought. Except for Shep, and that was giving her hope, but what could a minister turned gardener do for her now?

The big glaring wound she couldn't avoid looking at was the two-inch "X" one of her hooded attackers had carved on her stomach.

"My signature baby, so you don't ever forget me." The husky voice hadn't sounded like Derek, but she couldn't tell. She was too scared. While Derek was a major jerk, he wasn't too much into blood. She knew he'd killed a few people here and there, but slashing was not his style. Still, somebody was getting jittery. The "X" looked more like a cross, or was that her imagination? Marine knew it would scab over and maybe disappear, at least on the outside.

In the early years Derek had been her pimp, and she was his gravy train. But he was stupid, the elevator not going to the top, as it were. They'd been kids out on the streets together and she tried to take care of him. She gave him the illusion she was working for him but he was just her muscled protection. At some point Derek got hooked on drugs and that made him violent. So when he had a big bunch of meth to package and sell she turned him in. By then she was pregnant and it was the incentive she needed to make a break.

Then she asked around, looked for someone to help her and got Shep's name and address. Lucky for her, the case against Derek had gotten him six years in jail. That combined with her pregnancy helped her break free. That was right around the time Father Alphonso made her an offer she didn't refuse.

Who was behind this? Was it Irma who'd always wanted money? Or Derek who was pissed at her for turning him in or was it that priest? Last week Palikowski and his priest Gestapo came around asking questions. But none of this seemed big enough to have her kidnapped and left for dead. She took a long soak in the tub then when the water was cold she pulled the plug with her toes. She'd lain in the blood-tinged water long enough. When the tub was empty she filled it up again, this time with warm water, to rinse the blood and salt off her body.

After towel drying her hair she put on clothes she'd left behind six years ago. T-shirt, jeans, bra, underpants and socks, all a little big since she hadn't eaten much except that wrinkled apple with peanut butter and strawberry rhubarb pie in four, or was it five, days.

"Ok, girl, gotta kick you out of here." That's what Shep would say when she had to get to work and she'd overstayed her welcome at the greenhouse.

"One more thing," Marnie said, opening the closet door and removing a fake panel in the floor that she'd put in when she'd first inherited this room. Out of the hole she took a zip-lock plastic bag that held money, credit cards, fake ids, a key and passports that she'd hoped to never need again. She lingered over the stack of letters from Al's guys that she'd moved into her safety hole after she'd shown them to Brenda and Pammy Jo. But where was the book? She'd hid it here the last time she visited when no one was at the house. A wave of panic swept over her until she felt deeper in the hole and there it was, still in the packaging and ready to be delivered. Keeping this a secret had not kept Max safe. She would need to use it now. She gave the

room one last look, and left the door wide open with the key still in the lock.

~~~

"Have you heard from Crystal? How's Max?" I asked Rupert as he was making the morning coffee.

"Crystal came back last night. She said the sisters are having a blast with Max, so Crystal went to work this morning to assess the damage her time away might have caused."

This startled me. Rupert hasn't said anything about Crystal being back. Was he hiding something? Maybe he just wanted an evening alone with his wife without me asking questions. That would have been fair, but he could have told me. I wasn't sure what was up with him at the moment or why my hackles were up.

Returning from my outrageous adventures, I'd now been spending time on my grandmother's comfortable leather couch in the library. There were papers and post-it notes strewn everywhere. I was wracking my brain going over all the details but everything seemed a dead end.

Suddenly, the Woodstone front gate buzzer went off with a piercing sound that made me cover my ears with both hands. Rupert answered the buzzer. "Murdoch Residence,"

"Yeah, US Postal Service, I have plants and a package for Reverend—"
~~~

Rupert interrupted, "Jack is that you?"

"Yeah, Rup, what's up? You haven't locked the gate for years."

"Long story. I'll be right down."

A few months before Marnie'd disappeared, Rupert had suggested putting in a security system, but I wasn't into being my own gated community. So that meant that if you locked the gate, someone had to go down the long driveway to unlock it.

Rupert ran back in the door breathless, which was pretty strange for the usual cool, collected Rupert. "We got a delivery. Bulbs for fall—but look at this." He said, as he handed me the smaller package that was, it seemed hand delivered somehow.

"Those bulbs need to go in the cooler, don't you think Rupert?" I interrupted, laying the small parcel on my lap. "Give me a minute with this will you?"

Rupert was as curious as I was to know what was in the package. But his current behavior was making me cautious.

"Sure, whatever," Rupert turned on his heel and walked out of the house.

I waited until I heard the screen slam before I looked again at the package. The handwriting was hers and the return address was Marnie's house in Evanston, and it had a South Chicago postmark. That meant she must have been the one who called 911. Either way, as of yesterday, when she sent this package, Marnie was still alive. Oh my God, I hoped this was the explanation I'd been waiting for. Maybe there was a note saying "I'm sorry, please come get me."

I couldn't catch my breath. Up to this point it was all guessing. Now I would learn the truth. The envelope was an unremarkable, common-sized, pre-printed padded envelope from the post office. There was nothing unusual about the package itself, except for Marnie's handwriting on the front. I pulled on the embedded string but it broke in my hands. Then I ripped it open. My missing keys fell out but there was no car key.

There was also an exquisite small red leather book, about four by six inches, with the pages edged in gold, wrapped in a black silk scarf. I didn't recognize the scarf since Marnie never wore black—she hated black.

This book was handmade, in pristine condition, yet it seemed very old.

I lifted the soft leather cover. The paper inside was like a cross between parchment and onionskin. Thin enough to be elegant yet, thick enough so the pen wouldn't bleed through to the next page. There was an inscription inside the front cover, written with blue-gray ink. All it said was "PAX, Love A."

PAX was Latin for peace, but who was A? I was almost afraid to turn the page and see what this supposed book of peace contained.

Page one started with a list of names, addresses and phone numbers. Each had a number with a circle around it. I recognized the names of a few high profile politicians and clergy. I was too excited to sit down so I started pacing.

The ledgers found in Marnie's basement gave numbers, dollar amounts and dates, so maybe this book was the key? My heart was beating at what felt like a mile a minute. But why all the drama? Why didn't she just come home?

Whoever was setting up Marnie's meetings, must not have known about the red book, except for 'A' who seemed to have given it to Marnie as a gift. But did he know what she'd been writing in there? It would be too dangerous for the clients if this book fell into the wrong hands but the mere fact Marnie had it, must have meant she felt the need to protect herself. But from who?

I checked to see if there was a note hidden in the package. Nothing—no directions, no instructions. I had to believe Marnie was counting on me to help her, but I didn't know where to begin. The book could help unravel things, but could it help me find her?

Under normal circumstances, I would have been pouring over this book with Rupert, dividing up the names and asking questions. But something wasn't right there either. I needed Rupert's help but my gut wasn't trusting him. He should have told me about Crystal coming back from the monastery. What was I missing? I prayed to God I was being paranoid. But to not tell me about Crystal meant there was something wrong with our friendship or with

Rupert's relationship with his wife, and that, I couldn't even begin to imagine.

I took a zip-lock plastic freezer bag out of the kitchen drawer, and after re-wrapping the book in the silk black scarf I took a paper towel, wrapped up the whole thing, zipped the bag shut and wrote the words "unsweetened chocolate" on the white strip used to identify what was inside. And I stuffed it in the back of the freezer. I was the chocolate person in the house, and I doubted anyone would go into the freezer looking for chocolate. Rupert and Crystal knew everything about this house and would find anything I hid, if they were looking for it.

I ought to be ashamed of myself, I thought. Marnie would have known Rupert would receive the delivery. Why shouldn't I just go out there and show him the book? Why couldn't I stop acting like V. I. Warshawski? God help me.

Still, I couldn't ignore the warning signals my gut was shouting at me.

Padding out to the greenhouse, still in my pajamas and slippers, I shielded my eyes with my hand against the sun. In the greenhouse, Rupert was sitting at my desk looking both hurt and angry.

I held out the keys that Marnie had returned. He let out a slow whistle. I dropped the keys back in the bag but I didn't tell Rupert about the book.

"I guess this means she's alive." Rupert's shoulders began to relax, and he put his arm around me, hugging me. His forgiveness hug and open face made me feel guilty for mistrusting him. I decided to broach the sensitive topic again. "What did Crystal say about Max?"

He took one second too long to respond. I had the feeling he was being careful when he talked about his wife. Something was definitely wrong.

"Ah, Max is fine, I guess. She said he was having fun with the frogs at the edge of the pond and he was horsing around with a group of visiting brothers on retreat. But Crystal went right to bed when she got home and was off to work early this morning. She said something about running into an old friend from college who pissed her off."

"The stress of this is getting to all of us. We're all seeing ghosts around the corner."

"I guess," Rupert said, still fiddling with his pocketknife. "Crystal and I are going for dinner later." He shrugged his shoulders.

"Good idea," I said, wondering if he'd noticed I was talking to him more like a counseling client and less like my trusted old friend. His loyalty to Crystal was paramount—I knew that—and, to my knowledge, she'd never played games with him, much less played the field.

~~~

Besides my missing Subaru and the enormous Bentley, the only other vehicle at Woodstone was my battered but functional jeep. The old car was left over from the
~~~

days when I lived in Wisconsin and needed to get to my outlying congregants, rain or shine. Now I used it for small, messy greenhouse jobs like picking up old pots from a yard sale or gathering wild plants off road.

I had to find Patrick. After he rescued me from the police station in Gary, we were avoiding each other. He was mad and I was licking my wounds. But I had to at least let him know I'd heard from Marnie.

As I drove the jeep the few miles to Patrick's office, it dawned on me that we had two cars missing, Marnie's and mine, and she couldn't be driving them both.

As soon as I walked into the police station, I knew it was a mistake. The waiting area was clogged with people either waiting to be questioned or looking for information. I felt in the way.

"Lots happening today," I said to the young officer at the desk.

"Yes, ma'am," she said, "How can I help you?"

"Reverend Shepherd Murdoch to see Patrick Kelly, if he's free."

"I think he's taking a statement, but I'll check." The young officer picked up the phone and dialed.

"Reverend Murdoch here to see you." The slight woman behind the counter seemed too young to be a cop.

"Shep, this is my daughter Moira," Patrick said as he approached the desk. "And honey, this is Reverend

Shepherd Murdoch." I smiled and nodded at her, wondering if Patrick would have any other surprises for me today. I guess I wasn't the only one with secrets to reveal. But this was not the time to get ahead of myself.

"Moira is a recent graduate of the police academy and for some reason is doing temp work here until she finds a job somewhere else. Isn't that right?"

"Right, sergeant," she said, trying her best to stay professional.

"So what brings you out of seclusion?" He said, turning to me and pointing down to hall toward his office. Given that I'd been avoiding Patrick's calls since he dropped me at home following my arrest, I was uncomfortable that I was even there to ask for his opinion.

"I have something but I haven't quite figured it out." I said, as I sat down across from him.

"Yet," Patrick said almost smiling, hold his sharpened pencil as if ready to write down every word.

"I got this package in the mail today with my keys and a book." I handed him the envelope with my keys in it.

Patrick took a pair of gloves out of the box on his desk, gently took the bag by the edges, studied the address label and shook the keys out on the desk. "We're already looking for your car. So what's Marnie's point?" Patrick said, with an edge in his voice as he picked up the phone.

"Moira come back here with gloves and an evidence bag. I want you to run something to the lab for me," he said. He listened to her and then said with resignation, "Oh, honey, I'm not your sergeant, I'm your Dad....of course, I see you as my personal gopher." He smiled at me. "Besides you might like the young buff technician they have down there."

Patrick hung up the phone and checked over the package again, as we waited in silence for Moira to pick it up for the lab. Moira came in after a quiet tap on the door. I watched the efficient young recruit put the envelope and the keys in the bag, nod her head to both of us and close the office door behind her.

He tapped his pencil on the edge of the desk, "I have to meet with a family in 30 minutes but haven't had lunch and it's almost four. Wanna walk with me to the hot dog stand?"

"A hot dog? You know how much crap is in a hot dog?" I asked, pleased the conversation was lightening up.

"Fat and rat hairs. Oh, please don't you start. Moira moved in with me the day before yesterday to take care of me, she says. Right, I was happy eating absolutely whatever I pleased, now my fridge is cleaned out and I'm eating nothing but veggies and organic chicken."

He told yet another cop at the front desk that he'd be back in a half hour, and we walked out the door.

The hot dog stand just down the block from the station was famous, not so much for its hot dogs, but for the eighteen kinds of mustard they had to go with them.

"I'll have a char dog with everything, and so will the lady." Pat barked.

"Ah, no onions on mine, thanks." I said, nodding at him in acknowledgment. My kids loved this place. We came here after all the soccer games, win or loose, and Alex the owner never forgets a name or a face.

"You want fries with that, Pat, as usual?" Alex said, looking down at the char dog he was preparing.

"No, I'm taking enough heat for eating this dog." The middle-aged balding but not unattractive man with deep green eyes and a white apron spattered with grease and mustard pursed his lips and nodded like he understood Patrick's dilemma.

"And Shep, you want fries? How's that soccer player of yours?" Alex asked, as if they talked everyday and it was a normal occurrence to see the two of them together at his counter ordering food. Oh, the things he must see here.

"He's good, thanks. And no fries for me either, thanks. You know with that memory you ought to be a detective." He smiled, nodded and took the next food order from the teenagers standing in line behind us.

"Everyone's equal with Alex. Must be why everybody loves him." I smiled, taking one of the fries Alex had given Patrick anyway.

"You know why Alex would make a lousy detective? Because he won't tell on anybody."

"Some would see that as a great quality."

"Ok," Patrick said biting into his char dog, "Back to your friend. I'll run the prints on the keys and the envelope but we already know whose they are. If Moira is quick at the lab and is in the mood, she'll woo the guy into hurrying up and we'll have something tomorrow. But don't hold your breath."

"Ok and there was another book, but I left it at home," I said casually, as his cell phone started buzzing.

"Kelly," Patrick said into the cell phone he pulled out of the pocket of his sport coat as he looked at me with a wrinkled forehead.

"No, I'm down the street. Be right there." He closed the phone, and grabbed the paper tray and napkins left over from his lunch. "Gotta head back. You done?"

"Sure," I said, tossing my half eaten char dog in the trash, hoping Alex hadn't noticed. Patrick was moving fast and I had to jog a little to keep up with his long legs and quick stride as we covered the short half block back to the station.

"Shep, what were you saying about a book? Maybe you were going to ask me for dinner? I'll tell you the whole sordid story of my life start to finish, if you like."

"Ok. I think it could be the key we have been looking for. Dinner and sordid details, sounds perfect. How could I resist? When?" I said.

"Tonight at your place. With Moira parked at my condo, we'd have no privacy. And, after what happened at Le Petite Gourmet, I'm not sure we should go out in public for a while." He paused and looked off, "We're still not sure who was gunning for who or if they were stray bullets from a gang banger drug drop gone bad. All we have so far are the bullets they dug out of me, and the wainscoting of the restaurant. But this isn't for publication."

Patrick was losing the semi-gritty attitude he'd greeted me with less than an hour ago. "Ok," I said, "I'll see you tonight, about 7:30, my place?" I wanted Rupert and Crystal to be gone from the house on their 'date' so I wouldn't have to worry about any eavesdroppers of my own.

"Guess you've forgiven me my hiatus?" I said.

"Shep," Patrick said, giving my arm a squeeze, "I can't stay mad at you for long. Funniest thing..." he said, almost to himself, as if in amazement. We parted company as he turned toward the door of the police station and I walked to the jeep parked down the street.

At dinner I'd give Patrick the book. It might explain what she was up to, but it wasn't likely to help me find her any sooner.

That would give me enough time to try to catch up with Father Sawyer after 5 o'clock mass, see what he knows.

CHAPTER 23

Down in the kitchen she stuffed her blood-stained clothes from the barn in a plastic shopping bag she found tucked in between the kitchen counters, and took the clothes along. In a second bag she put the things she'd collected from their hiding place. She'd guessed that at least two hours had passed since the cops had taken everyone to the station, and it was time to get moving.

She wondered if Shep had meant for her to have her car. The keys were in the ignition and a cell phone was in the glove box. That wasn't like Shep.

The fishnet stockings and a skimpy black skirt tossed on the back seat spoke volumes. She still had no idea how Shep figured out to look at the Dream Palace in the first place. She'd been careful to destroy any clues about her past, except, of course, for those awful boxes in the basement. But even in there was no mention of the Dream Palace, so she must have missed something. Mistakes were something Alphonso hated more than anything else, but she must have gotten sloppy nonetheless.

It never felt right to keep things from Shep since, for the last six and a half years, she'd been her lifeline. Shep was too good at figuring things out and she hadn't been ready to be that transparent.

"I'm a minister," Shep would say. "Don't make a big deal out of the fact I knew more about you than you'd told me. All I had to do was fill in the blanks."

One thing for sure, Shep already knew things about her no one else knew, and now she knew even more. She threw the bags into Shep's car and sat for a few minutes just taking in that shabby old house one last time. Shep had taught her to say a prayer when she entered something new or left something old.

"Ok God here goes. I hope that the flowers keep on blooming until Brenda and Pammy Jo get out of here and the spirit of all those dead butterflies come to life and float this place away." That was the best prayer she could muster as she started Shep's Subaru wagon and pulled out of the long driveway toward the highway.

~~~

As I walked into Father Sawyer's office, there was that unmistakable churchy smell of old wood, dusty fabric and books. There was also this semi-permanent smoky odor embedded in the wood, from a time when almost everyone, coming or going, smoked. This old church
~~~

office was reassuring in a strange way. It reminded me of an easier time when a pastor was able to answer any question and was trusted by stranger and friend alike.

A few steps inside the door was a long work desk that took up one side of the room. The other walls were lined with a bookshelf, a supply cabinet and a gigantic old copier spewing out sheets of paper. To the left of the desk was a dark imitation wood sign with arrows guiding visitors to other rooms. To the right, "PASTOR" to the left it said, "CHURCH." All in fake gold gilt letters, worn off with age.

Behind the sturdy desk, built for wear not beauty, was an unsmiling middle-aged woman. Her curly brown-gray hair was cut short around her ears. "Afternoon, can I help you," she asked looking over her glasses at me, continuing to fold worship bulletins.

"I'd like to see Father Sawyer," I said, as I looked around the typical down-to-earth office.

"Not here. Can I give him a message?"

"Ask him to call Shepherd Murdoch." I fumbled through my purse for my business card, "Oh, and let me put my new cell number on that."

"Can I tell him what this is about?" The woman asked.

"I understand Father Sawyer has helped a friend of mine."

"Oh, and who's that?"

"Marnie Cooper."

The folding stopped and she looked at me. Curious. "I know Marnie. She used to be around a lot. I'm sure Father would like to talk to you. Marnie was one of his favorites."

"What do you mean by favorites?" I asked, surprised at the anger in my voice.

"Nothing, really."

"What did they talk about?"

"He liked to talk to her, ask her questions. I never eavesdropped. Don't keep your job long if you do that. Father leaves the door open when he talks to people. I guess I could've heard a lot if I'd tried hard enough. But I have my own troubles, don't need more. His office is far enough away I can't hear a thing anyway."

Methinks thou protesteth too much, I thought, but didn't say.

"Look I have to get these bulletins ready for 5:00 mass. Why don't you try back next week? Too bad you missed him. He left a few hours ago for retreat. He's due back day after tomorrow. I'll leave a message for him to call you."

"Thanks, that'd be great. Could you tell me what retreat center he's at?"

The secretary looked at me with a curious expression on her face, "Retreat, is time away from questions, phones and, well, people like you." She said, a bit too snitty, as she glanced at the clock and returned to folding the bulletins.

"I need to talk to Father Sawyer—soon as possible. It could be a matter of life and death. Can you call him?"

"I was instructed not to call – no messages, Ms. Murdoch. Even clergy need time not to be disturbed." Now she was getting irritated.

"Being one myself I would say especially clergy, Ms...?"

"Sorry, I didn't realize you were a minister," she said blushing, glancing at my card.

"No problem, happens all the time," I said, telling the truth. "I didn't get your name."

"Baxter, Clara Baxter."

"Ms. Baxter," I said, "Have you seen or heard from Marnie Cooper in the last two weeks?"

"I haven't seen Marnie for months." Clara spit out her words, ready to be done with our conversation.

"When she was in the office was there ever anyone with her?" I asked.

"No, just that cute little boy, Max I think, right?" Clara was nervously bouncing her knee up and down as she worked.

"Ms. Baxter, I am really sorry to interfere with your day, but Marnie has been kidnapped." The woman looked at me with big eyes. Now both knees were bouncing.

"Really?"

"Right. Tell Sawyer to call me ASAP."

"Sure. No problem," she said, staring down at her bulletins but she'd stopped folding.

"It's none of my business, but you ought to do something about that nervous habit," I snipped, not too minister-like, and she stopped bouncing her knees.

For no logical reason I was worried that Father Sawyer could be at the monastery where I'd sent Max. I couldn't help but wonder if his "retreat" had anything to do with why Rupert forgot to tell me Crystal was home. My imagination was going full tilt.

There were hundreds of places near Chicago where a priest might go on retreat. Why did I have to think that Father Sawyer would be at the monastery I knew about? And why was this thing with Crystal and Rupert gnawing at me?

Outside the church office was a small courtyard, tucked behind the huge stairs that led up to the massive front doors of St. Mary's. The building the office was in must have been a manse years ago but now was clearly administrative. Sitting on the bench in the courtyard I called Judith on my new cell phone. "Hey, Judith, it's me checking in. Is everything okay with Max?"

"He's great, Shep. Will you stop worrying? I can see him out the window in the garden picking lettuce and carrots for dinner with one of the visiting brothers. In fact, I sent Crystal home day before yesterday. She got a phone call and then asked if she could leave. I said we were fine, and she didn't need to hang around."

"What? Two days ago? I haven't seen her. I heard she got back yesterday. She didn't tell me about leaving early, isn't that strange?" Judith sighed loudly on the other end of the line.

"Ok," I said. "So, I'm not her keeper and we know I worry."

At that Judith chuckled. "I'm sure the one thing Max wants now more than anything is to get his mom back. He talks about her nonstop."

"Judith, has he said anything that makes you wonder?"

"Max has a marvelous imagination, as you know. I don't judge."

"In this case, Judith, nothing too strange should be dismissed. This is all bizarre. Try to listen for names, stories about people Marnie knows, things like that."

"Ok, if he says anything significant I'll let you know. What else can I help you with?"

"Ok. Do you know a Father Alphonso or a Father Sawyer from St. Mary's Church?"

"Sure, Sawyer's pretty well known. I've never met him in person but I've heard he's an egghead with heart. He's well known in educational circles, whereas I'm with the march-for-justice types. Totally different crowd."

"Thanks, that's a start and what about the other one, Alphonso?"

"I do know a priest who sometimes fills in at St. Mary's named Alphonso. He's good people too, but I haven't seen him in years. I do remember that Al was always trying to help people. I'm not sure at what. He's kind of secretive. Why'd you ask?"

"Just checking out ideas." This was the first time I realized there was a connection between our fathers Alphonso and Sawyer. So, as they say in the kid's guessing game, I was getting warmer.

"Where's Father Alphonso and how can I talk to him?" I asked my colleague and spiritual director way too fast. But Judith didn't seem to mind.

"He's a Dominican. Just call the House of Studies in Chicago and get his number. We in the church are all still pretty trusting when it comes to giving out phone numbers. He shouldn't be too hard to find. What could these priests have to do with Marnie's kidnapping?"

"I'm not sure. I'm just following my nose from one idea to the next. I shouldn't say much. No need to tarnish a reputation for no good reason. Sorry."

"Right you are. Never mind, maybe the less I know about the specifics the better. But I'd hate for my colleagues to be involved."

"Well, Judith, someone is stinky somewhere."

"Shep?"

"Yes?"

"I wasn't going to say anything, but when Max isn't chattering away he just stares off into space. It's as if he's retreating into another world. Then it's hard to get his attention."

"I'm doing my best to hurry this along, but I'm no detective. It does seem that because Marnie and I are friends that I've been appointed by her to find her, or is that anointed?" Judith laughed a little, but she sounded uncomfortable.

"You sound a little worried yourself." I said, wondering if sending Max to Judith and out of my sight had been the best idea. I hated the thought he was emotionally disconnecting. Maybe he needed a therapist and not just a loving group of sisters?

"Max could be in danger. Make sure someone you trust is with Max 'round the clock. And maybe have him talk to someone with a counseling background to keep him from disappearing out of sight. If you know what I mean?" I made a note to ask Patrick to see about surveillance at the monastery, something I was sure Sister Judith would not allow, but it was worth asking.

"Sure, honey, but are you getting a little paranoid?"

Judith never used sappy words like 'honey' but today I liked it.

"Don't you think worry, if not paranoia, seems to be appropriate here?" I said.

"Too much worry can kill you. Never mind, wrong turn of phrase, enough about you. What are the police saying?"

"I haven't heard if they know anything or not. I'm having dinner with the detective in charge of the case tonight."

"Marnie's lucky to have you out there pulling for her."

"Well, a girl's gotta do what a girl's gotta do," I paused, "and thanks for not giving me that lecture about how everything wrong with the world is not mine to fix."

"Shep, don't be so hard on yourself. And we both know any lecture would do little good." She spoke in that comforting voice I'd learned to trust.

"Judith I have the sinking feeling that even if Marnie survives this ordeal our friendship will never be the same. How could it?"

"My dear Shep," she said, in her most therapeutic and supportive voice, "stop the 'what-ifs,' or you'll make yourself crazy. You can be your own worst enemy and you don't have time to second-guess the future. Don't worry about Max. We never let him out of our sight."

"Promise me you'll keep him close," I said, whispering. "I've got a bad feeling—like I'm the only one who cares enough to find her. The cops are trying but there are no real clues to follow, no lights on the path."

"Maybe so," Judith sighed, "but as a minister you have to knit clues together in a spiritual way to figure out all kinds of mysteries. This can't be that different. You have sensibilities others don't have. And you don't judge Marnie guilty because of her past. It'll take someone who loves Marnie to find her. You know what I mean?"

"Not sure. I'm doing my best, but I admit I am out of my ken."

"Well, sweetie, all I can say is keep at it. And for heaven's sake, no heroics."

"Little late for that but I'll try to be more careful. Give Max a hug for me. Talk to you later."

Back in my jeep I headed toward Magnificat University to see if I could find Father Alphonso. My phone rang just as I was merging in traffic. Glancing at the caller ID I could see it was Judith calling again. I figured that if it was important enough she'd leave a message.

CHAPTER 24

She knew she'd have to ditch Shep's car soon since, in all likelihood, the cops were looking for it. Besides the possibility of doing time for whatever the cops would dream up, she suspected Irma could get someone to kill her for real this time. She shivered involuntarily. Either way she might never see Max again, and that was all that kept her going. If she was lucky, that car Howard said was hers was still in storage and she could get it today.

Grant's in Highwood was an upscale car garage where the Chicago Bears and Bulls players, as well as other North Shore notables, stored their high-end sports cars for the winter. Marnie was pretty sure there was a Porsche 936 at Grant's just waiting for her. But it would have been there for over six years and she wasn't sure how long they would have kept it. That was the deal she and Howard agreed on.

Howard Schwartz was an old trick Marnie had known since her early days on the street. Not too long after his wife died in a fire, Howard Schwartz had gone to the Dream Palace and was reacquainted with her. They became a regular hook up. He looked like a paunchy middle-aged businessman with a bad comb-over; she was dressed in spandex and sequins, with false eyelashes, a plastered on embarrassed smile and long hair flowing down her back. The whole look cried 'call girl and john walking to the hotel for a trick'. And that was how Howard liked it.

Instead of the grimy Dream Palace, she would meet Howard at the Hyatt Regency Hotel on Michigan Avenue in Chicago, first for dinner. He was happy to spend money on her. He paid her lots extra for staying all night. This was a 'pretty woman' gig as her friends called it, but there was nothing pretty about it. Tricking in a hotel, of course, was always better than being at Ogden and Division or at the Dream Palace. Sometimes in that hotel Marnie tried to kid herself into thinking she wasn't tricking at all.

Howard liked face-to-face sex, missionary style. He wasn't too rough with her, but then again he wasn't gentle, no one was gentle. Often Howard fell asleep with her in his arms and called her by his dead wife's name, Georgia, which was an odd comforting charade for both of them.

It seemed that Howard got off having her with him in public. She wore those cheap clothes that made it look like he was rescuing her instead of buying her services, but no one was fooled. She was one of those women who was drop-dead gorgeous with or without make-up. After Howard had met up with her again he'd made a separate deal with Irma at the Dream Palace—a deal Irma couldn't refuse. He had wanted proof of her health. Lucky for her she didn't yet show symptoms of any of the life-

threatening diseases like AIDS and TB that plagued some of her sisters in the work. Howard liked that and he paid her and Irma well, even though they all knew it could have just been an illusion of health for her or any of them.

Howard had never gotten over the death of his wife, at least not in his sleep. But during the day Howard was one nasty man and anything but bereft. He was a slimy lowlife whose comb-over was dyed black and it didn't cover the top of head. He did have beautiful teeth, and if he ever let you see it, a fine smile. When Howard was in a good mood, he was generous.

Howard wanted her to be his pretty girl on his arm. He took her with him on 'business-trips' to Japan. She'd seen Tokyo, Kyoto and Hong Kong and the money was good, but it wasn't her style to go so far from home. She was always afraid Howard might dump her in Tokyo, so she tried to avoid these trips, unless Irma made her go.

She didn't know who else Howard might have been seeing. Part of the survival strategy for her was being ever vigilant, and never forgetting that women in her business got killed by pimps, johns or drugs, but more often than not, by a jealous wife or girlfriend. It was always best not to get too close to know too much about any of these guys. They all had somebody who could get mad enough to hurt her. So she kept a good distance from the personal lives of her 'business partners.' Another good reason she avoided drugs at all cost.

All she knew about Howard was that he was a small-time gangster who had an enviable penchant for making lots of money. One night they both got sloppy and she heard a deal take place and happened to see the transaction. That's how she got the car.

She had come out of one of the bathrooms of Howard's suite at the downtown Hyatt when a couple of thugs came in, trading the title for the Porsche plus some cocaine for a suitcase of laundered cash. When she heard the exchange she was sure she'd be dead in the dumpster by morning. She didn't know about Howard's 'business' but, at the least, she knew he was constantly paranoid. Or as he put it, he "could always smell a traitor." That made Howard a dangerous john—all the time.

She had to admit that when she was younger she got off on the excitement of manipulating men like Howard. She might not have a formal education but she knew about dangerous men who needed sex. She knew that being coy could get her hurt, or get her money. She'd lived on the edge of danger for a long time and knew when to play-act and when to lay it out straight.

"How much of that did you hear? And don't lie to me."

"All of it, Howard," She'd said, trying to be calm and cool.

"Come on sweetie," she cooed, trying to bluff herself out of this sticky situation. "Why don't you take little 'Georgia' to bed, come on, honey. Don't worry about this."

Letting out an explosive, evil laugh, Howard made her a deal, "Ok," he'd said, "as long as I want to screw you and you keep yourself clean – no herpes, no clap – I'll leave that car I just got to you in my will." He laughed some more, enjoying his little game.

"I'll get the title put in your name, get you a safe deposit box and we'll store it at Grant's. Deal? Now I own you. I'll give you

something for keeping your mouth shut about what you saw here. Call it my nooky indemnity." He knocked back the rest of the gin gimlet he'd been drinking and laughed again, this time grabbing her hair and yanking it back, holding her head taut enough that her eyes began to water. She looked at him, steeling herself—getting ready for the hits that would come next.

"But don't you ever pretend to be my Georgia, or I will kill you. Got that? You could never be Georgia."

"Sure, Howard, didn't mean any disrespect."

Laughing again Howard had said, "You are one weird hooker. You don't drink, at least not on the job, you go to the doctor for checkups and you have manners. That's why I'll keep you around. No more cash, just our little nooky policy."

"Sure," she said, again. What difference did anything make anymore? He could kill her in an instant for less than her seeing a deal go down.

Howard was a crazy asshole but he was always true to his word. The following week he'd given her a key to a lock box with instructions to go to Chase Bank on LaSalle and show the key to the teller in the advent of his death. As fate would have it Howard was killed gangland style, as they say in Chicago, two weeks after he gave her the car. She picked up the car key at the bank but when she'd made her run for a normal life, she'd left the key back in her room at the house. If she was going to go free, she figured she had to leave it all behind. But now all that had changed.

~~~
~~~

It wasn't hard to find where Alphonso lived, nor anyone else who lived at the priory on Farwell, a few blocks off Sheridan Road, not too far from the university. Sitting in one of the ladder-back white rockers on the porch I decided to wait and see if Father Alphonso showed up.

The slow rhythm of the chair helped me think, but just waiting was making me nervous. I needed to go to church. There was nothing to say Alphonso would be home anytime soon; besides I did my best thinking in church, any church. Judith had said the Father Alphonso she knew sometimes officiated at St. Mary's when Sawyer was gone, maybe this would be my lucky day. It had to be the same guy. How many Father Alphonsos could there be?

St. Mary's was a cavernous church with amazing Tiffany stained glass windows and old wooden pews that were handcrafted and imported from Italy generations ago. As the sun shown through the leaded, beveled glass, a myriad of colors danced together around the huge church as if they were fairy people dancing for God.

The life-size statues around the sanctuary were foreboding on purpose, common in churches like this. In a little grotto to the left of the altar were rows of candles and kneelers. Here was a place to give a little money for the cost of the candle and to say a prayer and ask for help from the Virgin Mary, whose beneficent plaster face loomed above lighting candles.

I could hear others coming to find a pew to pray in. The church began to fill up. I decided to stay for evening mass.

I could use a little worship, I thought, as I continued to pray.

I prayed for me, for Marnie and for Max whose little life had been tossed and blown like a leaf on the ground. I prayed for my friends and for world peace. I prayed for everything I could think of before I settled into that tranquil place it takes so long for me to find.

As the priest came out to the altar and started to speak, I recognized his voice before I opened my eyes. It was the priest from the Dream Palace, Father Alphonso. Interesting. Now my mind was racing. That small moment of meditative calm was shattered with the clicking of my mind as it flew around inside my skull, grasping for some continuity.

It was clear Marnie had friends in high places in the church, but I wondered if she had enemies as well.

Earlier in the day at the church office, I'd hoped to find Father Sawyer who'd given Marnie a break in the cost of Max's child care tuition. That was all I'd known about Sawyer's relationship with Marnie, but I'd been grasping at air trying to make a workable connection. As things were coming unraveled, I still didn't know what it meant.

I suspect if anyone knew about what was going on, or what had happened to Marnie, it could very well be the man reading from the second chapter of the prophet Isaiah, "He shall judge between the nations, and shall arbitrate for many peoples; they shall beat their swords into plowshares, and their spears into pruning hooks;

nation shall not lift up sword against nation, neither shall they learn war anymore."

First, he was at the Dream Palace with God knows what intentions, then Judith mentioned him and now he was talking about God being the judge, as he looked right at me. I avoided his gaze, and when I glanced up again I was grateful that he was looking at someone else.

The good father proceeded to offer the sacrament of Holy Communion to all the Roman Catholics in the sanctuary. It always irked me that most priests allowed this life-giving meal only to their own breed of Christian, but not mine.

Nowhere in scripture did Jesus or Paul or anyone else say communion was only for the church in Rome. In my church all are welcome to the table, because we invite anyone who chooses to partake of the bread of life and the cup of blessing. Not so here. While my liberal church had lots in common with the Catholics, especially around issues of mission and social justice, we'd never see eye-to-eye on communion, ordination of women or same sex-marriage. Here at St. Mary's, this sacrament was a members-only affair. If you weren't a member well, you could take it anyway but it would still be a sin in the eyes of the Catholic Church, and why add an extra sin over a bit of bread and grape juice?

Given the circumstances of my visit, this momentary irritant didn't matter much in the scope of things. As much as I disagreed with their policy, I would respect it. I would have to remind myself to go to church Sunday for my own communion. Moreover, it was better to stay put, watching to see what the good father was up to, besides officiating at worship at St. Mary's and being a regular at that seedy dance club in South Chicago.

Alphonso started to read the words of institution but he was being tentative, almost as if he were unsure he'd be able to finish. His resplendent robe of white and gold with many colors of metallic thread artfully woven in and out in a nondescript pattern was cumbersome and heavy, as if it belonged to someone else, or as if he had shrunk, as some older people do. This lone priest was assisted by one young woman who handed him the communion elements, walked with him, helped him down as he kneeled and then up again. She looked at the priest with worried eyes.

When I was a kid going to church with my Catholic grandmother, only boys were allowed up front with the priest. All us girls had to kneel in the back, our heads covered with lace doilies or, in dire circumstances, a Kleenex held on with a bobby pin.

Following the benediction the celebrant father moved in slow motion toward the door to the right of the altar. I stayed in my seat. I was sure he'd seen me and recognized me from the Dream Palace. If this man did try to save prostitutes from their fate he would come find me. All I would have to do is sit tight and keep praying.

As the people drifted out of the church, it wasn't long before I felt a hand on my shoulder, a hand that felt like love, like benevolence, like the hand of God, gentle and secure. I knew it was Father Alphonso.

"How can I help you, young lady?"

"Father, I need to talk to you."

"Of course."

"I'm not who you think I am."

"And who might that be?" He asked, as he sat next to me in the pew, lowering his body, then turning to look at me with his face open and compassionate. It was almost a shame to tell him the truth.

"I'm Reverend Shepherd Murdoch, and," I took a deep breath, "I'm trying to find Marnie Cooper. She disappeared several nights ago." At that the priest jumped a tiny bit, shifting his eyes over to the now empty prayer grotto and the life size statue of the Virgin Mary. It was as if he too was looking for advice.

"When I went to the Dream Palace, where you first saw me, I was hoping to get information about finding Marnie. But I got arrested instead."

"I see," the priest said, as he watched the young girl remove the elements and the Bible from the altar, then store them in their rightful place before she left the chancel.

Alphonso was getting pale and starting to sweat, even though the church was air conditioned. From the side door the young girl came into the church. Now she was wearing frayed, tattered blue jeans, the way kids like to wear them, with a white tee shirt that said "Ireland Forever." She hesitated, and then came toward us.

"Father, you are needed in the office."

He nodded at her and said, "I will be there soon Emma, and you go on home now. Tell Mrs. Bristow I won't miss dinner." Emma frowned, shrugged her shoulders and headed back toward the church office.

"She's a great young girl, isn't she? She lost her mother last year. Emma has six brothers, a sister and a father who's never home. I'm not sure we do folks any favors telling them to have so many children. But I'm sure you, as a minister, are in full agreement with me there. I'm Father Alphonso," he said, putting his hand out. I think his talk about Emma was buying time to switch gears from thinking I was a hooker, to being a colleague looking for Marnie.

Alphonso stood up, a bit unsteady, "Well, Reverend Murdoch I'm sorry to hear Marnie's missing. I had high hopes for her." He wobbled a little and grabbed the end of the pew for balance. "There is more to all this than meets the eye. It's not as bad as it looks."

"How does it look Father," I said, irritated at his nonchalance. "What are the details?" I continued, "Marnie's smarter and more attractive than the average girl down on her luck who ends up pole dancing in a lowlife strip club, and then she disappears, leaving behind a young son. But she can't think her way out of this now, can she – no matter how smart she is." I was beginning to lose it.

Arguing with a man who was clearly not feeling well, in a sanctuary no less—what was wrong with me?

"Why not let the police handle it?"

"The police are working on it," I quipped.

"Just not fast enough for you?" he said, with a little smile.

"Right."

"Ok, I've known Marnie since she was a young girl. I worked with her mother in the early years of my call. Her mother was one hard woman, not soft around the edges like Marnie, nor as smart. Looking back, I'm not sure I did either of them any favors."

As if responding to a signal managed off stage, the young Emma again came back into the church to help the obviously ailing priest. Alphonso with a quick jerk, turned towards me and whispered, "Come back tomorrow at 3 o'clock and meet me at the coffee shop across the street from the university. Don't tell anyone."

He reached out to shake my hand but it was different than before. Now, this was a perfunctory handshake that was the result of good manners and social convention. The old priest's hand was cold and clammy. He was genuinely sick and not feigning illness to get out of talking to me. Leaning on Emma, he was stooped over as he made his way through the chancel and then into the church office on the other side of the sanctuary.

As I walked down the long aisle toward the door I decided to take Father Alphonso at his word. We could talk tomorrow. At least he was willing to talk. I couldn't stand to wait one more day, but I wasn't going to argue.

Outside of the dark church the sun was setting. Through the narrow spaces between the apartment buildings across the street I could see slivers of what must have been a spectacular sunset, but the full effect was hidden from me, like so many other things.

Piercing the air was a shrill anguished cry from the church office.

Scrambling down the remainder of the steps I ran around the church's grand staircase and up a few stairs to the office. I pushed my way through the cheap aluminum screen door with such force it clattered when it hit the wall behind it. Emma, who'd minutes earlier helped the priest out of the church, was kneeling down next to a crumpled figure on the floor and praying out loud. Father Alphonso's robe was thrown, haphazard, across the secretary's desk, and he wasn't making it home for dinner.

I knelt on the other side of the keening young woman who couldn't be more than sixteen or seventeen years old.

"Did you call 911?"

"He told me not to call."

I nodded my head, "Let's lay him flat and get something for under his neck." Taking the secretary's small embroidered pillow off her chair we got the priest comfortable. I took his hand in mine and put my other hand on his forehead and prayed, "I lay my hands on you in the name of our Lord and Savior Jesus Christ, beseeching Christ to uphold you and fill you with grace, that you may know the healing power of Christ's love." He squeezed my hand when I said, "Amen."

"Bad ticker for a long time now, reverend," Alphonso whispered, as he opened his eyes and looked at me. "Guess we're not having coffee. You understand. You're a woman of the cloth." He surprised me by winking and squeezing my hand again.

"Well, Father, I do believe you're flirting with me." I smiled. I took my cell phone out of my purse and dialed 911. "At some point I'm going to have a talk with God about disobeying orders, since I am ignoring your wishes. But we have to at least get you comfortable. Then, if you don't want to stay at the hospital, you can ask them to take you home, okay?"

Father Alphonso nodded again, and closed his eyes. That little spurt of energy seemed to make him even more tired. His lips started to turn a cold shade of the lightest blue. Emma was still on her knees and looking at him. She'd stopped crying but was still gasping for little bits of air. Emma kissed Father Alphonso on the cheek, "I'm going to get Mrs. Bristow," she said, grabbed what looked like her school backpack and ran out of the office.

"God bless you my child," the Father whispered to her, "God bless you." But I don't think she heard him.

CHAPTER 25

Now, the key to the car was in the bag with her cash, credit cards and passport that she's brought with her from the hiding place in her closet back at Brenda's. She had no idea if Howard had really left her the car. But checking it out seemed like a good idea. She could sell it, get some real cash, get Max and leave to start over somewhere else. Easy peasy.

She could have gotten that car years ago when she'd left the Dream Palace and moved uptown. If she had, maybe she wouldn't have had to keep babysitting Alphonso's sexually confused, sweet wanna-be priests, saving them for the church. But the car was still dirty money and she had wanted a fresh start for herself and her son. At the moment, however, she had very few options. So dirty or not, this car could offer a way out.

She didn't know, nor did her friend Shepherd Murdoch, that Sergeant Patrick Kelly had checked with the DMV when Marnie had gone missing, and her name had come up as owning a 936

Porsche, as well as the Toyota. He ran the VIN number at the half dozen car storage facilities in the Chicagoland area and found the car at Grant's Automotive, a business that always registered their cars by VIN number. He'd alerted Grant's and they were watching for her in case she'd show up.

Living as a sex worker you couldn't afford to think too deeply. She couldn't watch for hidden messages. It was all on the float-up, as the girls would say. On the next good day, something good would float up. That was where all decisions had to be made, on the surface, fast, with little time allowed to think about the consequences. If it was a set-up, a sex worker like Marnie almost always walked right into the trap.

Cops would bust up a sleazy motel and send the johns packing, wagging their fingers at them, like you would a bad dog or naughty two-year-old. The arresting officers would bark things like "get the hell out of here," as the guy struggled into his pants. But the cops would have their fun with the women, saying things they couldn't say to any law-abiding citizen. Putting the cuffs on the girls, they muttered things under their breath like 'stupid bitch' and 'disease-ridden crack head.' But that was where they were wrong, about her at least. She wasn't stupid, diseased or on drugs. And she worked hard at that.

She had been lucky that she hated drugs. They made her sick, as if she were allergic to them. Alcohol, however, had sometimes been an ally. She could drink anyone under the table and still be able to think and function, or so she told herself. The numbing properties of alcohol could be helpful with any john, violent or not. She'd drink just enough to get numb, but not so stupid drunk that she couldn't remember what she did. Good genes, little shit, her mother would say, as she taught her how drink with a john, watch him pass out, and take the rest of his cash.

~~~

Waiting for the ambulance with Father Alphonso, it was hot. They must have the air conditioning on a timer because it was getting stifling in this small office. Father Alphonso was silent, his breathing now a raspy undertone. He would squeeze my hand every so often and seemed to know I was praying for him.

The EMTs arrived and got to their tasks with their usual efficiency. As they checked Father Alphonso's vitals and started an IV, they were asking me questions I could not answer.

"Sorry, I don't know anything about his medical history, except that he told me he has a bad heart," I said, shrugging my shoulders. "Are you taking him to Evanston Hospital?"

"Yes, ma'am."

"Ok, Father," I said, leaning close to his ear I whispered, "you are in good hands. I'll stop by later and check in on you, okay?" He nodded a tiny bit but never opened his eyes. "You hang in there."

As I walked back to my car I knew there would be little chance I'd be able to stay with Alphonso. The emergency room staff were protective of their patients, especially if they hear the words "heart attack." That's when the Red
~~~

Sea parts and you go right in front of others who have been patiently waiting their turn to see a doctor for their pain.

Dusk had turned into night there was a damp breeze. It wasn't one of those soft warm nights by Lake Michigan. But instead it had that awful sudden chill in the air caused by a strong wind off the lake. As I walked to the car I prayed, "Gracious God, please don't let Father Alphonso die before he tells me about Marnie."

How selfish of me. But Alphonso looked as if he'd rather die than tell me what he knew.

I'd go back to the hospital, but first there was dinner to think about. I ducked into an eclectic Asian take-out place just a half block from where my car was parked.

"A large order of Pho soup, please. Vegetarian Pad Thai and Chicken Green Curry extra hot," I said to the diminutive, wrinkled woman behind the counter. "Oh, and two Thai coffees, almond cookies, and fortune cookies both. Thanks." She nodded, and said, "Twenty minutes."

With my new cell phone, I called Patrick at the station.

"Sergeant Kelly has left for the day, ma'am," said yet another young voice. Must be the season for new recruits.

I dialed Patrick's cell. When he didn't pick up, I left a message.

"Patrick, a slight change of plans. I'm waiting for carry out but I was wondering, could you meet me at Evanston Hospital before we have dinner?

"Father Alphonso, who knows Marnie, I think I told you about him. Anyway, he's had a heart event. I'll be on my way to the ER in about 15-20 minutes. I hope after they get him hooked up to all those monitors they might let me talk to him." His cell phone cut me off. Guess that was enough of a message anyway.

"Any chance you could hurry up my order?" I asked the woman behind the take-out counter, "I'm in a little hurry." She shook her head and again and said, "Twenty minutes."

I checked the messages on my home phone. One from Patrick confirming his arrival for dinner, one from Rupert telling me he and Crystal were still going out for dinner and a movie. And there was the message Judith had left earlier in the afternoon.

"One more thing Shep, well two," began Judith's voice. "First, Max needs you, so please, please be careful. I don't know what you've been up to, but you were so evasive on the phone I have to think it's something you are afraid to tell me, for fear I will try to talk you out of it.

"But two, I want you to know how Max is doing and not just with the sisters. He has grown fond of the three seminarians working in the apple orchard this week. I think the male influence is so good for Max and these are very nice young Dominicans finishing up at Magnificat or De Paul, I can't remember.

"Max doesn't like it when they put on their collars, not sure what that's about. Oh well, bye sweetie and be safe. And please keep checking in with me. Bye."

Nothing would happen with Judith watching Max, but I didn't like this.

I paid for the takeout and jogged to the car.

As I arrived at the emergency room, I'd had no trouble getting to see Father Alphonso. But he didn't look like he'd been able to speak his last confession out loud. He was unconscious and looked close to death. There were several priests crowded around him in the small cubicle, one having just completed what appeared to be last rites. Emma, the young girl I met at the church, was also there, her face wet with tears. Another priest with a stole on squeezed into the circle around his bed, and it didn't seem to bother anyone that I stood and prayed with the others.

Dying, for the confessed soul of any faith, is said to be a joy. I know that. Confession and absolution leave no untidy loose ends to clean up. After being pardoned, it becomes time to move on to the next part of the journey. I wonder if Alphonso had told one of the priests at his side anything that would help me. But, even if Al had confessed something, I knew I'd never hear it. It's against the rules for all clergy to share anything said in confidence, so I was pretty sure that attempting to get any information out of that confessor would be a dead end.

"Maybe a day or two," the young doc said to the room, and not to anyone in particular. "I doubt he'll regain consciousness but it's not unheard of. He can, of course, hear you, so now would be a good time for you to say your goodbyes. We can have the ambulance take him home. I understand that was what he wanted."

Standing on the fringes of the small group in Alphonso's room, Patrick slipped in next to me. We gave our condolences and turned to leave the emergency room.

"Excuse me, Sister, could I talk to you?" It was Emma again, the young girl from the church. I smiled at Emma's presumption I was a nun.

"Of course, my dear," I said, steering her toward the consultation room where I had counseled many a family member in years past. Patrick followed us without saying a word.

The small, dark and sparsely furnished room had seating for four. It was around the corner from the hustle and bustle of the busy emergency room. It was a place of temporary comfort where families could hear the bad news, or just find a quiet place to collect themselves before moving on without the loved one they came in with.

"Well," Emma began, after the three of us sat down, "Father Al told me to talk to you. He's sure you don't understand his work very well. I'm not the best one to tell you. You should get in touch with his assistant, Brother John Leonardo, but he's gone for a few days."

"Let me guess, he's on retreat at a monastery?"

"Right, how'd you know?"

"Never mind, honey. What do you want to tell me?"

"It's a long story."

"I'm sure it is, Emma." I checked my watch, it was 9 PM. "Do you want to have some dinner in the cafeteria and then we can take you home. Where do you live?"

"Right now she lives at our residence," a tanned, attractive priest said, as he opened the door to the consultation room. "Maybe you should talk tomorrow, I think Emma is tired. This has been a long day for her."

"Of course, Father, you're right." I nodded and said, "and you are?"

"Palikowski, John."

"Reverend Shepherd Murdoch." I said, as I put out my hand and he withdrew his. This has happened to me before when I met priests of the high and mighty kind who disapproved of any kind of women clergy. But now was not the time for that conversation. I'd ignore him, but the little move was not lost on Patrick.

"This is Sergeant Patrick Kelly," I said, to the offending priest, "from the Evanston Police Department."

The priest looked as if he'd been expecting us, or if not us in particular, someone who'd come to talk about Father Alphonso.

"Is this a police matter?" Palikowski asked Patrick.

"Yes, we think Father Alphonso may have information about a woman who was kidnapped from her home several days ago." As Patrick was discussing the details of Marnie's disappearance with Palikowski, I put my arm around the shivering Emma who was listening to the conversation between Patrick and the priest. Palikowski indicated that he wanted to talk to Patrick alone, so they left the room.

I was glad to have a brief moment with Emma. "No matter how hot it is outside it seems that they keep it cold in these places on purpose. Keeps you awake," I said. But she just nodded, looking at me with huge frightened eyes.

"Here's my card. Call me anytime, day or night." I paused, "Emma, I have a feeling you know lots more than Father Palikowski is going to want you to tell me. I just want you to know there's a woman, not too much older than you, who's missing and in serious trouble. Anything thing you know will help. But time is running out, she has already been gone for five days. So, call me as soon you can talk, Ok? It's important."

Emma nodded, and without looking at it, she stuffed my card into the front pocket of her jeans.

"Emma? Could I ask you one more question? What does Brother Leonardo look like?"

"Oh, he's young and cute," she said. "He used to be an engineer or maybe an architect but decided to give his life to God and work in street ministry with Father Al.

Leo's got red hair and blue eyes, kind of funny for a guy with an Italian last name. He's a great guy and a great listener, like Father Al, but Leo also talks to you. I think his real name is John but everyone calls him Leo." Her eyes filled again with tears, and she shuddered both from the sadness and the cold temperature in the room.

As Emma walked back to Father Palikowski, I shivered too. Less from the air conditioning and more from the realization that she had described the man I had met with Alphonso at the Dream Palace. The one who got Pammy Jo to talk about God. I also realized that the man Emma had just described had the same attributes as little Max. Maybe this John Leonardo was related to Derek somehow? Or even Marnie? Now I was speculating. Lots of folks have red hair, blue eyes and talk a lot.

"Could you both come to the university tomorrow morning, at ten? I'll have the people there you need to talk to," Palikowski was saying as he handed us both a business card that read, Director of Public Relations, Magnificat University.

"Father Alphonso was a man with a mission," he said, choosing his words with care. "We were a bit stymied at his approach but proud of his attempts to save the lost. Father Alphonso has been retired from teaching sociology for some time now. But we take care of our own and the university will, of course, cooperate in any way with you on this matter."

"You have forgotten one thing," I said, to the cool talking priest.

"What's that Ms. Murdoch?" I wondered if he was forgetting the 'Rev,' or was he trying to put me in my place?

"Well, *Mr.* Palikowski, you are talking about Father Alphonso in the past tense, and, as of ten minutes ago, he wasn't dead yet. And a young woman is still missing."

The priest nodded, pursed his lips and looked at me with disdain as he turned to leave, not responding to my cryptic remark.

"Patrick, I was close to something with Alphonso. Now it will be glossed over by Palikowski and the university's PR department." Patrick slipped his hand over mine as we walked toward the exit doors.

"Gee, and I thought you and Palikowski seemed to be hitting it off so well." Patrick cracked a grin.

"I bet his pompous self can't wait to be relieved of Alphonso's embarrassing ministry. It must be the worst nightmare for a public relations guy, priest or not. He doesn't seem too broken up about Alphonso being on his way out." I was talking to myself again, as much as to Patrick.

The outer doors of the hospital emergency room opened into a hot muggy Chicago night, when a couple hours ago it was chilly. Chicago weather was too hot or too cold but unpredictable most of the time. We headed toward the parking lot in silence. I had parked in the emergency chaplain's spot and his RX was right next to my Jeep.

"Did the girl say anything helpful?" Patrick asked, as he opened the door of my car.

"No, like most teenagers she just stared at me and nodded when I asked questions. I think she heard me, though. I told her to give me a call, but she's scared. What did you learn from the PR guy?"

"This priest is protective about Alphonso and the university, and that young woman, Emma O'Donohue. I guess they took her in not too long ago. She's living with the housekeeper at the priest's residence until she finishes high school. I think they're hoping she'll go to college next fall. She's kind of like their pet. A little creepy if you ask me."

"When you were talking to Palikowski, Emma said I should meet with Brother Leonardo, who I think I met at the Dream Palace, but I think he's at a retreat with the rest of the boys. Shouldn't we try to talk to her tonight? Marnie is still missing and time is not on our side here."

"No doubt, but Marnie is a survivor, don't forget that, if that helps you worry less. But this late, Emma's protective fathers would make it nigh impossible to talk to her without paperwork. I'm not sure it will make much difference if we talk to her tonight or tomorrow, unless of course she runs away or overdoses on crack."

"That's not funny Patrick. She could be..."

He put up his hand as if to signal me to stop.

“First, let’s see what kind of dog-and-pony show the university PR department can put together tomorrow. That is less than twelve hours from now. Hell, we might not be able to talk to her until then anyway. After that we’ll see if we need to talk to both Emma and the housekeeper. People always talk better on their terms. Something about jail bars is intimidating and shuts people up. Always better to catch the fly with honey, honey.”

“I can’t believe you said that. My father used to say that all the time when I would get all mouthy. *Catch more flies with honey than vinegar*. I looked it up once – Poor Richard’s Almanac.”

“It’s late, if you’re quoting Ben Franklin we might never eat. What’s for dinner?”

“Vietnamese takeout, in the car, I bought it hours ago. We just need a microwave, unless you’re not up for it?” I was hoping he’d take a rain check.

“Takeout is perfect. I’ll meet you at your place in a few.” Patrick looked tired as I felt, and this might not be the time to reveal the book in my freezer. This could be more of a chow-down meal, before absolute exhaustion set in, for us both, but c’est la vie.

CHAPTER 26

She parked Shep's Subaru around the corner and out of view of the expansive entrance of Grant's. Going around to the service entrance, she saw someone she knew. He was an old trick who apparently worked at Grant's Automotive these days. She'd remembered back then he was a mechanic for one of those quick oil change places.

"Hey, Freddy, got a minute?" He was dressed very sharp and clean for someone who got under the hood of a car for a living. But, then, people loved their cars, and his boss must have paid for him to look the part.

"Ah, do I know you?" He asked, as he looked over his shoulder to see who else was around. She took off her sunglasses but left on the big floppy hat she'd grabbed at the last minute off of Shep's back seat, "Yes, you do."

Whistling low under his breathe, looking around for witnesses and seeing none, he picked up the walkie-talkie that was clipped to his belt,

"Carlos, I'm goin' out for a smoke, be back in a few." At that he opened the door and they went back outside. It was getting dark, but this place was open late."Keep your head down, there are cameras," he said, as they walked down the alley behind the fancy place that was not your ordinary automotive shop.

"Ok, I don't want to hear you say a word and I'll deny any of this," he said.

She put her hand on top of her head to keep the wind from blowing off the ridiculous straw hat.

"Everybody's looking for you—cops and private dicks. I don't know what you're into now, but shit, this is deep." He looked over his shoulder again, satisfied no one was following them.

"You always were one for the drama, Freddy."

"No talking, I'm not kidding." He said, looking scared.

"You watch too much T.V., lighten up. Tell me why my name came up, and I'm gone. I never served you nothing at the Dream Palace, never met you before. Your wife will never...!"

"You never did follow directions Shana—no talking." He said snickering, in spite of his tough guy posture.

"Ok, here's what I know. A 926, stored here for years, had a VIN that came up registered in your name and we're supposed to call the cops if you try to claim it. My advice is get out of here and go

to your plan 'B,' and I don't want to know what any of this shit is about. You understand, right? I gotta get back to work."

"Didn't you forget something?"

"What?"

"You told Carlos you were gonna have a smoke, I thought you quit."

"Things change, Shana, lots of things. That's all I know. Are we even?" He asked almost like a little kid hoping for the best.

"Even as can be Freddy, and tonight be sure to tell your wife you love her. It's important."

"You always were the strangest hooker, Shana. But leave my wife out of it, she's too good."

"Aren't they all? Ok Freddy, I'm out of here, but one of these days I'll get my car."

If the cops were looking for her she needed to move fast, and she hoped the Subaru wouldn't be spotted as she headed in the only direction she could think of. Time to see if she could clean things up, since running away with her Porsche wasn't going to work.

~~~

Patrick was waiting for me. Rupert had locked the gate when he left and it took me a minute to remember the code to open it.
~~~

Rolling down the window of his RX7, Patrick watched as I punched in the wrong code a couple times before I got it right.

"If I didn't know better Rev, I'd think you were trying to break in."

"Yeah, that's funny. No more B & E in my future," I said, touching the back of my head where it was still tender. The big metal iron doors clicked and slid sideways, fitting into the casement that then turned into a tall wrought iron fence that curved, ending at the beach on both sides of the property.

"So, you live in a gated community all your own." Patrick said, after we'd both parked in the back of the house, near the kitchen door. He was carrying the now quite cold Vietnamese food into the house.

"I don't like locked gates," I said, making a face. "I don't have much use for them, too much trouble. Did you ever see that play 'Fences,' by August Wilson? I saw it in New York City years back. With James Earl Jones, who was fabulous, of course." Patrick shook his head as he busied himself, heating up the soup on the stove and opening cupboards, looking for suitable microwave containers for the rest.

"*Fences* is all about the reasons we have fences in the first place. That is, of course, to either keep people in or to keep them out. I figure if the bad guys are gonna get in here they're gonna get in. I think the sheer size of that fence deters the average cat burglar, but if you are willing to jog through brush to the beach and climb over some big wet, slippery boulders, well then you can swim in."

"I hope you don't feel the same about the alarm system on the house," Patrick said, as he placed the food on a big tray he'd found in the pantry.

"What? Oh, I never set that thing. I'd have to change the code for sure. Rupert knows how to set it." Patrick made a face.

"Show me where it is, I'll set it. At least until we get this squared away, Shep."

"Oh, for heaven's sake, I'll just set off the alarm myself and bring Evanston's finest for no good reason. To say nothing of ruining my hearing until you all get here."

"It's gone off once and that was my fault. After that I left it alone. But whatever, if it makes you happy go ahead and set the thing." Of course, Patrick wasn't looking for my okay. He called the alarm company, got a new code, using his official credentials and set the alarm.

"You want wine with dinner? I have some downstairs. Be right back." Unlike Marnie's basement, mine was well lit. There was a wine rack built into the sidewall. I guess my grandmother liked her wine, or hated it. I couldn't be sure given the number of dusty bottles of vinegar I'd found when I moved in. I had added a few of my favorite wines and tonight I couldn't decide between a light Pinot or a heavier Cabernet, so I brought up one of each.

Patrick had set the table on the sun porch, lit candles on the old oak table. I handed him the wine, "One California, one French," I said, as I sat down and started preparing my soup, squeezing fresh lime juice, adding sliced hot red finger peppers and mung bean sprouts to the chicken soup. Patrick opened the Cabernet and poured the wine.

"You look tired," he said, handing me my glass.

"More like weary I think. You must be accustomed to this yo-yo life, where one minute you think you're getting somewhere and the next you're back to square one. I like the one-step-at-a-time approach that leads somewhere." The Pho was divine. I ate the noodles and then drank the spicy liquid. "Food tastes so good when you're hungry and tired." I said, managing a smile.

Patrick had taken off his jacket and still had his holster on. "Do you know how to use a gun?" he asked between bites of fried rice, curry and Pho that he ate at a more civilized pace than I did.

"Right. I'm a pacifist, I think handguns should be outlawed. Are you nuts? You think I'm in that much danger? My God how could that be? I'm locked and alarmed in. Me shoot a gun? Right."

"I should've known," he said, more to himself. "Ok, let me put it to you this way, if you want to learn how to shoot a few cans off a fence, we could go out to the range one day and I could give you a lesson or two."

"I know this sounds funny, after what I just said, and since I hate guns, but I confess, I've always wanted to learn to shoot one. I also want to skydive and be a vegetarian too, doesn't mean I would. Guns are too powerful. You can change things in a nanosecond with a gun. And guns, like condoms and big car engines make you forget your manners."

Patrick leaned back, and laughed. "Guess I'm batting two for three with the gun and the RX7," he said smiling, leaning toward me, almost grabbing my hand and then thinking better of it. "Guess we have to work on the last one, maybe after this mess is over."

"Patrick, I had something else to tell you. About that package." He sat back and went back into cop mode. I was almost sorry to burst our little romantic bubble, but first things first, and he was right. Besides, isn't there a serious boundary violation about getting attracted to a cop with a gun when you're a pacifist?

"What about the package?"

"The package had keys alright but there was also a book." Before I could finish explaining, the alarm system went off making screeching noises that would scare me right out of my own house, much less frighten away an intruder.

Within minutes Evanston's finest were at the gate, which I of course had left open but Patrick had locked, having watched me punch in the code earlier in the evening.

Against Patrick's wishes, I ran down the driveway to let in the cops and Patrick went out into the back of the house, gun drawn. Whoever had tripped the alarm was gone by now, tipped off by the ear-splitting racket. Unlocking the big front gate for the two Evanston Police Cars in my driveway, I was thinking that if this nonsense went on much longer, I just might take Patrick up on those shooting lessons.

So much for one's values when it hits close to home, but who was I kidding? Even if I learned to shoot a gun I could never point it at a person. Never.

"Sergeant Patrick Kelly is on the other side of the house," I blurted to the young cops as they drove in.

"Get in the car, Reverend Murdoch, no use running into the alarm-tripping fox out here. We'll drive you back up to the house." I could tell they questioned the idea of a human intruder just as much as I did.

"My employees aren't home and if there's anyone stupid enough to still be here, they're in the yard," I said, as I swept my arm over the large expanse of woods and lawn that I could never get used to as belonging to me.

The two cars drove up to the house in a hurry and several officers got out, and began to comb the property. One was Moira Kelly, Patrick's daughter. In the dark, with the moon and flashlight to see by, they came up blank. I wondered what Moira had thought when she saw her father's black shiny RX7 Mazda in my driveway after midnight? And I wondered how they'd all gotten here so soon, unless they were still watching the house from the cemetery across the street. Who needed an alarm system with this set up?

"Maybe it was a raccoon, Reverend Murdoch," the young Moira Kelly said as she looked at me and smiled. I sat on the steps still shaken. So much for no dinner interference from Patrick's daughter.

"That's why I hate those things, you can get scared out of your wits and waste everyone's time after the sensor gets tripped by a bat or a raccoon."

"Or a kid," Patrick said, coming up from the beach with a gangly teenage boy in tow. The kid, about 16, was belligerent but scared. And from the looks of how scared he was, it didn't appear he was a hardened criminal, not yet.

"Let me go. I just came to go swimming. We do it all the time, never had no alarm before." His dark hair was straight and cut just above his ears and flopped every which way hiding his good looking face.

Patrick had caught what appeared to be a shirtless potential skinny-dipper in cutoff shorts and no shoes. Not a threat worth pressing charges over. But Patrick had him firmly by the arm. The kid was out of his league with a cop who still lifted weights and claimed a washboard six-pack for stomach muscles. But slight as the kid was, Patrick's recent shoulder wound had to be throbbing nonetheless.

"I have this covered. You all can go back across the street," Patrick barked at his colleagues, answering my question of how they'd arrived so fast. "I'll take care of this. I'll call you if I need you."

"You," he said to the boy, "sit down."

"Stupid kid," Moira muttered under her breath. "He'd be better off with us, than my old man," she mumbled to one of her young colleagues as they headed back to their car.

"I heard that young lady."

The three of us just sat on the stairs watching the cars leave.

As we began questioning our interloper, Rupert and Crystal arrived home from their night out.

"Hey, waz up?" Rupert said, a little too forced, with his shoulders hunched and hands stuffed in his pockets. From his strained smile it appeared that all was not well between him and Crystal at the moment.

"Salvador, what are you doing here?" Crystal asked as she came into the light of the porch shocking everyone. We all looked at Crystal surprised, except for Sal.

"You know him Crystal?"

"Sure, Sal does yard work over at the church, where the daycare center is," Crystal explained. "So, Sal?" Crystal repeated, waiting for an explanation. But the young intruder just sat still and stared at her.

There was a rustle in the trees to our left as a young woman stepped out, "I asked him to come with me," said a second intruder, coming to Sal's defense.

"Emma?" We all said together.

PART III

CHAPTER 27

“Everybody in the house. And Patrick, put that gun away.” Now I was in my element. I knew how to manage this group. “Sit down.” I pointed toward the huge formal living room I rarely used, because it was so big.

“I'm sure there's a lot I don't know about what's going on,” I said, walking around the room and turning on all the lights in hopes of keeping everyone awake. “Here's what I do know, short and sweet. Marnie's missing and each of you has some information to contribute to the puzzle. And you, Sal and Emma, get to go first.”

“I don't know anything.” Emma looked scared. “I know Marnie and Max because I help out at the church and the daycare center.” Emma was half an inch from hysterical. “And that's how I know Crystal and Sal.” She finished.

“And Father Alphonso?” I asked.

"Right. All the Fathers and Mrs. Bristow took me in after..." She broke off.

"After what?"

"My mother signed me over to them." Emma was clipping her answers short.

"So, your mother isn't dead." I asked, trying to follow her.

"She might as well be. She's in jail."

All the *do-gooders* in the room, Patrick included, moved toward Emma to comfort her. I put my hands up, indicating the three of them needed to back up.

"That doesn't explain why you're sneaking around my house at midnight?" I continued.

"We go swimming here all the time," Sal interrupted.

"I don't buy that, Sal. Except for the small stretch of sandy beach on the other side of the jetty, this is a dangerous place to swim even in broad daylight because of all the undertows, to say nothing about the rocks. Try again." He just shut down, as teenagers do, and didn't answer my question.

As I looked around the room I tried to be objective. Emma had big circles under her eyes, from crying about Father Alphonso, and who knew what else. She sat on the couch next to Sal but not touching him, sitting forward, with her elbows on her knees, staring at her inward pointed toes as she chewed the tips of her fingers. Emma had the same jeans and shoes from earlier today but she'd changed to a tee shirt that said *The Pope is my Homeboy.*

Then there were Rupert and Crystal. Something was very much wrong there. But I was not sure what their troubles had to do with the renegade teenagers in my living room or with Marnie's disappearance.

I caught Patrick's eye. He gave me an inquisitive look and turned his palms up, suggesting I get on with it. Then he sat back and waited.

"Just a second, I'll be right back." I went to the kitchen, grabbed a six-pack of Orange Crush from the fridge and got my "chocolate" out of the freezer and put it under my arm.

Back in the living room I handed out the cans of pop to the silent room. I took the baggie out from under my arm, unwrapped the paper towels and revealed the exquisite red leather book with its gold embossing. I set the book on the coffee table for effect and Crystal gasped.

Now, no sound, from any one. No slurping of Orange Crush, no coughing, no fingernail biting.

"Marnie told me she kept a ledger." Crystal started. Her gasp had revealed her complicity, if not in Marnie's disappearance, at least in knowing about the book and maybe about what the book represented.

"I work at the church and have since I was a kid. The fathers sent me to college at Magnificat, which I think is their plan for Emma here." Crystal recited her story as if she were reading the bible in church, with no affect – just repeating the story. "I've been at the Early Childhood Center since then, first as a volunteer, now as the director."

"Father Alphonso gave Marnie my number. When she called me, she needed a place to stay and someone to talk to. I told Marnie I thought you could help." We were all watching Crystal unload her secrets. Everyone was wide awake, except for Sal, who was closing his eyes and nodding off.

"And you didn't tell me all this, because, why?" I asked, sounding more curious than peeved.

Crystal took a deep breath. "Years ago I fell in love with a seminarian preparing for the priesthood when I was in college. Father Al met with us and tried to talk us out of seeing each other." Crystal looked at Rupert. "Sorry honey, I promised to never tell anyone." Rupert looked disgusted, hurt and angry all at once, more at the secrecy I'd guess, than anything else.

"Keep going," Rupert said, "I want all the dirt out on the table." Rupert's first reaction, until he'd reconciled the information, was always defensive anger. This looked like a big confession on Crystal's part and I hoped their marriage could survive all these years of deception.

"Father Al saw himself as a kind of Robin Hood for the church," Crystal kept talking, "Saving celibacy for the priests, or at least getting the errant younger ones back to being celibate before they would take their vows. But sometimes sex can be a powerful detractor from one's path. For all of us." Crystal was starting to wobble.

"So," I said, jumping in, "Father Alphon... Al was attempting to save prostitutes and set them on a better path, as well as trying to help erring priests stay celibate? You're kidding. How crazy is that?"

"Right, but priests who had, well, problems, they came first," Crystal was stammering.

"Save all Catholic clergymen from their sexual urges, but women be damned," I asked?

Crystal nodded a little. Emma stared off, and I got mad. "And was he setting up the women? Finding women for theses guys to screw?" Even Sal was wide awake now, looking confused, like when you fall asleep in a movie and can't figure what is going on.

"Well, the hope was they would just talk, Alphonso had instructed her..."

"So, Marnie gets pregnant from one of these consorts and...hey, wait a minute. I know what this is." I picked up the book and read the names that undoubtedly corresponded with the numbers on the other ledgers we had unearthed from Marnie's basement. I handed the book to Patrick, but he was way ahead of me.

"Marnie's insurance policy," Patrick said, flipping through the book. "These must be the names of the men, priests and seminarians who paid Marnie for her talking time – or more."

"I also recognize a few politicians. Once we break this story Marnie can come out of hiding and come home," I said, sitting on the floor.

"Shep, this isn't Hollywood," Patrick said. "Even if you're right about all this, things don't quite happen that fast in the real world. Marnie's still missing and in big trouble. Maybe she's in even more trouble now without Father Alphonso to run interference.

"Revealing a dying priest's interest in saving young seminarians from their primal urges could be seen as a good thing." Patrick was on a roll now. "Who knows, maybe in the media it could say he *saves all those youngsters from homosexual pedophilia priests hiding behind a collar.* A kind of rescue and intervention program. He could be seen as a hero ..."

"Oh, for God's sake, Patrick, now who's going off half-cocked?" I interrupted. "Priests who abuse young people, or anybody are, heterosexual. Only the unenlightened think pedophiles are gay, even though many priests are. Gay, that is. Shit, let's get real here." I walked around the room a few times and then sank to the floor again, sitting with my legs crossed yoga style, reminding myself to breathe.

"I think you're right about one thing, Patrick. All we have is a sensational story. We are no closer to finding Marnie than we were two hours ago. Unless, of course, one of you knows something and you're too afraid, or loyal to share." No one was catching my eye, except Patrick.

"Or maybe all of you are hiding something," Rupert said, looking at Crystal. "Sure is a sad state of affairs when you begin to question your...friends." Sal, Emma and Crystal each studied their cuticles or concentrated their gaze on the rug.

It was late. I knew there was 'more yet to be revealed,' as we say in church, but my brain wouldn't work any more, and no one was talking.

Patrick took over. "That's enough for tonight. Under normal circumstances I'd have the lot of you at the station by now, but tonight I'll be *mister nice guy*. Sal, you sleep on the little couch over there, I'll take the big one. Emma in a guest room and Shep, you in your room. Nice of me, huh?" I thought he winked at me. Now, I was seeing things. I couldn't be interested in a man who winks at me.

"I'm arming the alarm system and I've changed the code so escape is out of the question," Patrick said. "But this is more comfortable than jail, so enjoy. Rup and Crystal, go home but I wouldn't go anywhere. Crystal, you're on your honor here, but we'll need a statement from you tomorrow." She nodded, as an errant tear slid down her face.

"Hey, Crystal," I said. "There's much to admire about a person's ability to keep a secret, unless it hurts other people. I think you know more but maybe you don't even realize how what you know is important."

"Preach it sister," Crystal said, in a nasty tone of voice I'd never heard from her before. I was not sure what to think. Was this another friend I only *thought* I knew?

"I might not know much, Crystal," I said out loud, "but it is obvious to me that you are hiding something. I just hope you're smart enough to tell somebody what you know," I said, as she turned around and slammed the door behind her.

By the time my head hit the pillow, I didn't much care anymore about any of it. I just prayed nothing tripped the alarm. All I wanted to do was sleep. I hated the feeling of being locked up in my own house with police cars across the road and another cop on the couch downstairs. I had to pray.

God, keep Marnie be safe. I'm tired. Even my prayers are so weak. I sure could use your help.

CHAPTER 28

There was a gentle tap on the door. The clock said it was three in the afternoon but I felt like I hadn't slept. I was in that half-awake-never-quite-having-fallen-into-a-deep-comforting sleep-place as my gentle intruder came in, set down a steaming mug of coffee before he sat at the foot of the bed, and began to massage my foot.

"You must be kidding Patrick, I need to sleep. I don't care what's happened."

He didn't answer me but kept rubbing, pressing on the pressure points on the bottom of my left foot then moving on to the right. The sensuous touch of his hand combined with the smell of fresh coffee talked me out of trying to sleep.

"I got a call," he said in a quiet, gentle voice. "Remember that body that showed up several days ago? It was positively identified an hour ago as Derek Johnson."

"Derek?"

"Derek."

"Well, that's confirmed. I'm awake yes, but I'm still so tired. I might forget all propriety, and say things I shouldn't, like, 'why don't we just get under the covers and forget about all this for a few hours?'"

Patrick's hands moved slowly up my ankles and calves. "Probably not today Rev, not today. Right now we need to talk."

"Hey, isn't that my line?" His hands kept creeping up my legs, stopping at my knees.

"What are the details, and how are Sal and Emma?" I asked, sitting up and reaching for the coffee.

"But before you answer that, will you open a window? It's getting warm in here." Patrick got up and opened the two windows on either side of the bay window that gave an unobstructed view of Lake Michigan. This gave me a chance to collect myself.

"I sent the kids home hours ago. All of them," Patrick said, as he opened the last window. "I had Moira and her partner drive Sal and Emma to the police station to give statements. We'll run fingerprints, in case either one has any priors. Minimum they'll get is a lecture about trespassing. My daughter is a decent interrogator and she might come up with more."

"Did she learn that interrogator thing from you?"

"She's a natural, she taught me."

"Go on. What else?"

"Derek was discovered the day after you were arrested with your new girlfriends, in a shallow stream, that runs behind Brenda's property. If it is her house? Not sure who actually owns the place, but we're looking into it as a part of the murder investigation."

I kept sipping coffee and nodding. "How'd they find him?"

"Some hunters and their dogs found him. He was all bloated from the water and the heat but it appears he'd only been dead a few days. He had a series of random slash marks on his chest and that was what linked him to our case and why they gave us that heads up. Coroner says the slashes were superficial but probably spurted some blood, hence the mess in Marnie's kitchen."

"Superficial cuts. So, what killed him?" I asked.

"One tiny bullet directly into the heart. Well placed by a killer who knows both their weapon and human anatomy. Small caliber weapons usually only kill people when the killer knows the fastest way to kill his, or her, prey and they are very close. And there was another bullet in the groin. For effect. But of course you know it was Irma, right?"

"Right, Irma had that little gun. She threw it under the porch just before the cops came to the house." I tried to be nonchalant

"Did you tell anyone this?"

"No, no one asked me too many questions at the police station, once they knew who I was. And, if you remember, I was just trying to get out of there, not interested in chit-chat. You sure I didn't mention this already that she'd done this? I think I did. Guess I just forgot to tell you about her hiding the gun. Sorry."

"Let's go over all this again."

I nodded. Patrick's hand was resting on my ankle, as if he and I did this sort of thing every day. I pulled my feet back and tucked them underneath me.

I'd sworn off love. It was too messy, too much work and too unpredictable. Besides, I didn't like the negotiating part. But still, I was enamored with Mister Cop from Cork, and surprised he wasn't angry I'd forgotten to tell him about Irma hiding that gun.

"I'm awake now, no rest for the weary as they say," I said, yawning and pinching my cheeks.

"I thought that was no rest for the wicked."

"Well, that too." I said, biting my lower lip.

We were both quiet. Smiling, knowing that any other time this would have been a perfect entrée for an intimate moment. Being playful seemed so tempting and so out of place given the circumstances.

I was out of bed now getting dressed, pulling on my jeans and going to the closet for a shirt. "What's the weather?"

"Hot," Patrick said with a little smile as he watched me dress.

"So," I said, buttoning my shirt and smiling at my fingers trying to concentrate on the conversation, "This is all pretty cut and dried. Irma killed Derek, done deal."

"Depends. He was about 6 feet and skinny. They found a lot of drugs in his blood, meth and valium for sure. She shot him up close, but maybe he was already dead or on his way. Irma herself is pretty small to drag Derek to a secluded spot."

"But he was a drug addict. Meth to get high and crazy, valium to stop the shakes. Old recipe. In college my friends would raid their mother's pill collection doing diet pills to cram for finals and then pop a valium to help the coming down. Now, it's the same except they don't study."

"Why Rev, you're a regular font of knowledge, but we know nothing. It's all circumstantial, except for what you saw."

"Patrick, don't get high and mighty. While we were raiding the medicine chest, you were smoking the good stuff in those overseas rice fields."

"Not me."

"No hash, no weed?"

"At first maybe, then I swore off it." Patrick looked off and waited a bit before saying more. "Drugs like both sides the same. It makes killing a lot easier. I never wanted killing to be easy."

"You and Marnie have that in common."

"What do you mean, Shep?"

"You'd both rather feel the pain awake, than sink beneath the fog and let the world have its way with you."

The room was quiet. As with most vets, the memory of that terrible jungle so many years later still cut deep. Patrick stood up and looked out the window at the lake, "I hate to be out of control. You do things when you are out of control."

"Now, you sound more like me," I said, smiling at him.

I scooted in front of him, taking his arms and wrapping them around my waist and we both looked at the lake water, lapping back and forth with no care for our worries.

"Being around you is hard," Patrick said, almost in a whisper, "I say things to you I never talk about."

"It's my curse," I said, and at that Patrick flinched, and let his arms drop to his sides.

I turned back to face him. "I'm not meaning to make light about what you said, but all my life, well, people just tell me things," I said, putting my fingers on his face. "But, no matter what, stuff like this is an honor to hear."

"I hate it." Patrick was struggling with the conversation.

"Look, getting back to what I said before, Marnie is like us too. We're all a bunch of wanna be control freaks. A hooker gone underground, a cop about to retire and doing what scares him the most, and a minister who tried to quit the pulpit but it won't quit her...like I said we're quite a team."

"What are you talking about?" He asked, as a fresh breeze blew strong off the lake fluffing the curtains and giving the room a clean smell.

"Well, you and me aside, Marnie hates drugs. She isn't like most hookers, who turn tricks to pay for their pimp-induced drug habit. I think not doing drugs gave Marnie a fighting chance, a leg up, a head start. Besides she's so pretty. But honestly I am not sure that's a plus for anyone trying to survive a shitty life."

Patrick put his strong arms on my shoulders, hugging me toward his body. "Marnie not doing dope meant that every time someone bought her for sex she felt everything. She remembered everything they did to her."

I shuddered and couldn't quite catch my breath. I knew what Patrick was saying about Marnie was true. "You're right. Maybe doing drugs to cover the pain and disgust she must have felt might have been better. But just in the short run."

Pulling back from me and staring at me, as if my answer really mattered, Patrick asked. "And you?"

"Drugs? Never touch the stuff. Not for a long time. Never the hard stuff – just little pot, but that makes me sleepy and I did Leary acid in the '60s, the real stuff, not the street acid made out of strychnine that killed people. I stopped all of that crap once I knew the war in Vietnam was going to be over. It was pretty clear at that point we were all going to have to get back to living, and not flirting with death ourselves, but that was many years ago. Now a glass of wine once in a while is all I can lay claim to." He was tall enough that he could rest his chin on top of my head. Patrick pulled me to him again and held me there for a quick hug, then he pulled away, shaking his head and smiling.

"Once a hippie, always a hippie," I said, ready to kiss him for real this time, but an ear-piercing squeal ended our reverie as the security alarm went off again.

"Get in the bath tub," Patrick said.

"No, I want..."

"Do it. It's the safest place to hide from stray bullets."

"Stray bullets?"

"No arguments. Stay down until I get back."

I was glad I'd gotten dressed before the dreaded security alarm went off and Patrick had banished me to the bathtub. Scrunching down in the recesses of the deep but not too long claw-foot tub I was uncomfortable and pissed off. The longer I lay there, the more irritated I got. Shit, that alarm must have been tripped by a young fox or a deer wending its way home after a drink at the lake. That's why I hated the stupid thing; it scared the critters as well as me.

The alarm stopped and at the same time my cell phone started to buzz from deep in the recesses of my jeans pocket. Fumbling from my half sitting, half lying position I got the phone and answered before it went to voicemail.

"Reverend Murdoch," I said, trying to act as if I was at my desk.

"This is Mrs. Bristow, Father Alphonso's housekeeper?"

"Oh, hello Mrs. Bristow. How are you? How is Father Alphonso?"

"That's why I am calling. He would like to speak with you, here at the residence."

When I didn't respond right away, she said, "Is that okay?"

"Sure. I'm sorry–I was just surprised. Last time I saw Farther Alphonso they were giving him last rites. So, what time does he want to see me?"

"Could you come right now?" She said, in a voice that was quiet, but insistent.

"Sure, I'll be right there," I said, as I climbed out of my hiding place in the tub.

"Thank you. It will mean a lot to him."

Watching me come down the stairs, Patrick didn't look too surprised I was disobeying his order to stay put.

"Are you done sweeping for little foxy gatecrashers," I asked?

"False alarm," Patrick muttered.

"You think?" I said, way to sarcastic for both of us. He didn't say anything. We walked to the kitchen where Patrick was still looking for our phantom intruder.

"I know you're trying to help me," I said," but playing the damsel in distress who needs a chivalrous, if dashing, knight isn't my thing. It makes me nervous. And on that note, I need to go. Pastoral call."

"You know what, Shep?"

"What, Patrick?"

"There is one thing worse than a wise old hippie."

"And that is?"

"A wise, feminist hippie."

"At least you know what a feminist is. You're miles ahead, my friend. Just don't try to lead me across the street or order food for me at a restaurant. That would be grounds for –"

"Got it *Ms. Steinem*," he said, cutting me off and leaning against the kitchen counter. Patrick looked like he belonged in my kitchen, in my house. Right along with my grandmother's homespun tablecloth and the fresh-squeezed orange juice in the crystal pitcher on the table.

"Patrick, if my independence makes you nervous, angry or embarrassed, you'd better get out of this kitchen before we both burn up." I took a breath and went on. "I'll never be an overly careful, sensible person who can't think for herself or take a risk or two." Patrick just stood there with a smile on his face, staring at me.

"Shep. I said, I've got it. I'm a cop and protective by nature. Just who I am. Now get wherever you are going."

"That I can do," I said, as he watched me lock the door and we both walked to our respective cars. To his credit Patrick didn't ask where I was off to, but I know it made him nervous.

"I'm going to the station, then home for a little shut eye. I never sleep too well on the couch. Call me," he said.

"That I can do." I said, with a little wave. "And, I appreciate you didn't ask, but Mrs. Bristol called and I am off to see Alphonso, one last time, I presume."

CHAPTER 29

Alphonso was gray around the edges and hanging on. I was surprised he was still alive. Last time I saw him the priests around his bed had given him up for all but dead. In my business I know people can cling to life and live on for reasons known to them alone.

Coming to the bedside of the dying is all part of my training, but I would never get over the incredible feeling when sitting with anyone, stranger or friend, as he or she was about to die. It was as if I was right there with the holy of all holies, participating in the most important part of life – the moving on to the next part – what an honor it was.

Alphonso's room at the residence was sparse, a single bed up against the wall, bedside table with a light, and a chair that Mrs. Bristow must have just vacated when I rang the doorbell. She was obviously more than a housekeeper, more like a housemother.

"I came right away. How is he?"

"He's been waiting for you, Reverend."

I gave her a quizzical look. "He doesn't even know me."

"I beg to differ," Alphonso's soft voice could just be heard from the corner of the room.

"You know Father," Mrs. Bristow said, to him in a hushed voice, "Palikowski's spies have probably told him Reverend Murdoch is here now." Alphonso, in a slight movement, shrugged his shoulders.

"Mrs. Bristow would you please leave us, for just a moment."

"Of course, Father," she said, looking worried and sad.

I sat down and took his hand. "Let's pray," I said

"I don't have much time."

"I know, but God will wait.

"Almighty God, by your gentle power you raised Jesus Christ from death. Watch over this brother. Hear with compassion the yearnings of your servant Alphonso. Release him from all fear and from the constraints of life's faults that he may breathe his last in the peace of your words: 'Well done, good and faithful servant,' may he enter into the joy of you, our beloved God. Amen"

"Thank you. You're a good pastor. I would like to make my confession to you."

I nodded, "It would be my honor."

Father Alphonso grimaced. "Can I get you something for the pain," I asked?

"Just listen to me. Please. I've not always done the right thing. I have sinned in front of God and others. But I have tried to do better." Alphonso paused to catch his breath.

"I know," I said, as I lay my hand on his hand. Father Alphonso turned his hand over to hold mine.

"For the past 35 years I have tried to make up for my earlier indiscretions but the albatross never left me." His grip on my hand was strong for a man so ready to die.

"Do you want to tell me what you are talking about?" I asked.

"As penance for my sins I worked with women in prostitution. I wanted to save them. I didn't save any. I was always too late. The damage was done before I got there.

"They are selling sex long before their first arrest." He gasped for air, but pressed on. "Not too far behind was someone...a man, a pimp." Alphonso started coughing. Mrs. Bristow appeared that the door but he waved her away. "The men took the money, doled out a small amount of drugs, and bits of money to keep the women serving them."

Alphonso was almost animated now in spite of not being able to breathe very well. “No sex worker chooses the life they lived. No hooker, pole dancer, call girl, or even pimp woke up and said. *Gee, I think I'll sell sex for a living.* This awful life of sex, drugs and violence was always chosen for them by a mother, father or family friend. *And call girls?* My friends would ask? *Same thing for the most part, but more complicated.*

“So, I learned to love them.” He paused again to breathe, gulping in big chunks of air as if he were trying to hold on to the oxygen and get it to stay in his lungs..

“I tried to give them information and not talk them out of the only life they knew.” He looked at me with big eyes. His shrunken face, made his eyes enormous, I think he was trying to see if I understood. His lips were cracked and parched.

“How about letting me moisten your mouth?” I asked. He nodded and closed his eyes, as I took the soft wash cloth from off the bed stand and dunked it into a large porcelain bowl of ice water, put there I was sure, by Mrs. Bristow. I daubed his lips with the cool water, and Alphonso took a large breath, nodded to me and continued.

“Marnie was different. I got lost. I committed more sins. Oh, not like before. No, this time I tried too hard to change things. I introduced her to Max's father and,” now he was whispering, “he shouldn't be a priest. He doesn't have a calling to it, not really. I was trying to save them both, to help. But I failed.”

Father Alphonso was having a hard time talking, he was tired, or more like bone weary and he seemed more ready to die with each word. I was going to have to be content with what he was able to eke out. I had to read between the lines as to why this was a confession worth hanging on for? What was I missing? Or was it just this simple confession that I'd already figured out and he just had to say it aloud, one more time. But he wasn't finished.

"I failed," he repeated, "and I failed the church." A tear slipped out of one eye, making a small circular wet spot on the pillowcase.

There was a clattering noise of hard shoes on the wooden staircase. From just outside the door Mrs. Bristow's voice came into the room high and shrill. "Father Palikowski, he asked to not be disturbed."

Palikowski strode into the room exuding bureaucratic power and confidence. The tall officious priest and university public relations director was the same one I'd met yesterday at the hospital. "I heard you were here. Why this looks like a deathbed confession, pretty irregular for a woman to hear the confession of a Catholic priest, isn't it. You missed our meeting."

"News travels fast, Ski." Alphonso, with tears still on his face, managed a little gray grin, as if he enjoyed making Palikowski uncomfortable.

"I got a call telling me she was here. What else could it be but confession?"

"Still watching me, Ski?"

Palikowski shrugged, "Ms. Murdoch I must ask you to leave."

"No," barked Alphonso as he started to cough. His grip on my hand was weaker. "Come here," he whispered. I leaned my ear to his mouth. I couldn't hear him—his breath was so labored and shallow. Most of what he was saying was in Latin, he must have been praying. The words I did understand were *Miss Crystal*. My heart leapt into my stomach. I was dizzy and my head ached at the same time.

Then as if he didn't care who heard him, Father Alphonso said in a loud voice, "It's my fault, I'm sorry. Can you help?"

"Of course," I said, hoping I could help and I wasn't even sure what he wanted me to do. Of course, he was, even in his dying breath, trying to make his nemesis Palikowski squirm. "You rest now." I wish I could have pressed him more, but that wasn't the kind of minister I was. As much as I wanted Marnie home safe, and knowing full well Father Alphonso was the key to the puzzle, I wouldn't interrogate a dying man. Damn.

"Thank you," Alphonso said, closing his eyes. His face, that had been so haggard and gray when I'd walked in the room, was now brighter. It was as if God was already opening up heaven for him and changing the color of his skin from ancient sallow to glowing—letting the old way die and a new one take over.

Leaning down, I kissed his cheek, "Go toward the light now." I said, as I laid his hands on his chest, one on top of the other. "All is well, God is ready for you, you have nothing to be sorry for, you are a good and faithful servant. There is nothing to be afraid of."

Laying my hands on Alphonso's head I prayed aloud as Mrs. Bristow and even Palikowski closed their eyes. *I lay my hands on you in the name of our Redeemer Jesus Christ, beseeching Christ to uphold you and fill you with the grace of God, that you may know Christ's redemptive power now and till the end of time. Amen.*

Palikowski followed me out of the room, as Mrs. Bristow sat in the chair next to the bed, laying her gentle hand on the hands I'd just released. "I'll stay," she said.

"That will mean a lot to him," I said, as I patted her shoulder.

Palikowski shut the door behind us, opened his mouth and looked like he was going to start talking, but I put my hand up. "Shouldn't you be in there praying with him, and not out here talking to me?"

"What did Father Alphonso tell you?" the public relations troubleshooter asked, ignoring my question.

"He told me where the Gospels of Mary, Martha and Elizabeth are buried, and what Jesus really meant about loving your neighbor." I said, pushing past him, leaving the residence.

As I sat alone in my old battered gardening jeep, where there was no need to be the caregiver or the protector, I cried.

I punched the numbers to the Evanston Police Department into my cell phone and I think Moira answered. "Can I speak to Patrick Kelly, please," I asked in a quite voice, wiping the tears from my eyes. Tears like these inevitably come after I sit with anyone who is dying—whether I know them well or not. I tell all my chaplain friends that their work, dancing in the last moments of death with so many people, makes them closer to God, both in the short run as well as the long. They laugh at me, and say I'm too into the mystical. Maybe so, maybe so.

"Sergeant Kelly," he answered, using a tough cop-like voice that I found comforting in its strength.

"Alphonso confirmed my suspicions," I said, without introducing myself. "He knew a whole lot about Marnie and Max, that's for sure." I choked up. "I'd guess he'll die tonight or early in the morning. It's obvious that he's already held on longer than his body had wanted."

"What can you tell me?" Patrick asked.

"Do you remember that Marnie had always led me to believe that Derek was Max's father? Well, she seems to have lied. Alphonso gave me the impression that a young priest is the father, and that Crystal is involved more than she's let on."

"How deep?" he asked.

"Up to her eyeballs, I would guess," I said, as my cell phone buzzed to tell me I had a call waiting. "Can you meet me at Woodstone later? I'm in the car, I have a call coming in, looks like Mrs. Bristow on the other line," I said, as I clicked over and answered, "Reverend Murdoch."

"He died, just a few minutes ago. I thought you would like to know."

"Thank you for calling me, Mrs. Bristow, I know you were family for each other. He was blessed to have you care for him."

"For twenty years, Reverend Murdoch. He took me in after my husband died and I had nothing. For twenty years I have cooked and cleaned house for these fathers, but this one was special. He's not so much in his head, but he's always caring about others and trying to help them, especially the women."

"Mrs. Bristow you must be very sad, I am sorry."

"There is no time for that. I have many things to do – I'll grieve later. The funeral will be in three days at St. Mary's. I know he would like it if you were there."

"I will be there, Mrs. Bristow."

"Thank you, Reverend Murdoch. I'd appreciate it."

To sit with someone who is dying is always a privilege, but in this case, also a burden. The passing of Father Alphonso left me grieving. Not so much his death but the fact that with him died all the little bits and pieces of information that might help me find Marnie. Bits of information I doubted were written down anywhere.

"He shouldn't be a priest...and Miss Crystal," was what he'd said.

Crystal?

It was dark as I pointed my jeep toward home. By now Crystal must have given her statement to Patrick. I was pissed. What was the point of Crystal not telling me she already knew Marnie before I did? We were friends. Or maybe I was just a simple dupe that both Marnie and Crystal had seen as an easy mark.

I was hungry and had no interest in cooking. The Faith Café was a few miles from Woodstone and I needed real food. There was a parking space right in front, and it was after nine so I didn't have to feed the meter. I ordered miso soup, a house salad and a large carrot juice. There was a great folk band playing and I decided to stay for a few songs.

The people in the band were all friends of mine from way back and I was glad to listen, laugh, let my head go into the music, and forget the mess I had found myself in. Sue, one of two women in the Sons, came over at the break and gave me a hug. "Rev, what a great surprise, haven't seen you in ages."

"Been nutzy busy, Sue."

"Right, well give me a call we should catch a coffee." She was such a love, and as much of a bleeding heart as me.

"Sure, maybe in a few weeks. But I gotta run. Kiss, kiss," I said, and blew her a kiss. The rest of the band waved, as I paid my check and left the restaurant. They usually played much bigger venues but tonight they were trying out new material and, I loved every new tune.

As I pulled into my driveway I saw Patrick's unmarked police car. He and Rupert were already in a heated discussion.

"She's gone," Patrick said, as I got out of my car.

"I know she's gone," I said.

"Not Marnie," Patrick barked, "*Crystal.* Rupert says he has no clue about any of this, do you believe that, Shep?" Patrick's anger helped me stay centered. I could see Rupert was broken up.

"Nothing can surprise me." I gave Rupert a hug. "She was good," I said. "Marnie and Crystal both are. But this isn't about us being lied to. Something serious is going on. Given all that's happened I wouldn't assume Crystal left on her own free will—though she may have."

"You are so Pollyanna, Shep," Patrick said, "this *looks* like a huge scam gone wrong."

"But what's the point? You know what, Patrick, I was beginning to doubt Rupert a few days ago, but never Crystal. I had it backwards."

"Didn't I, Rupert?" I looked at my right-hand-man, the one I'd counted on to take care of everything at Woodstone. "You don't know any more than the rest of us, do you?" Rupert looked both embarrassed and angry.

"If I am naïve, so is Rupert," I said, placing my hands on his shoulders and looking him in the eyes. "You are thinking that her strange behavior contradicts how much she loves you. I know for a fact that's just dead wrong. This is all about payback, or greed, or cover-up, or shame. Maybe someone wants Livy's money, to which I have no access. Maybe it isn't Marnie or Crystal at all. I think someone else is walkin' this dog." I could tell by the looks on Patrick and Rupert's faces that what I was saying made sense.

"I don't know what Crystal's up to," Rupert said, after an uncomfortable silence, "but I don't think she knows either. She's been screaming in her sleep and not eating. Just says it's bad dreams, but I'm worried."

"Me too, me too," I said. "Let me ask you this, Rupert, did she say anything to you about Alphonso dying?"

"Sort of. She said an old priest she'd known for a long time was dying of heart problems. I remember asking her if they'd been friends. All she'd said was, *not exactly*."

"Reading between the lines," I said, putting my thoughts together, "I'd hazard a guess that at one point or another, Alphonso might have helped Crystal too, and she's afraid of something real or imagined. Shame combined with the fear of what might happen, makes you the kind of scared that lets you mistrust even the ones you love. With Alphonso dead, the house of cards, and all he was protecting, is up for grabs. I refuse to believe Crystal is doing anything to hurt you, Rupert, but she is in trouble.

"All I have to go on are the dying words of a man I hardly knew. Not much, to be making such presumptions, but it sounds like Crystal is involved, at least somehow."

"How long has she been gone, Rup?" Patrick asked his old friend.

"I was out when she was due home, but I could see she'd been back. Since Patrick had told her to go to the station and give a statement, that's where I thought she was. Then I noticed her overnight bag was gone and I knew she'd taken off."

"Has she done this before?" I asked

"Not in a long time." Rupert said shivering, even though the day was warm and humid.

Patrick held out a pack of cigarettes he'd taken off those kids last night. "Without more information we're stuck at the moment for a game plan," he said, as we all sat down on the porch and lit up.

"If this was anything other than two missing friends, an abandoned child and a dead priest I'd kick myself for smoking," I said, to myself, as much as the others, taking a drag of the acrid smoke into my lungs. "Isn't this stupid?" I said, shaking my head.

"Rupert, when'd you quit?" I was chatting.

"Six years ago, same time I quit everything else."

"Patrick, when'd you quit?"

"Three months ago, when the doc gave me an ultimatum."

"It's been ten years for me. Here we are a bunch of dumb asses smoking, but I love to smoke, too bad it kills you."

Nobody said anything. Then Rupert started laughing, "Crystal *would* kill me if she knew I was smoking. But she's killing me anyway." Rupert was tearing up, and he wasn't one to show his feelings in front of people. "Look, I'm going home," he said, "This is making me crazy. Pat, call me if you hear anything, promise?" I knew he had to go punch pillows or walls or whatever he did to get himself to stop hurting so much.

"And Shep," Patrick said, snuffing out his barely smoked cigarette in the dirt, "I have to get back to the station. I'm on tonight. Between the basic crap that comes in, I'll try to see what I can figure out about Crystal's disappearance. I'll put out an APB out for her car, but at this point, even that may be premature. Maybe there's an explanation, maybe she's just shopping?"

"This late? Nothing is open. And she didn't give her statement and her overnight bag is gone. Now who's dreaming?" I said, finishing the last of my cigarette, smoking it down to the nubs. I was feeling sick already, but wanting another one.

"I'm just suggesting we might be jumping to conclusions. The last words of the priest might not indicate Crystal is implicated in Marnie's disappearance," said Patrick.

"You don't sound convinced."

"Either way, you stay put, Reverend."

"Right," I said, "I'm tired enough for one day." I was tired, sick-and-tired, especially if I was being taken for a ride by my so-called best friends. But something wouldn't let me buy that. The explanation all had to be more complicated than I'd been able to figure so far.

"Hey," I hollered after Patrick, "leave me a smoke." Patrick tossed me the almost empty pack, and I waved him off.

Inside the kitchen I poured myself a small snifter of Bailey's Irish Cream and went back outside, this time to the front porch, to smoke a last cigarette. Gosh, they tasted good, even after ten years. The moon was high and far away, and the clouds were sliding across the moonlight, making it easy to see one minute and almost pitch black the next.

A week ago Marnie called my house and asked me to come get her. Her kitchen had blood all over it, Marnie was nowhere to be found, and Max was hiding behind a chair. I started nosing around, found the books, and the photo. Where was that picture? I crushed out the unfinished cigarette and went upstairs to find it.

The picture had been torn in half and whoever had been with Marnie ripped away. I rummaged in the drawer where I'd been putting all little clues of my search. I'd been given the ledger-type books, Rupert had gotten out of Marnie's basement, gone to Patrick to see if some expert could figure out the code, but the picture had been in my bedside nightstand drawer along with the notes I'd been taking since this started.

Even before I got to the drawer I knew the picture would be gone. On the way up the stairs I stopped. Shit. It had all been right in front of me. I always thought it had been some guy next to Marnie, in that picture. On the back it had said *the Dream...*" How stupid could I be? That other person must have been a woman, not a man. For the most part the men who went to the Dream Palace were running from something, and would not want their pictures taken. I would bet dimes-to-donuts it had been Crystal in the photograph. That might explain a bit of why Crystal, a woman I'd never seen wear her heart on her sleeve, shed unexpected tears last night and then ran away today. But why? I was making giant leaps here, but it was possible.

As, I'd guessed, both the picture and my notes were not in my drawer where I'd left them.

Were Marnie and Crystal friends from the neighborhood, the Dream Palace or what, maybe sisters? Crystal had known everything about this investigation from the get-go, but she didn't look or act the least bit like a sex worker. I'd trusted Crystal with Max and she'd taken him to Judith at the monastery. My heart began to pound. *Shit,* that was it. I'd bet the farm that's where she went. Maybe Crystal was going to get Max. But, why?

Dialing Judith, I grabbed car keys, my purse and jacket and headed for the jeep. Starting this rattletrap of a car, I wished I had my Outback. The phone kept ringing at the monastery, and there were no phones in any of the rooms where the sisters slept. Rupert must have heard me leave, but I didn't want him to come with me. If Crystal was at the monastery I wanted some time to talk to her, alone.

The monastery was a 90-minute drive northwest out of town. Crystal was well ahead of me, but if Marnie had called anyone for help, she probably would have called Crystal and not me. Maybe Crystal told Marnie where Max was. If I were Marnie, I'd do everything I could to get my son and run. Not very smart, but it would be something Marnie would do. If Marnie had called Crystal she would have told her everything she knew. In my hurry to leave I'd not locked up the house or closed the gate, but if I was right that would't matter, not now.

Lots of "ifs," but Crystal's connection to Marnie was the only reason I could think of that Crystal would leave Rupert so upset and out of the loop. If I was right, Crystal knew Rupert would go to the authorities to protect her, and that would be like going to the enemy. I wasn't a hooker, but even I distrusted cops, so I imagined that would be a logical fear for Crystal, if indeed this made any real sense at all.

There was little or no traffic as I entered the highway at Old Orchard Road and headed north, just an occasional sports car racing another on this strip of highway that was rife with street racers, late at night. Patrick had one of these little pocket rockets. I'd have to ask him if he found this section of road enticing. Why else have a car that goes fast, if not to drive it fast? Of course, there was always the joy of knowing you could go fast if you wanted.

The fresh cool air from my open window was noisy, chilly and welcomed. The anger and the hurt were gone. This wasn't about me, and my feelings. This was about two women trapped in something dangerous and a little boy caught in the middle. Racing toward the monastery, I called Patrick and left messages on his office machine and on his cell. I couldn't wait for him.

As I drove up the long driveway toward the monastery residence and retreat center, all was dark, as would be expected this late at night, except, that is, for the light over the front door that was set on a timer to stay on during the nighttime hours. It was a keyless entry setup like a telephone pad and opened by punching in a code that was changed from time to time.

Judith set the code and always tried for number combinations that made some religious sense. It was the same lock system for all the outside doors at the retreat center. Inside no locks were needed, since trust and faith carried the day. The last time I was here the code was 5853, of course that translated as *Luke*, so I tried it, but the huge carved door didn't budge.

I punched in 6275 for *Mark*, 6279 for *Mary* and every combination I could think of that might open the door. Then I tried 5683 *love,* and the big door clicked open. Judith was reminding me of something I already believed—it was love, not judgment, that always came first.

Two steps at a time I made my way up to Judith's room and opened the door. And there was my spiritual counselor tied to a chair, with duct tape over her mouth, and very much alive. I hugged her as I held the phone to my ear and dialed 911.

CHAPTER 30

"This is going to hurt, Judith, but fast is better," I said, as I tore the duct tape off her mouth.

"They're gone," Judith said, blinking from the sudden pain as I untied her thin arms and released them from their awkward position behind the chair.

"Who's gone?"

"The ones who tied me to the chair, who'd you think? I heard them leave in a car." Sister Judith rubbed her face as I took a robe that hung on the back of her door and handed it to her. I knew she'd be embarrassed being naked in front of me. She nodded a thank you.

"I figured that," I said. "How long ago?"

"I think about 45 minutes. There were three of them, with bandanas around their noses and mouths. Two acted and dressed more like boys, one might have been a girl. I think they took Brother Leonardo and Max. I heard their voices outside. Then someone else drove up. I could hear fighting and then two cars, one after another, peeled out of the driveway.

"Oh, Shep, that poor little boy. What's going on?"

"I'm not too sure, but how are you?"

"Mad is all. A houseful of nuns is a poor defense against three scary looking kidnappers."

"Lighten up on yourself. People determined to do something like this will do it. How did they get in?" I asked, as I could have kicked myself for putting Judith and the other women in harms way by bringing Max here in the first place. We both looked at each other, as the sirens and swirling police car lights woke up the night and, of course, the rest of the people at the monastery.

"The front door. Like you, someone with them must have been here before and just guessed at the code." Judith said, as she pulled her robe even closer around her and retied the belt.

"Or someone told them," I said. "Most people think the code is just random. Who knows about your choosing words of significance and translating them into numbers?"

"Come on, Shep. That's no secret."

At that point a well-mannered state police officer came to Judith's open door and stood with her hat in her hand. "I'm sorry to bother you sister, and...?"

"Reverend Shepherd Murdoch," I said, extending my hand, which she ignored.

"Reverend Murdoch," she said with a little nod. "Would you both please meet the others in the dining hall?" The officer was wearing the full regalia of equipment including a bullet proof vest, that must have added at least fifteen pounds to her body weight. She touched Judith's elbow, steering her out of the room, "We need to check your room for prints. Again, I am so sorry."

"My room?" Judith started, then shook her head in disbelief and nodded as if she understood. Nuns have such little privacy when they live in a residence. This invasion of her space must have been disconcerting to Sister Judith.

Heading down the stairs and into the dining hall the officer turned to me, "Reverend Murdoch, we need you towards the front door for just a moment, then you can rejoin the sisters if you wish."

As the officer led me down the hall, I asked her, "Were you raised Catholic?"

"Yes, I was." This officer had appeared uncomfortable. Seeing Sister Judith in her robe must have given the young officer pause.

"I thought so." Our childhood learnings, both good and bad, seem to stick to us like glue. I found her respect and deference to Judith a pleasant comfort.

Cops were everywhere, searching the premises and taking statements, while technicians were trying to get prints. Then, of course, there was the strange vision of a group of nuns in their nightclothes, sitting tense and nervous in the dining room.

"Not wearing habits anymore is one thing, but sitting in my bathrobe in the monastery dining room is quite another," I overheard, as a woman officer guided me toward the front reception area. Patrick was waiting for me and, of course, Rupert was with him.

"Hey," I said, "Why don't we let these folks do their job? Anybody got a cigarette?" They both shook their heads, as we walked outside into the crisp night.

Outside waiting for the officers to get statements and clear the premises, I was getting antsy. "This watching the sun go up and down with you two is getting to be a habit. Either of you mind if I go for a walk?" I had been waiting for daylight. "I need to walk – nervous – let me know if anything happens," I said, raising my cell phone.

This property was familiar territory for me. Patrick and Rupert would do their best to keep me hanging around them when it was dark, but they'd be less protective in the daylight.

"You've got to be kidding? The perps could still be here, hiding in the trees." This time it was Rupert with the sage advice, not Patrick.

"Spoken like a true city boy," I said. "Look, the path goes over to a few houses in the distance across the pond, and to the hermitages just over that small hill there. I heard these have already been checked out," I said, stretching the truth. What I had heard was one of the sisters telling the officers about the property, and I *presumed* they'd checked them out. I had to go see for myself. What no one had mentioned was a tree house on the adjacent neighbor's property. I had eyed this wonderful structure on my walks in the past when I was at the monastery on retreat myself. It was built between two trees and had what looked like several additions to the original structure. It looked like the kids who'd built the original tree house had grown more proficient over time in their building skills and had made several improvements to their original construction. Regardless, it would make a great hiding place and I wanted to check it out.

Last autumn I'd talked Marnie and Crystal into coming with me for a silent retreat. Marnie and I had a hard time not talking, but the required quiet seemed to fall fresh on Crystal, and she glowed in the silence. The dense calm did the opposite to Marnie and me. We both got jittery and nervous at not talking, so we took little walks away from the monastery, and Crystal would came along. On one of those walks, we discovered the tree house and, breaking the silence, had all remarked on how much fun it might be to live in one.

By this point in my discovery I had no reason to doubt that Marnie had called Crystal, who'd told her where Max was. But someone else must have found out, too. Otherwise why tie up nuns, and what about Brother Leonardo and Max? This didn't track. Could this be some diversion? Or did Judith not understand what she was hearing?

Marnie, or anyone hiding close by, would be flushed out. The sisters must have told the officers about the various nooks and crannies of the property. If any of them were still here, the search teams would have found them by now. But if she hadn't left before the cops arrived, and if she was going hide, my bet was on the tree house. That is, of course, if she came at all, or if all this nonsense with sirens and flashing lights hadn't scared her off.

First, I took the paved road over the first hill to the north of the retreat house, the sun just rising up over the hill. After about five minutes of walking, the path switched from blacktop to gravel and then, once in the woods, to a path covered with composting leaves. I was pretty sure that the tree house was down the hill and to the left

Up over the ridge, in the distance, I caught sight of a figure walking slowly toward me. Even in the dim light I could see it was not Marnie, as I had hoped, but Brenda!

"I give up. I give up. Take me in." Brenda was wild-eyed, like she was speeding on meth or tripping on bad acid.

"Brenda, what are you doing here?"

"She made me come."

"Brenda, are you okay?" I asked, as I noticed she had blood on the front of her shirt.

"No, I'm not okay, she shot me."

"Who shot you, Brenda?" I asked, but she kept walking and muttering, "I give up. I give up. O, God I'm going to die." Then she fell to her knees, slumped to the ground in a heap. I reached out to her but she growled, and said in a deep low voice, "Don't touch me, or I'll kill you." Her words were without merit, as she toppled over and fell sideways on the grass.

"Brenda, this is Reverend Shepherd Murdoch," I said to her, not sure that she even recognized me. "I'll call for help, you stay right here." Her eyelids fluttered as if she had heard me. "Stay right here."

"Fuck you," she whispered.

"Yeah, right. Just stay right here and don't move, or you'll make it worse." By this time she'd passed out, but she was still breathing in little irregular bursts. Lifting up her shirt, I saw a wound that looked recent, but not from today. It was oozing dark blood. Lifting her eyelid I saw that her pupil was not reacting to the light. No fever. I checked the pulse in her neck; it weak but constant. Maybe, she was hallucinating from losing all that blood, or drugs or both.

I took off my sweatshirt and covered her clammy shoulders, then moved in towards the woods. I dialed Patrick's cell phone, which went to voice mail. I was sure he had it on 'silent' and would get a message when the phone announced the message by vibrating.

"Patrick, go north of the monastery on the inner blacktop drive. It turns into a gravel path. Just before the path ends at the woods, you'll find a woman who's been shot. Her name is Brenda and she's angry, but she'd protect Marnie, and I would guess, Crystal, at all costs. Brenda is from the Dream Palace, go easy on her." I breathed heavy into the phone, as I jogged toward the woods, "I'm heading into the woods toward a tree house on the southeast edge of the sisters' property. No time to wait for you. Call an ambulance for Brenda," I clicked the cell phone off.

It was dark inside the cool forest. I shivered, and I tried to acclimate to the change in temperature. Inside this thick stand of pine and oak, I shuddered again, not at the chill, but the dark shadows, where anything could be lurking.

I walked quick as I dared, not wanting to alarm any creatures, or they me, or to slip on the wet, decaying leaves that littered the ground. The tree house, I remembered, was at the end of the woods, on the edge of another clearing where the forest wasn't so dense.

Just as my eyes were beginning to see a little better, I heard a noise behind me. It was either that mountain lion folks had been talking about, since one was seen near here last month, or it was a human. Instinct told me to jog sideways off the path. A few yards behind me I made out the shapes of not one, but two people. I thought I'd have better luck with a mountain lion. I ducked under a branch and backed my way into a thicket. Instead of staying put, which might have been the wisest thing to do, I ran, and went deeper into the forest toward the direction of the tree house.

My pursuers were kids, and they were faster than me. In one sudden movement they jumped out in front of me, grunting like football players, each grabbing an arm, throwing me backwards. Dark as it was, they were close enough now to see that one was the James Dean look-alike who'd clobbered me with a baseball bat and still reeked of Old Spice. The other was younger, and it was Sal, who'd slept on my couch last night. They were carbon copies of each other, one older by five or six years. Brothers.

Remembering a bit of the self defense training I'd learned in a workshop for clergywomen years ago, I managed to twist and turn out of their grip, and run back out of the woods. Praying I wouldn't trip on any logs, or slip on the wet leaves, I made my way back out. The boys ran after me at first, and then stopped, as if they knew they might be running into a trap.

As I'd hoped, the state police officers and EMT's were taking care of Brenda. Patrick was pointing instructions to two young state cops, who jogged to the east of the woods toward the tree house. As Patrick combed the area with his eyes, he saw me, as I ran out of the woods about 500 yards away. At a loping kind of run Patrick came towards me, with Rupert not far behind.

"I sent a team to the tree house," he said.

I bent over, trying to catch my breath from this sudden sprint, "Two teens in the woods, one was Sal," I said, as I pointed into the darkness of the forest, but Rupert, and Patrick had already spotted them.

CHAPTER 31

Déjà vu. Just like the other night, when Emma and Sal were discovered at my house, coming out of the woods was Patrick with Sal, and Rupert had collared the older boy.

"We questioned that one last night," Patrick said, to the state cop, who was putting plastic zip strips around Sal's wrists. "It was circumstantial. We had to release him, he's sixteen. This one, the one who doesn't look the least bit contrite, well, I've seen before too, as a witness at a crime scene," Patrick gestured to the older boy. "I'd like to question these two when you're done, if that would be alright with your sergeant?" Patrick said, to the trooper who nodded, as he marched the boys down the hill.

The morning sun had gone under the clouds and the wind was kicking up. Patrick and Rupert filled in a bit of information for the officers, and I stood a few yards away to wait for them to finish.

Where was Crystal, this mysterious John Leonardo, Max and, of course, Marnie? What was I not seeing? It occurred to me that I'd been looking at this all wrong. What if they weren't running away *or* lost?

When our dog Bailey used to take off running I'd panic, and say he was lost. My son would remind me that our Bailey dog wasn't afraid or lost but he was having fun. Right. Maybe the people I was looking for were in deep shit as far as the authorities were concerned, but they didn't know it. They didn't consider themselves lost.

I was sure Leonardo was Alphonso's protégé seminarian, the one who caused Al to delay his rendezvous with God, and tell me he'd tried to do the right thing. What else did Alphonso say besides he didn't think this guy was called to the priesthood? What had the good, if misguided, father been trying to tell me? Was it in some kind of code, since he knew, or presumed, that Palikowski was close by? Or were they just the confused last words of a dying man?

"Penny for your thoughts."

"Hi, Patrick. Rupert." I said, as I noticed my teeth were chattering. "Guess I'm in a little shock, huh? Once more with feeling. This routine is so tiresome."

"Maybe you are just cold. How about some coffee?" Patrick asked, as he wrapped his sport coat around my shoulders.

"Sure, the kitchen is this way," I said.

As we turned to walk back toward the monastery Patrick slipped his hand in mine, and Rupert dropped back to walk behind us. We were lost in our own thoughts as we retraced our steps back to the monastery. All was quiet now. The ambulance had taken Brenda to the local hospital. The two young fellows would be questioned by the State cops and then Patrick would get a call if there was any new information.

All evidence and statements had been taken from the nuns. As we passed the chapel I could see they were now dressed and doing what they do best, praying.

The kitchen was warm from the big industrial-sized oven where someone was already baking bread and cookies for lunch. The young cook, with his red pony tail pulled back with a hair tie, was chopping onions for the Moroccan stew he'd planned for the evening meal, adding to the great smells already coming from the kitchen.

"You all look pretty cold," the boy-cook said. "Can I get you some tea, or maybe spiced apple cider?" The three of us agreed that the cider sounded good. "Why not go sit in the dining room, and I'll fix it for you."

As we sat around the table cupping big white ceramic cups of cider, I wondered if we were all afraid to say out loud what we were thinking.

"I'll start." Judith's voice came from the door of the kitchen, and we all jumped.

"I hadn't figured it out right away," she said, pulling up a chair. "Most people think nuns are dense when it comes to relationships, I would say it's quite the opposite. We just don't talk about it that much. It's not unusual for people to come here and say they want to learn more about the Benedictine way. Or, if they are already religious, to find some time to pray, work, and reflect. Like you do, Shep," Judith said, turning her beautiful mom-eyes on me.

"As you know, Crystal and Marnie had been here before, but so had Alphonso and John Leonardo. They weren't regulars, but every so often they'd come for a few days to rest. Alphonso called the young man his beloved, like Jesus in John's gospel."

"What are you saying, Judith? Were they lovers?" I blurted out, with a gasp. "Don't get me wrong, I don't care if they are or were, it just hadn't occurred to me."

"Well, yes and no. I don't know for absolute sure, but I'd say the young man reminded Alphonso of someone, maybe a brother or even a son. In that way they were beloved, but that's a hunch. Alphonso wouldn't want this to be out in the open, especially to Palikowski, who everyone knows does priest damage control for the university. And this friendship or connection would be a serious public relations nightmare for Palikowski."

"Did Alphonso know who he was before John started working with him?" I asked.

"I don't know. Like I said, this is a hunch. But I'll tell you this, when John and Al came here for a retreat—nine times out of ten, so would Crystal."

"What? Why didn't you tell me this before? Was this before or after she came with me? I trusted you Judith to be honest with me. I told you all about my friendship with Crystal."

"Forgive me for not telling you. I felt it wasn't my place to fill you in on Crystal's whereabouts, nor she yours."

"Come on Shep—you know all about clergy-client confidentiality," said Rupert, as he stared into his empty cup.

"So, Rupert, does this jibe with what you know?" I said, recovering just a bit, but still wondering if Judith had told us everything she knew about my so-called friends.

"Crystal and I have been together for a long time," he said, choking up. "Until a week ago, I was sure she was honest with me about everything and that I knew everything there was to know about her. Remember a day or two ago, when you got suspicious of me and called me on it? Crystal was acting so strange, I needed to try to help her first."

"And?"

Patrick's cell buzzed, "I'm gonna take this, wait a sec," he said, as he opened his phone and stood up. "Kelly here, what have you got, officer?" We sat listening to the one sided conversation, while Patrick paced the room and listened as the State Trooper filled him in with what they found.

"And what about the tree house?" Patrick listened to the answer and shook his head toward me. "Thanks, we'll be in touch." He closed his phone, and sat back down.

"They are finished, took everyone in for questioning and no one is still on the premises who doesn't belong. No sign of Marnie or Max. There was no one at the tree house, but it looked like there might have been some recent activity, but hard to tell if it was today or not." Patrick sighed, took a long gulp of water and said, "Where were we? Rupert, I think you're up."

"Right. Well, I knew Crystal went on retreat from time to time, but I didn't know she came to the same place you went to, except for that one time when the three of you went together. In fact, I never asked her where she was going or who she was doing it with. We have a very trusting marriage. I had no reason to doubt her, or she me. For the record, I still don't." Rupert stopped for a moment, and stared off before he continued. "After Marnie disappeared, I noticed that Crystal started to act strange."

"There's no doubt she loves you," I said, reaching across the table to squeeze his hand.

"I agree, Rupert. When she was here she talked about you more than she talked about herself," Judith said.

"Patrick, you must have something new after listening in on the interviews of Brenda and the two boys?" Patrick raised his eyebrows at me, as if he was wondering whether to reveal his responses to the group or tell me in private.

I nodded toward him, "At this point we've got to trust each other, don't you think?"

"If their stories are to be believed, this is a family affair of sorts," Patrick said. "According to a very high Brenda, she and Pammy Jo have the same mother, that would be Irma, but Shep you'd already guessed that. The two boys are brothers, not sure about who *their* mother is, but they may have the same father as Marnie. Brenda was pretty loopy at this point, and the EMTs were not happy I was questioning their patient. She did say, when I asked her, that Irma runs the prostitution road house in South Chicago, and the father..."

"Not Alphonso?" I gasped.

"No, Shep," Judith said, as put her hand on mine, "Alphonso, could be John's father, but I think that is the extent of his transgressions. And for the record, the one reason I am telling you any of what I know, is because Max is missing."

"Ah, thanks Judith, didn't mean to put you in a bad place. Being a mandated reporter is tough. So, as this goes, sex with Leonardo's mother was the 'old sin' Al was alluding to just before he died." Judith didn't confirm or deny this, but her corroboration didn't matter on this since it was all speculation anyway.

"Anyway," Patrick continued, "The father of Marnie and one or both of the boys was not mentioned in Brenda's ramblings. "The best I can figure, from the preliminary reports I ran after last night's incident with Sal and Emma, is that the father of Sal and his brother is some cop downstate who gives Irma security at the Dream Palace—conjecture is that he is using off-duty police officers for her protection, and Irma is paying them all under the table. After checking I found out that the Illinois Bureau of Police Internal Affairs has had these cops under surveillance for some time now."

"I can't help but think about that nasty breast-fondling cop who booked me when I was arrested with Irma, Patty and Brenda. Maybe he has something to do with all this. I remember his pocket flap was covering his name tag."

"Possible, Shep, and his name isn't on your arrest paperwork either. You know an internal investigation is a sensitive thing for all concerned. How this ties together isn't clear. I'll check into it, you might be right."

"What about Max?" I said, as I poured myself more spiced cider from the carafe on the table. For a few heavy minutes no one spoke.

Then Judith began, "I am very concerned that he is missing from us, but I suspect Max is where he belongs, with his mother and father, Marnie and John. And I could be wrong, but I suspect all the players from Marnie and Max, to maybe even the nasty cop, will be at Alphonso's funeral at St. Mary's."

"Oh, that should be a very interesting affair, don't you think?" I said, with a wry smile.

I hugged Judith, we said our goodbyes and drove back to Woodstone.

~~~

Patrick dropped Rupert and me at Woodstone. “I'm going to the station, and see if anything new has come in I haven't heard about yet. Go to bed, Shep. You too Rupert, you look beat. I will see you both at the church tomorrow. And don't either of you get any wiseass, hotdog ideas, and go pursuing any tangents without checking with me. I'll have my cell on.”

“Not to worry, I'm too tired to go off on any Marnie hunts. But I can't speak for Rupert here, who's pacing up and down, wearing a hole in my driveway.”

“Well, wouldn't you be a little nervous if your wife was missing?”

“Pat,” Rupert said, as his friend of many years climbed back into his squad car, “follow your own advice, man. Get some sleep. I'll be fine.”
~~~

CHAPTER 32

Walking into my house exhausted, I smelled something I hadn't smelled in weeks. It smelled exactly like roses, a little on the sweet side for me but it was the perfect scent for Marnie. I appreciated the olfactory heads up but I jumped, none-the-less, when I heard Marnie say my name.

"Oh my God." I dropped my coat on the floor, reached out and held on to her. We were both crying. "Oh, my God... oh, my God..." I kept repeating as I held her tight in my arms, as if I was afraid she would evaporate. Marnie held on too, but I could feel her distance. As the immediate relief subsided, I started getting irritated, but I was too tired to be angry. We pulled apart and stared at each other.

"Well, look who's standing in my kitchen, plain as day."

Marnie clasped her hands in front of her and looked down at her feet, like a guilty child.

"I'd like to ask you where the hell you've been, but by the looks of things, you have been through hell."

She just stood there.

"I'm going to make us some tea," I said, which was what I always did in a bad situation. I ran filtered water into the teakettle and put it on the stove. I stood there staring at the kettle.

"I think you need to turn it on," Marnie said, with a small smile in her voice.

"You don't look so good, Marnie," I said. Her hair was dyed black, her face was pale and drawn. She had big, almost purple, bags under her eyes. Her usually well-manicured fingernails were chewed to the quick. Undoubtedly, she was taking me in at the same time.

"I'm sorry. I should have told you everything. But how could I, you..."

I interrupted, "First, don't presume what I would have done since you never gave me a chance. But you're right, we both look like shit and something tells me you've been through a lot more than me." We sat down at the table, listening to the water start to simmer.

"Why don't you just start from the beginning. Or don't you trust me?" I said, sounding much too whiny for me. "But first, where's Max?"

"Asleep upstairs."

"And John?"

"You figured out about John? He's up there too, on the floor, in case Max wakes up and gets scared."

"Well, that's a relief, glad someone's thinking about Max," I said, regretting my tone of voice almost immediately. "Sorry, I don't mean to be such a jerk but ..."

"I deserve it," Marnie said. "Shep, I never thought this would get so bad.

"Years ago, after I found out I was pregnant I couldn't tell John or anyone the truth. I knew he felt connected to me, maybe even loved me, but John always said he wanted to be a priest. All his mother had ever told him was that his father was a priest, and it wasn't that his dad didn't love him, but he loved Christ more."

"So, John thought he'd be a priest too, since it had worked out so well for his mother and father? Oh, sorry, snotty voice again. You know, happens when I'm tired."

"I guess that's right. But I knew John was Max's father all along. After all you don't get pregnant from lap dancing, handjobs or..."

"Spare me the graphics Marnie, but continue," I said, waving her on. The kettle was boiling but the whistle had been lost long ago, so it just spit steam into the kitchen.

"A few months before I got pregnant with Max, Father Alphonso made me an offer." She got mugs from the cupboard, along with my favorite teapot. After her earlier sudden burst of information, Marnie was quiet, as she busied herself with making tea.

She took the blue ceramic teapot my mother had made me years ago, and she rinsed it out with hot water, just as I'd taught her. I watched as she measured tea into the tea ball and dropped it into the pot. I appreciated the silence. It gave me a chance to listen for that faraway voice inside me and try to think more clearly, and maybe even pray. Those few moments of prayer slightly rejuvenated me, and would, I hoped, keep me from ranting and raving about how scared I am for Marnie and Max, and, if I was honest, for me.

"Keep talking," I said, waiting for the tea to steep.

"Alphonso said he would pay me to talk to seminarians who were uncertain about their sexual urges. You know, those who were wondering if they should really be priests. Since he was their social justice professor teaching about urban street ministry, he had access to all these priests who were second-guessing their call. Al also had this thing about saving all of us.

"He thought I'd be perfect for the seminarians and priests to talk to, and he wanted to help me too."

"What *did* you talk to them about? The weather? Movies you'd seen?" I said quietly, without sarcasm this time.

"At first. Then, as we got to know each other, they asked more pointed questions. And we talked. These guys would test out their feelings about women. They'd ask questions they'd never been able to ask, that sort of stuff.

"I wanted away from Irma and Derek so bad, I hated my life. So, I took Al up on his offer. Definitely a no brainer. I talked to these guys—seminarians, ordained—gay and straight. I talked to whoever Al set me up with.

"They were all nice to me and grateful. Father Al planned the meetings, usually at nice places like the Drake or the Palmer House. For the most part all we would do is talk and have dinner. So, I began to save the money he paid me and hide it from Irma."

"Why didn't you just leave when you could, when you had such a cushy new job?"

"I was afraid to leave the Dream Palace. I knew Irma would track me down and I'd be back at it, so why try to leave? Then I got pregnant. By this time the only person I was having sex with was John. Funny that his name's John, isn't it?"

I only nodded and poured more tea into our mugs.

"Well, when I told Irma I was pregnant, she was actually happy. She has this crazy notion that for some reason we should have kids. Somewhere in Irma's thinking she draws the line at abortion. Must be because she'd had a few herself, I couldn't tell you for sure. Anyway, I told Irma it was Derek who got me pregnant. I hated him and thought she'd get rid of him if she thought it was him. But instead she wanted us to live together. He was one mean fucker. Oh, sorry, I know you hate that word."

I nodded, "Fuck means *to brutalize* and in this case I guess Derek was a brutalizer. And so, you were protecting John, since he was a priest and, instead, you lived with Derek who you hated and who abused you? But you couldn't take it, so then you came to me for help, turned Derek in, and tried to start over?"

"I never told John that Max was his son." She looked down at her lap. "Maybe things would have been different if I had."

"So, how'd he find out?"

"John said Father Al called him two weeks ago, and said he needed to put a few things right. That was also around the same time Derek tracked me down. Derek came to find me after he'd been out of jail for a few weeks, and he needed money."

"Let's get back to how John found out about Max."

"Well, for the most part everyone at St. Mary's is really good at keeping secrets. I mean all of our lives depended on keeping secrets. I'd told Al that the baby was John's but to keep it a secret. John was going to be a priest, and it never dawned on me that John might change his mind. If I couldn't have him free and clear, I didn't want him to know. You know what I mean?"

I nodded again.

"What I didn't know all these years," Marnie said, "was that John loved me. It was his relationship with me that had him slow down his ordination process. He never took his final vows," she said, with a little smile.

"So, after Father Alphonso told John that Max was his baby, then what?" I asked yawning. "Sorry, go on."

"That wasn't all. Alphonso also told John he was pretty sure DNA would prove that Al could be *John's* father."

"This just never ends, does it?"

"John and Al don't look anything alike, and I think that was a bit too over the top for John, and wishful thinking for Al. But when John heard about Max he came looking for me."

"When did you hear all this?"

"Last night. It was the first time I'd seen John since before Max was born. But we both feel the same as before. John told me he looked for me after I left the Dream Palace, but when he asked Irma she said I was dead. And to her I was. Alphonso finally decided to tell John about Max, when he'd heard I'd been kidnapped."

"Kidnapped...*kidnapped*. You must have been terrified. I couldn't imagine you leaving Max, but kidnapped? Oh, Marn..."

"Actually they took me after a bit of a knife fight in my kitchen, where I got Derek's blood all over the kitchen with a butcher knife. I got him a little in the chest and only a little nick to his neck, but that one really bled. Then those boys held me down and one of them carved an "X" ion my stomach." Marnie pulled down her loose fitting pants reveling a four inch, semi-healed wound.

"That looks bad. Tomorrow I think you need to see a doctor and get some stitches to keep that from opening up."

"It wasn't until they threatened to hurt Max that I stopped fighting and agreed to go with them—it all happened so fast. I got cut, we heard your car and one of the kids said you went around back. I knew you'd take care of my baby." Her eyes filled with tears that splashed down her face. "I sure hope he didn't see anything. Oh God, do you think he did?"

I shrugged my shoulders.

"So, anyway," she said, in a resigned voice, "I just went with them. I didn't know what else to do."

"Oh God, Marnie," I said, shaking my head, trying to make sense of this sad story. "I can't help but think I might have been able to help you, if you'd told me the truth."

"Well, I didn't, did I?" Her eyes flashed with anger, as if I was asking just a little too much.

"No," I said.

"Secrets don't matter anymore now. Al told John to call Crystal, and she told him where Max was, so John went to be with Max, assuming I'd do my best to get there. And I did."

"How?" I asked.

"I called Crystal. I told her I had to get Max, but I was so worried you'd be mad at me or, keep me from him, say I was unfit or, whatever, so I made Crystal promise not to tell you. I'm sorry..." Marnie said, as a tear ran down her cheek.

"I'm listening." I got up and ran some water in a glass and held it out for her. "Water?" She slowly shook her head, side to side.

"Let me get this straight," I said, "Alphonso told John to call Crystal. Was this before or after he talked to me?"

"Not sure," Marnie said.

"If what you are saying is true, Al knew Crystal had taken Max to the sisters. And after Crystal tells him how to get there, John goes to Judith's and he hangs out with Max—how am I doing so far?" The tea wasn't working so well at keeping me sharp.

"What do you want from me, Shep?" Marnie must have heard something critical in my voice, "I'm not really happy this is such a mess. It's not like I tried to get kidnapped, tied in a cellar naked for three days while one or both of these boys raped me and..."

I melted. "Oh God, you're right. Come here, honey," I said. I held her in my arms while she cried. "Right, you're right, sorry." I patted her back. "Oh, honey, I'm so sorry. No one deserves what you have been through."

"There's more. Just try not to make me get all the details right."

"Sorry. I'll try not to be such an..."

"Asshole?" Marnie said, recovering her composure and smiling a little, as she wiped her tears with the back of her hand. "Let me at least finish this, you deserve it...

"So, a few days later I get away—not easy—but one of the kids felt sorry for me and untied me. Probably the same kids Irma had with her at the monastery this morning, I never saw their faces. Anyway, I needed to get away from Brenda's place fast as I could, I saw you and I was gonna holler, but then Irma came. I was afraid of what Irma would do. So I called 911 with a phone one of Derek's boys lost. Later I called your house and Crystal answers, like I said, then she tells me she took Max to the sisters—are you following me, Shep, you look..."

"Dizzy from this, but go on,"

"John and Max are at the monastery, but Judith hasn't yet figured out the connection. John seemingly just happened to go on one of the recent Benedictine work retreats, and he tried to spend time with Max, getting to know him and stuff.

"Only problem was Palikowski and his goons were monitoring who came to see Father Al. John thinks they followed every visitor Al had, and Palikowski sent these horrible guys to the monastery to find us. I don't think they knew why, just that Al had told us some things. Anyway, thanks to Crystal's fast thinking, we all got away, they missed the fork in that winding road at the bottom of the hill and we never saw them again. No one got hurt."

"Except someone tied up Judith, and shot poor Brenda. I suspect you've left out a whole lot of this story, but I get the general idea."

"Brenda?"

"Seems she was looking for you, too."

"No, somebody must have brought her there, thinking she'd help them find me, which she never would have done. She's like my sister."

This made no sense to me, but by this point I didn't care about the details. "I've heard enough for now, I'm beat. We all have a funeral to go to. Let's talk more later. If you're still going to be here that is. You did bring my car back, right?" I said, as I pushed my chair away from the table.

"I deserved that. I don't know how I'll make this up to you. But before we go to bed I have a question, a favor really."

"Depends."

"Will you marry John and me tomorrow at the church, after the funeral?"

"Sometimes I just don't know about you, Marnie. Where is your brain, your sense of decorum? What is this, a movie? You have to have a marriage license for it to be official and besides, isn't that a little in bad taste? At a funeral? And what about pre-marriage counseling? Guess it's too late for that, huh," I said, with a little smile.

"After we got away from the monastery I begged John to marry me. He said, *yes,* and we got the license at the courthouse in Waukegan just before they closed. I know this is goofy, but everybody will be at the funeral, and Alphonso would have loved it. I want to do this to honor his passing. All you need to do is clear it with Father Sawyer. Being that you are a Protestant and St. Mary's is a Catholic church, he'd have to give permission."

"Seems you have everything figured out. So, John is leaving the priesthood or expecting special dispensation from the pope? And what about the little matter of Derek dead in the woods? I imagine you could be brought up on charges for that one."

"Derek was a nasty man and hurt me plenty, but I didn't kill him. My money is on Irma, or one of her boys, somebody he pissed off. Like I said, Derek was mean to everyone, but both Irma and Derek thought I had money stashed."

"I actually saw Irma shoot Derek. But it is possible he was already dead. This is all too bizarre, I have to go to bed. But, one more question...where's Crystal?"

"We dropped her at home. She's with Rupert."

"Another all-nighter for Rupert...at least everyone is where they are supposed to be." I wanted to ask more about Crystal and her life before I met her. But that could wait.

"Shep," Marnie looked at me with those big eyes, "will you talk to Sawyer?"

"I might, I just might, but you are one crazy girl if you think marriage, especially to an almost priest, is going to solve your problems." I had no intention of going through with this wedding silliness tomorrow. We could save that for another day.

"I love you, Shep, you are the best thing that ever happened to me," she said, clutching at my neck. "Without you..."

"Marnie," I gently pushed her away. I wasn't sure I was ready to say, *I love you too.* I didn't know what I felt at the moment. "It's late. I think we both need to get some sleep."

As Marnie turning to go up stairs I dialed Patrick, who picked up his cell phone right away.

Going over the high points of Marnie's story, I left out the part about them wanting to get married. "This crew plans to go to the funeral. Will you let them do that before you bring them in for questioning?"

"I don't see why not. At this point there is only minimal interest in Marnie Cooper's shenanigans now and we are actively looking for Irma."

CHAPTER 33

For the first time since Marnie disappeared, I slept soundly. Waking up, I heard little clinking sounds in the house, like someone was setting the table in the kitchen. And I knew by the smell of things that Rupert was making breakfast.

I splashed cold water on my face, grabbed my robe and went downstairs. Marnie and John, Rupert and Crystal ate without talking at the kitchen table, all dressed in requisite black, ready for the funeral. Through the kitchen door I saw Max in the den watching TV.

I poured myself some coffee, and no one spoke.

"John Leonardo," I said, to the attractive man dressed in a black suit, white shirt and red tie, he must have borrowed from Rupert. "We haven't been formally..."

"Yes, ma'am," he said, standing up, looking nervous. Marnie and Crystal cringed—they know how I hate to be called ma'am. I acknowledged their look with a lopsided smile, and they smiled back.

"Nice to finally be properly introduced. You sure have caused quite a fuss."

"Yes, ma'am," he said, again.

"First, we have a funeral—we'll catch up later. I understand that the three of you will be under police observation from the time we leave the house until you're questioned at the station after the interment. Rupert and I will undoubtedly be left out of this initial round. We'll keep Max and, with any luck, you'll be back before dinner. Crystal, when the dust settles, I presume we'll clear the air between us."

"Marnie and John, this other thing has to wait 'til you are cleared." They nodded as if they'd expected their little silly little bubble to burst anyway.

"Good coffee," I said, wistfully longing to interrupt Max from his cartoons. But hugs from him would make me want to sit on the couch all day and watch mindless TV.

"I need to get ready." They nodded again, glancing at each other like children worried they'd angered their mother to the point of no return. Admittedly, I was still miffed at last night's revelations...but not really angry. I don't do anger for very long.

"You drive everyone Rupert. I'll be your chauffeur next time, promise." The room was quiet except for the sounds of Grover and Cookie Monster coming from the den.

"I'll go with Patrick, who should be here at any moment, and I'll fill him in. And before you try it again you two, enough with the nodding."

Then we all jumped, as Max shrieking with joy, and ran to me, "Oh, Mama Shep, I missed you. Mommy said I couldn't wake you up."

"That was nice of your mom," I said, getting down on one knee to hug him. We both rocked back and forth.

"Why are you crying, Mama Shep?"

"I'm just so happy to see you. I missed you. You and I have lots of playing to do, but now I need to get ready. Looks like you need to get dressed, too.

"You know where we're going this morning, Max?"

"Mommy told me a friend of hers died and he..." Max said, pointing at John, "told me that the man went to be with God."

"That's it, sweetie. If you have any questions after the funeral just ask me, or..." I turned to John, "ask him. He knows lots about this stuff. But I've got to get going. Can't go to church in my pajamas, now can I?"

Max shook his head as he grabbed a banana off the table and headed back toward the TV.

"Love you," he said.

"Love you, too," the rest of us said in unison.

Max turned around and smiled at all of us, and said, "Love you more."

As I went upstairs to get ready, I heard the sounds of Crystal and Rupert getting the kitchen cleaned up, and Marnie cajoling Max away from the TV and presumably into some suitable clothes for church.

I rushed through my shower and put on my high-necked starched white shirt and black suit with a fitted jacket and swingy skirt. In the mirror, I saw a somber sight so I put on lipstick and blush to try to brighten myself up.

By the time I got back downstairs the kitchen had been tidied and the rest of them had already left for the funeral and I had a few minutes before Patrick was to arrive.

Thankful there was still hot coffee in the carafe, I went outside to the fabulous porch that always reminded me of what a fine house this was. I sat on the small wicker couch and waited for Patrick. The porch was a throwback to the Queen Anne wrap-around porches that were popular in the late 1800's, and had been a particularly favorite place for my grandmother. Rumor has it that it was the first thing her architect friend Leona had designed.

The porch had an open deck and was painted bright white so the many hanging baskets of fuchsia could show off their hot-pink and purple flowers and tight dark green leaves. A tip of her hat to the west of Ireland – where fuchsias were huge hedge bushes, not little plants in a pot.

This morning especially, I appreciated the peace and quiet of this gorgeous space as it faced the incomparable beauty of Lake Michigan.

The sun, now well off the horizon, sparkled up the water and made the whole world seem alive with joy. Thinking that Alphonso would get a lovely day for his funeral, I heard footsteps around the side of the house.

"I'm on the porch," I hollered, presuming Patrick and was coming around instead of thru the house.

"So you are, little chicky."

I froze.

"Irma..." I said, recognizing her voice and getting quickly to my feet—instantly on high alert. Irma was about six feet from me and she was holding another smallish-sized gun, bigger than the gun she had dropped under the porch at Brenda's place, but still small enough to fit in her hand.

"Nice house..." she said, using her free arm in a sweeping gesture. "But I guess you won't be enjoying it for much longer, will you now? Why, you're already dressed for a funeral...your own maybe?" At that, Irma cackled.

"I'm expected at a funeral at St. Mary's." I said, reminding myself to breathe normally, and act as if this was a normal conversation.

"Anyone I know?" she asked, her curiosity piqued.

"Actually, yes." I needed to stall her until Patrick arrived.

"And who might that be?" Curiosity seemed to have gotten the better of her.

"You know that old guy that came to the Dream Palace?" I could feel my pulse beating hard in my neck, but I knew that I desperately needed to stay calm. I'd seen Irma's moods swing before—it was imperative I stayed calm.

"Lots of old guys, little missy," she said, her voice edgy with aggravation.

"You know the one you didn't like. The one who paid really well but just wanted to talk...well, he died. He was a priest." I wanted to keep her talking. Where the hell was Patrick?

"I'll be damned...what a pervert...coming to watch half-naked girls dance and him being a priest. That's just not natural. I never did like him."

"He was a little weird but he was trying to help..." Clearly that was the wrong thing for me to say. Irma lifted her gun with one smooth motion and shot off one round... the bullet whizzed by me, inches away from the side of my head but close enough for me to realize she didn't miss—she was playing with me. If her point was to keep me scared, she was succeeding.

"You damn do-gooders have ruined everything. The palace got closed down last night, thanks to you. You stupid..." She pointed the gun at me again, and I froze.

"I should kill you right here," she said.

"I don't think you..."

"Shut up, you slut."

"No, you shut up." I said, in an angry voice. "You can kill me with that little gun there, but no one calls me a 'slut.' You might have bullied desperate women and men but neither they nor I..."

Irma didn't let me finish, she just started laughing—a high-pitched, hysterical laugh that was both distressed and frantic but only lasted for a few seconds.

Squinting her eyes into two long narrow slits, Irma was motionless. It seemed she was losing a battle with herself. She was assessing her next move. Apparently I'd thrown her off by raising my voice. But she looked different than when she'd started this. Irma could obviously kill me, but now she seemed a little scared. I suspected that this was when she was most dangerous.

Irma was maybe about five feet tall, and she had made the mistake of standing to the right of the porch so she couldn't see who might be coming up behind her. Over the top of her head, I saw Patrick ready for the funeral in his dress uniform casually walking around the side of the house. Patrick saw Irma, pulled his weapon and indicated with his free hand, I should keep talking—

"Irma, you could kill me, but that wouldn't help you much. So, why..."

"Shut up. You just shut up."

Patrick was slowly moving in on Irma. She must have noticed my eyes move behind her. She began to turn around, and was ready to shoot, but I stood up, and directed her attention on me.

"If you kill me," I said, in a loud voice walking closer to her, "someone else will come to prevent you and people like you from..."

She cocked her gun and pointed it at me. But there was a noise behind her, she turned and just started shooting. Patrick was in the open but too far away for the trajectory of her little gun. I grabbed the small wicker table next to me and hurled it toward Irma's gun, but she held on to it, turned around and she shot toward me. I kicked at the chair and again jumped sideways. She stumbled over the wicker chair and shot toward me again, but the bullet hit the tree behind me with a thud. That threw her off enough to let me grab her arm, and hit it against the porch railing. She dropped her gun. I kicked it away and pulled her arm behind her back.

Irma twisted out of my grasp but fell to the ground from the force of trying to get away. She scrambled to her feet and attempted to run. I tripped her again and she fell flat, yelling obscenities. Patrick reached the porch, grabbed Irma by the arm, over powering her, and walked her around the other side of the house to a waiting police car that had come to accompany us on our drive to St. Mary's.

Irma no longer looked even remotely threatening. Instead she looked like the defeated old woman she was.

CHAPTER 34

Patrick recovered Irma's gun from the grass in front of the porch where I'd kicked it, handed it to another officer who'd come back with him and Patrick put his arms around me.

"I know you're trying to be nice, Patrick, but I don't need this right now." I shrugged out of his arms. "This is a mess, Patrick, so much to do. I've got to get to Alphonso's funeral."

"Relax, Shep," Patrick instructed, "you're starting to hyperventilate. You have just been shot at. Just give yourself a minute." I tried to force myself to breathe more regularly, to prove I was fine. I heard more footsteps come from around the house and started to tense up.

"Sergeant, we're taking the suspect to the station, you need anything else?" said the officer.

"Check the gun we recovered and see if it was the same gun that was used in that shooting yesterday at the Benedictine Retreat Center.

"Otherwise, Izzy, I think we're pretty good here, but would you send one of the EMT's that must have come with you, to take Reverend Murdoch blood pressure?"

"No, please I'm..." Patrick pointed to the chair. Feeling foolish, I did what I was told.

"This is a precautionary measure, Izzy." Patrick said. "Will do." Izzy said. "Right away, Sergeant."

Within a minute a solidly built young man, with a great smile and gentle manner, was asking me a bunch of calm, but pointed questions as he slipped the blood pressure cuff over my arm. After a minute he said, "You've had quite a shock," he said, handing me a bottle of Gatorade. "While your blood pressure and pulse are high normal, I'd still suggest you go to the emergency room and get checked out by a doctor."

I'd already had too much up-close and personal time in the ER lately. "Young man," I said, "how about this? I promise to go see a doctor if I don't feel better in a few days."

"Actually, if you still feel light-headed and dizzy in the next few hours, you definitely need to go get checked out—do we have a deal?" The man's smile was so genuine—it was as if he was sincerely interested in my well being, even though he'd probably never see me again.

Patrick groaned, but he knew no one could be forced to the ER if they didn't want to go.

"You're good at what you do," I looked at the EMT's name badge, "Michael. I see you're named after an important angel—the name fits you. I feel lots better, and I so appreciate your concern, but really I've got to go. I'm late."

The young man gave me a *you better take care of this* look, and jogged off to the ambulance that must have been ensconced in my yard.

There was a loud noise, probably a truck backfiring on Sheridan Road, and I jumped. Patrick put his arms around me again and held me close to him. This time I didn't fight but instead leaned into the shoulder of his tidy uniform.

"I think you can relax a little, Shep. It's over."

"What's over? I'm so tired of crying," I said, tearing up. "This is so not me. I haven't cried this much since I was six. What's over?" I asked, breathing better even though my body was still shaking.

"Well, if the undercover detective I met with this morning has this right, it was Irma who killed Derek, not Marnie."

"Thank God, thank God. Tell me more," I said, as we walked down the porch steps, around the house and toward the end of the driveway, watching as the last squad car pulled out onto Sheridan Road.

"Irma's boyfriend or possibly husband gave up information to try and save himself."

"Some boyfriend..." I said.

"The detective showed me his picture—it wasn't the jerk who interrogated you when you were arrested; he was the big guy in the corner having dinner at Le Petite Gourmet. They're looking to see if there was someone else on staff at the restaurant working with them."

"I'd also seen that guy the night I was at the Dream Palace. Do you think they sat us at that table so they had a good view of you? Or me...you sat where they tried to seat me... they were trying to kill me?" I shivered at the thought.

"Not sure. Then last night, when they closed down the Dream Palace, Irma came gunning for you."

"That's what she said. I guess she was out of people to blame—so she decided I was the reason for her troubles." I said, shaking my head.

"Crazy people do crazy things. Apparently some of the women at the dance club had known where Marnie was living after she'd left, but they gave Irma your address instead."

"Not that Brenda or Pammy Jo are what I'd call friends, but I'd given them my card. I doubt that they gave Irma that information willingly. My suspicion is that Irma beat it out of them.

"And Derek?" I asked.

"When Derek got out of jail he went looking for Marnie. That set this whole mess in motion. After he'd bungled Marne's kidnapping and she escaped, Irma must have drugged, then killed Derek, out of frustration more than anything else. Then she just kept shooting people."

"Marnie always said Derek was one nasty guy. Still no one deserves to be murdered. One more question. What about the wooden boxes in Marnie's basement?"

"Interesting you should ask. Apparently, Marnie wasn't the only one keeping records. In the boxes were all of Alphonso's files. Years and years of files recently moved to Marnie's basement. Files on the wayward priests Alphonso had worked with for thirty or forty years.

"Palikowski, that obnoxious public relations guy at the university, has been trying to get his hands on these files, for obvious reasons. Now he's requested the contents of the boxes, claiming them as church property. That will be decided in court—it could take years to figure that one out. Marnie isn't out of the woods completely yet. Depends on those records."

I smoothed my hair, tugged my jacket over the waistband of my skirt, adjusted my shoulders and stood up straight. "Right, then, I've a funeral to attend—you coming?"

"Sure. First, can you stand one more bit of good news?"

"Not certain—but shoot...no, ah—go ahead." I smiled at Patrick, as he opened the car door, and I got in.

"Well, it appears that Alphonso had a large savings account, and a substantive life insurance policy—all of which has been left in equal amounts to John Leonardo, Marnie Cooper, and to their son Max."

"Wow. That will be helpful, Al must have taken that three wise ones' story to heart, not sure Marnie and John will be as wise as Mary and Joseph with their windfall. If we're lucky it's in a trust. With rules to parse it out. But hey, could this get any better?

"Patrick."

"Yes."

"Might be time for those shooting lessons. I guess if people are going to be shooting at me I probably should learn how to shoot back. Do they have classes for pacifists?"

CHAPTER 35

We were late to the funeral, but in the crowded church our late arrival went mostly unnoticed. Patrick and I scooted in next to my errant clan. I sat down, reached for Marnie's hand and squeezed it hard. She squeezed back with a big smile. At this point she didn't know that after the funeral there would probably not be bevy of officers carting her off to jail, nor would there be a wedding today. Nonetheless, it looked as if Marnie was in heaven and not the least bit worried about anything. John's lap was full with a snuggling Max, while his other arm was settled loosely around Marnie's shoulder. She was glowing. I'd never seen her so happy.

The church was filled to capacity with mourners, many obviously clergy and members of St. Mary's. Many were standing along the sides and at the back of the church—quite a tribute to the old priest.

I also recognized some of the women sitting in the pews. It wasn't their faces I recognized, but their short tight skirts, bright make-up and ratted hair. They sat in clumps together or alone, here are real congregants of Al's church.

Whether they had changed their lives and given up sex work I didn't know, and maybe that was never the point. But Al had obviously made an important impact on each of them, even though he thought he'd never helped a one of them. Now I hope he knows different!

I was glad to be there, to say goodbye to the complicated and, some might say, rogue priest I had only just met. But I was completely distracted. My mind whirled as I tried to fit the pieces together. I wasn't paying attention to exactly what was going on in the service. I stood when the congregation stood and knelt when everyone else did.

But I woke up from my thoughts when I heard Sawyer say, "Today we will be celebrating open communion in honor of Father Alphonso, and his congregation."

I went up for communion, as did the women of Alphonso's flock. Many teetered on high heels, and they were not sure exactly what to do, but they came forward and received communion. In this simple act, they were there for Father Al. I was pleased that Father Sawyer had given a nod to the other celebrants to serve all who came forward, Roman Catholic or not.

This was a radical gift Sawyer was giving to honor his friend and colleague, and I knew I was going to have to change what I thought about priests and communion. I could hear him say, "the bread for the journey and the cup of forgiveness" to each person who came to partake of this ancient ritual.

Finally, we came to the place in the service where Father Sawyer was to give the eulogy. He looked around the sanctuary, until his eyes stopped at me. "I would like to ask Reverend Shepherd Murdoch to come forward and say a few words." After my initial startled response, I stepped out of the pew, and made my way forward...it never occurred to me to decline the request. I would just speak from the heart. Thankfully, I'd had a little practice at this.

The congregation, from the vantage point of this high pulpit, were like any other group of people mourning the death of a loved one. Many were crying and leaning on each other's shoulders, or dry-eyed from too many tears already shed, or from an inability to cry at all.

"While I'm surprised at the request to speak, I will let you know that I have actually been thinking a great deal about this very amazing man." I started, gathering my thoughts, "I'm honored to be here, and to say a few words about a man that many of you knew much better than I did." I looked around slowly, stopping to look directly into the eyes of one or two people, as I began to preach.

"Father Alphonso was not a perfect man. Many of you knew him as a university professor, but his real call was as a pastor who tried to give understanding and consolation and to not impart judgment. He loved God without a doubt, but he admittedly quarreled mightily with the tenets of the church.

"At first Father Al was ill prepared. As a young priest he made a few mistakes that would forever haunt him and greatly impact his ministry.

"Alphonso was more honest than most of us, maybe not always with his superiors about what he was doing in his ministry, but always honest with those living in compromised lifestyles, always honest with himself, and always honest with God.

"No matter what anyone might think of Father Alphonso's unorthodox, some would say renegade ministry, one could never believe he was acting alone. He obviously believed God had forgiven him his transgressions, and he was passing that forgiveness on to others. He also knew that God was with him in his work, at his shoulder all the time.

"Many here were touched by Father Alphonso. In his last conversation with me, he wondered if his ministry had made much of a difference. But as I look at your faces gathered here today, I can see that he most certainly made a great difference in your lives and in mine.

"Others found Father Alphonso a difficult do-gooder and a thorn in their side...a priest whose sense of good works went way overboard when it came to helping those who needed him. Some of you who disapproved of Father Alphonso may think that your workload will be lightened as a result of his passing, but I think you will be wrong."

My eyes had found Palikowski, who was now obviously uncomfortable.

"There's no doubt in my mind that as a result of Father Alphonso's courageous work, others will take up this unconventional ministry and run with it." At that there was a burst of applause, and someone in the back yelled, "Preach it, sister."

"When a vacuum is created, we know others will come forward and take up the cause. In that knowledge, Father Alphonso Leonardo will rest peacefully." There was a loud clap of thunder outside, providing divine punctuation and heralding yet another summer storm.

I smiled at the crowd who had settled into that place of gentle quiet that pastors love. "I have said enough, and by that thunder clap, I would say that God clocked in with loud and affirmative *amen*—heralding the life of this man, this pastor, this good and faithful servant.

"There's little more to say, except, perhaps, to once again be reminded of how many lives Father Alphonso touched and what amazing work he carried out among us in the name of our God—our Creator, our Redeemer and our Sustainer.

"In his death may we let him go—sending him off with the prayers of our hearts. I, for one, will miss him very much."

I went back to my seat and Patrick took my hand, and smiled. He shook his head back and forth, "Shepherd Murdoch, you are incredible. Absolutely incredible."

After the service we all tumbled into the Bentley and followed the hearse from the church to the cemetery across from my house, leaving Patrick's daughter to fetch his car from the church parking lot. I pulled my grandmother's enormously ridiculous car in my own driveway, parked it and we all walked across back across Sheridan Road to the cemetery. It was a hot August day, and as is normal for Chicago at this time of the year, the storm that was threatening rain had passed us by. It seemed silly to stand out in this mid-day heat for too long, but I knew we would only be here for a few minutes, as these things are generally brief, and to the point.

All who had come to the cemetery from the church gathered around the casket as it sat just above ground, tethered by strong straps attached to a temporary rectangular chrome frame that encircled the grave. Even Max stood patiently and listened to the words spoken by Father Sawyer.

As Alphonso's simple casket was lowered, ever so slowly into the earth, I looked at the faces of those gathered around and I prayed that this ending would be a new beginning for all of Alphonso's friends, especially Marnie and John. And for Max.

The casket touched the bottom of the hole with the slightest thud. Then for a few less than sacred moments, the cemetery workers removed the straps used to lower the casket before they respectfully moved away from our gathering and waited for us to finish.

The next task for these nameless workers would be to shovel the dirt to close up the hole. I whispered a request to Father Sawyer, and he took a step back, nodding at me. I picked a few roses from the flower arrangements brought from the church, and handed them to Marnie, John and Crystal...others followed taking flowers until the flowers were gone from the arrangements.

There is rarely music at an interment, which I have often found unsettling. And, while I was not the officiant, I began to sing quietly, as much for myself, as anyone standing there. *Be now my vision, oh God of my heart, nothing surpasses the love you impart.* Father Sawyer and Judith, as well as the other clergy gathered around the perfectly sculpted hole in the ground joined in with me. A few of us knew this song by heart, *you my best thought by day or by night, waking or sleeping your presence my light.*

As a farewell gift, some people who had picked from the flower arrangements, roses, daises, calla or star-gazer lilies tossed them on top of the casket, others kept their flowers with them, as a last remembrance of Father Alphonso. The crowd began to dwindle as the mourners headed toward their cars, and the rest of their lives.

As we turned to leave the cemetery, an imperceptible and tender late August breeze began to blow around us, continuing to blow away any threat of a summer storm back across the lake.

This welcome breeze against my face felt like the breath of God brushing against my cheeks, assuring us all that everything was as it should be. At least for the moment.

This tender message was a perfect and fitting way to say 'goodbye' to the dead, and 'hello' to the living.

God was blowing love all around us, and, for this little moment in time, all was right with our world.

We left Alphonso's casket covered with flowers, and some, as they walked to their cars, continued to quietly sing, *Heart of my own heart what ever befall, be Thou my vision O Ruler of all.*

Amen and Amen

CPSIA information can be obtained
at www.ICGtesting.com
Printed in the USA
FFOW03n1350090417
34320FF